Sarah Dunn has moved from ⬛⬛⬛⬛ times, and from New Yor⬛⬛⬛⬛ which means, at the mome⬛⬛ only resi⬛⬛ York. Her first novel, *The* ⬛⬛⬛⬛, has been translated into twenty-three languages.

Also by Sarah Dunn

The Big Love

secrets
to
happiness

SARAH DUNN

sphere

SPHERE

First published in the United States by Little, Brown and Company
A Division of Hachette Book Group, Inc. in 2009
First published in Great Britain in 2009 by Sphere
This paperback edition published in 2010 by Sphere
Reprinted 2010

A CIP catalogue record for this book
is available from the British Library.

ISBN 978-0-7515-3830-4

Printed and bound in Great Britain by
Clays Ltd, St Ives plc

Papers used by Sphere are natural, renewable and
recyclable products sourced from well-managed forests and certified
in accordance with the rules of the Forest Stewardship Council.

Mixed Sources
Product group from well-managed
forests and other controlled sources
www.fsc.org Cert no. SGS-COC-004081
© 1996 Forest Stewardship Council
FSC

Sphere
An imprint of
Little, Brown Book Group
100 Victoria Embankment
London EC4Y 0DY

An Hachette UK Company
www.hachette.co.uk

www.littlebrown.co.uk

For Peter

a happy marriage

Do you want to know the secret to a happy marriage?"

"Tell me."

"Put your wife on Paxil."

People told Holly all sorts of things. She didn't know why, really. Maybe it had something to do with her face, which was wide open and promised kindness. Holly's face was much kinder than she actually was. She had big green eyes and extremely pale skin and an easy, forgiving smile, but the real problem was probably her dimples. Holly was one of the seven grown women left in Manhattan who still had them, dimples, which meant that strangers were always asking her for change for a twenty or to watch their laptops in Starbucks. Once, a woman she'd never met before asked her to hold her baby while she strapped a car seat into the back of a taxi. Part of the reason Holly had trouble with men was they mistook her face for the truth, they felt she had vast untapped reservoirs of understanding and ended up telling her all of the sordid and shameful bits of their histories, and when they saw not so much as a flicker of judgment pass over her features, they kept right on going. It was, Holly found, a great thing for a writer, to have people tell you things, but it could wreak havoc on relationships.

"Amanda's taking Paxil?" said Holly.

Mark nodded yes and lowered his voice to just above a whisper. "She's a completely different person. It's like I woke up one morning and suddenly found myself married to this sweet and lovely woman. She's always been a bit of a, well, I don't want to say 'bitch' but—" He looked up in the air for a second, searching for the word. "Let's just go with *difficult*. I mean that in the best possible way, she's really intelligent and impressive and opinionated and I love her, I really do, but it was getting pretty tough to live with her."

"Yeah, but, isn't that kind of alarming? I mean, that a pill could make that much of a difference?"

"Alarming? Are you kidding? It's the best thing that ever happened to me."

Amanda came in from the kitchen carrying a small bowl of black olives. Amanda was one of those women who start out thin and spend their thirties getting progressively thinner. Holly couldn't figure out how she did it. It was almost like she'd discovered a magic pill, or was involved with some sort of spooky voodoo that she insisted on keeping to herself. Amanda kept getting thinner, and her hair kept getting shorter and spikier, and her eyes, defying all known laws of human biology, kept getting bigger. Amanda was beautiful, Holly had to admit, but she was in danger of turning into a bony, bug-eyed elf.

"I didn't know you started taking Paxil," said Holly.

"I love it," said Amanda. "You should try it."

"Why? I'm not depressed."

Amanda and Mark just looked at her.

"Why is everyone convinced there's something wrong with me?" said Holly. "Last night I was on the phone with my step-mother, and I told her I was thinking about getting a dog, and she said, 'Oh, good, that means you're ready to receive love again.'"

"She said that?" said Amanda.

"She did. And I said to her, Oh, Ellen, don't you worry about me. I've been receiving love," said Holly. She popped an olive into her mouth. "I've been receiving love in, you know, multiple orifices."

"You did not," said Amanda.

"I wanted to."

"What's she even talking about?" said Amanda. "You've *been* ready to receive love."

Mark was sitting on the edge of the couch with the bottle of Pinot Noir Holly had brought and one of those rabbit-ear wine openers. "What kind of dog?" he asked.

"I haven't got that far," said Holly. "I'll probably just go to a shelter."

"When we rescued Peppo," said Amanda, "I did all sorts of research about dogs that are happy in apartments and breeds that do well in New York, but when it came down to it, I wanted the kind of dog I grew up with."

Holly gave Amanda a look.

"What?" said Amanda.

"He's a pedigreed Portuguese Water Dog. You had to fly to Oregon to pick him up from the breeder. How is that a rescue?"

"That's how it works with purebreds. People who adopt them have to sign a contract that they'll return them to the breeder if they don't want the dog anymore. Then the breeder finds a rescue home for it."

"Yeah, but that's not really a rescue. I mean, you didn't 'rescue' him from anything. That's just a used dog."

"Peppo's a rescue, Holly."

Holly looked over at Mark to get some backup — he'd spent a thousand bucks plus airfare on the dog, Holly knew for a fact, because he'd complained quite loudly about it at the time — but he was hunched over the coffee table, fussing with the wine opener, oblivious. She knew from experience that pursuing this line of reasoning with Amanda was futile, so she decided to change the subject. "What exactly is your husband wearing on his feet?"

"Oh. You noticed Mark's slipper socks. Attractive, aren't they?"

Mark's slipper socks were just that: oatmeal-colored wool socks with a brown leather outsole stitched onto the bottom, like feetie pajamas without the pajamas.

"I mean, I know I'm like family," said Holly, "but I don't think you should inflict those things on family."

"The astronauts wear these," said Mark. "These are *astronaut's* slippers, standard issue since nineteen eighty-two."

"Have you become an astronaut?" said Amanda. "Did I miss something? Have you given up investment banking in order to explore outer space?"

"Hey, I love these slippers," said Mark. "I want to be buried in these slippers."

Amanda looked at Holly and gave a little marital "what can you do" shrug of her shoulders.

"Oh. I almost forgot," said Holly. "I have to show you something. Can I borrow your laptop?"

"Of course."

Holly sat down on the couch with Amanda's computer and managed to open up her email. "Listen to this," she said. "'Dear Holly. This is going to sound strange, but I'm writing regarding Spence Samuelson. I have been dating him for about eight months, talking about a serious future together, and now something catastrophic has happened. I don't know how you might feel about talking with me about this, but I would love to hear your perspective. Thank you. Cathleen Wheeler.' And then she leaves her phone number, with a Colorado area code."

"Oh my god," said Amanda.

"Who is Spence Samuelson?" asked Mark.

"He was the ex before the ex," Amanda explained. "The guy before the ex-husband. He was before your time."

"Wait." Mark turned to Holly. "He's the shitty guy in your book?"

"Exactly," said Amanda.

Holly said, a tad formally, "The character of Palmer was fictional, but sort of loosely, in the broadest possible way, based on Spence."

Amanda rolled her eyes at this. She knew the truth, which was that Holly had changed exactly two details about Spence when turning him into Palmer, his name and the color of his eyes.

"Did you call her?" said Mark.

"Not yet."

"Are you crazy? Do it now," said Amanda. "Put her on speakerphone."

"The woman said something catastrophic happened," said Mark. "I don't think we should put her on our speakerphone."

"You know, after I got this email, I had an epiphany," said Holly. "*This* is why I wrote a novel. For this exact experience. To have girlfriends of men I used to date track me down and ask me for advice. It'll be like being a therapist without having to get a degree."

"Lord," said Mark.

"What?" said Holly.

"That poor, sad schmuck," said Mark. "He has no idea what he's in for."

Holly Frick had had the worst kind of divorce: the kind where you're still in love with the person who is divorcing you. Not "fond of," not "still attached to," not "building a life together"—hopelessly in love with. And it was a year ago exactly that Alex had left her, a fact that had somehow slipped her notice up until earlier that evening, when she went to hail a cab and saw the dried-out Christmas trees heaped in sad piles along the sidewalk. Alex had left her on January third. Kind of like a benevolent CEO who holds off on the pink slips until after the holidays.

Alex had left Holly abruptly, more or less out of the blue, not for another woman, not even for another man, but for, it would seem, *women*. As many as he could get his hands on. The rumors came back to her throughout the spring and summer, trickling in from various gossipy sources, stories about his fling with the frosty Thai hostess at Tao; a graduate student who worked in the basement of Shakespeare & Company; the "model" who sold lingerie at Barneys. Holly's therapist claimed she'd metabolized the breakup of her marriage like a trauma victim, that it happened so suddenly and so unexpectedly it was like she'd been in a car accident, or the subject of a violent crime, which Holly figured was as good an explanation as any as to why she'd spent the past year of her life feeling like she was underwater.

She knew that what she was going through was nothing

special, just garden-variety heartbreak, the sort of thing that poets and novelists had been writing about for hundreds of years, but she also knew, from those same books, that there were people who never recover from it, ones who go on through life beset by a dim and painful longing. It wasn't until that day, when she saw the Christmas trees littering the street and was shocked to realize a full year had gone by, that she started to fear she might be one of them.

Amanda and Mark had a baby, a thirteen-month-old named Jacob, who was asleep in his room for most of the evening but made a brief cameo appearance around the time of the last moo shu pancake. Jacob was huge. At his six-month birthday party he was the size of a small two-year-old, but seeing as he had only about a thirty percent chance of transferring his pacifier from his fist to his mouth on any given try, he seemed vaguely retarded. He wasn't, though—he was just too big. Holly and Amanda had, years earlier, come up with a name for just this sort of baby—blond blob (because, and you'll see that this is true, these enormous blobby babies are invariably blond)—but that was before Amanda had gone and given birth to one.

After Jacob went back down, Holly and Amanda settled in on the couch with a fresh bottle of wine while Mark dozed in his chair.

"Talk," said Amanda.

"What? I'm good."

"Good!"

"Not that good," said Holly. "But better."

"That's still good."

"It's weird," said Holly. "A couple of weeks ago, I woke up on a Saturday morning, and I hadn't made plans with anybody, so the whole day was sitting there, stretched out in front of me, this big blank, which usually makes me feel all panicky and anxious and bad about myself—"

"You should have called," Amanda interrupted. "You could have come over."

"Yeah, I know. Thanks. Anyhow, I got dressed and I made my way downtown, and I did some Christmas shopping, and then at around four I went to see a movie I'd been wanting to see at the Film Forum, and then I came home and made a nice dinner for myself with real cooking involved and I ate off the good plates and, you know, in the end, I had this really great day. And the whole time I was aware of the fact that I was by myself, but I wasn't bothered by it the way I would have been in the past," said Holly. She reached for the bottle of wine and refilled both of their glasses. "I *got* married. I tried that. It didn't work out for me. And maybe I'm just one of those people who are meant to be alone."

"You're going to meet someone, Holly."

"I don't know if I even want to. Honestly. I'm fine alone. I feel like this is the first time in my life I've been able to say that and have it be completely true," said Holly. "I'm. Fine. Alone."

"Of course you're fine."

"And it feels good, you know, to finally be in a good place with all of this."

"And you're not really alone."

"I'm pretty alone." Holly took a big swallow of wine and closed her eyes. "I miss Alex."

"No you don't," said Amanda.

"I do. I miss him," said Holly. Her voice got small. "I think I'm still in love with him."

"You're not in love with Alex."

"Okay, so what is it then, when you walk by a restaurant you used to go to together, you get tears in your eyes and your chest feels like there's a huge hole in it and you have to go straight home and crawl into bed and get under the covers? What can that possibly mean, other than I still love him?"

"That's grief. That's healthy."

"I don't know," said Holly. "It feels like love."

"It doesn't matter," said Amanda. "You guys weren't happy together."

"I think maybe we were."

"You were miserable, Holly."

"So? I'm miserable now. And I'm not sure it's all that much better to be miserable alone than to be miserable with another person," said Holly. She thrust her forefinger in the air as the thought came to her: "Misery loves company."

"You're drunk."

"I do like to drink."

"You can sleep over if you want."

"No. That'll just make me feel more pathetic," said Holly. She flopped back against the cushions and stared up at the ceiling, which was flickering in the candlelight. "God, I've fucked up my life. My novel was a spectacular failure, I'm back writing for TV—for the world's crappiest TV show if anyone's keeping score—I'm thirty-five years old, utterly alone, and the outer walls of my eggs are taking on the consistency of tissue paper as we speak. Meanwhile, Alex leaves me and his life is going great. I think he's dating someone pretty seriously."

"What makes you say that?"

"Nothing, really," said Holly. "I'm just pretty sure he is."

Amanda put down her wineglass and looked hard at Hollss"Are you still checking his email?"

"No."

"*Holly.*"

"I'm not. I promise," said Holly. "He changed his code."

Mark opened one eye and piped in from his recliner. "You were checking your ex-husband's email?"

"I'm not proud of it."

Amanda got off the couch and headed towards the kitchen with a few dirty glasses. "Don't take this the wrong way, but I think you should really seriously consider getting a new therapist."

"Hey, you can't blame this on her," Holly called after her. "I don't tell her things like this. Trust me. She'd be appalled."

A few minutes later, Holly rolled off the couch and joined Amanda in the kitchen. After briefly rallying, just long enough to suggest that Holly (a) consider Internet dating, because a forty-three-year-old at his office met a guy from Teaneck that way, and she was pretty fat, or (b) maybe take a salsa dancing class, Mark had fallen back into a slipper-socked slumber. Amanda was at the sink with the rubber gloves on. Holly picked up a sponge and went to work on the countertops.

"Your husband thinks all my problems would be solved if I signed up for a salsa dancing class."

"That's not the worst idea," said Amanda. "You like to dance."

"My friend Betsy took a salsa dancing class, and when she went out to the hallway during the break, one of the guys from the class was just standing there, leaning against the wall, perfectly normal, with his hand down his pants."

"Was he, like, doing things to himself?"

"Does it matter?" said Holly. "Really, with that story, does it matter why his hand was in his pants?"

"I see your point," Amanda said, and then she turned off the faucet. "I have to talk to you about something."

"What?"

"Well, it's kind of complicated."

"Did I do something wrong?" said Holly.

"No, no. Of course not. It's not about you."

"Well, then, what is it?"

"It's — now this is going to seem like a bigger thing than I meant it to be, and it's really nothing."

"Okay...?"

"About a month ago, I met a guy at this benefit thing I went to."

"Uh-huh."

"His name is Jack, and he knows my old boss Theresa. We talked about Theresa a lot at first — the woman is out of her mind — and we just got into this dynamic with each other. Then we had lunch, and, you know, a few emails back and forth. Nothing big."

"I'm missing the part that's complicated."

"Yeah, well, that's just it," said Amanda. "It's getting complicated."

"Spell it out for me," said Holly. "Are you sleeping with him?"

"God, no. No. Nothing like that."

"Good. Then what is it?"

"I don't know what it is. I'm a little confused," said Amanda. "Feelings are getting involved."

"Does Mark know about it?"

"No," said Amanda. "I mean, he knows there's a guy out there named Jack, I've mentioned his name a few times, but he doesn't know."

Holly put the sponge down. "So what you're telling me is, you're dating somebody."

"Of course not," said Amanda. "We've had a couple of innocent lunches."

"You shouldn't talk to me about this," said Holly. "I'm no good with infidelity. I always overidentify with the cuckolded party."

"This isn't infidelity, Holly."

"Then why are we whispering in the kitchen?"

Amanda opened the cabinet and took out three coffee mugs.

"What are you telling me this for?"

"I want you to meet him."

"What?" said Holly. "Why?"

"I don't know," said Amanda. "You'll like him. You'll like each other."

"I don't think I want to meet him," said Holly. "I'll feel complicit. I feel guilty even having this conversation."

"Why should you feel guilty?"

"I don't know," said Holly. "Somebody should feel guilty, and I tend to feel all the feelings in the room."

"Just meet us for lunch next week, will you, please?"

"We'll see."

"Is that a yes?"

"It's a 'we'll see.'"

the ex before the ex

Some forty blocks uptown, on the thirty-seventh floor of the Jocastan, a monstrous glass-walled midtown apartment complex that blocked the sun from a healthy stretch of Forty-sixth Street for several months of the year, Spence Samuelson — the ex before the ex, the guy before the ex-husband, aka the shitty guy in Holly's book — was spending his evening alone, drinking vodka and messing around on his computer. He'd read a while back that scientists in New Jersey were building a particle accelerator the size of a sports stadium in order to create a black hole, a black hole which would then, presumably, swallow the scientists and the stadium and the state of New Jersey and the rest of the known universe, and he thought they could save themselves a lot of trouble simply by combining a high-speed Internet connection with carefully titrated amounts of 80 proof grain alcohol. When he heard the phone ring, he looked up from his screen and saw it was nearly ten o'clock. He'd forgotten to have dinner.

"I can't believe you," said an angry yet sniffly voice.

It was his girlfriend Cathleen, calling from Boulder, and it didn't sound good.

"What? What did I do?"

"What did you *do?* I don't know, Spence. Why don't you tell me what you *did?*"

"I don't know what you're talking about."

"Oh god, I'm seriously going to lose it if you keep lying to me."

"What do you want me to say?"

"Why don't you go open up your email."

Spence clicked on his email. He could hear Cathleen through the phone line. Angry breathing. Fuming — that was what she was doing. He opened up a file of digital photos she had forwarded to him. Oh, shit. Shit shit shit.

"Oh my god, Cathleen. I'm so sorry."

"I don't want to hear that," she said. "I want to know *the truth*."

"Did I sleep with her?" Spence said. He looked at the picture on his computer screen. Did he dare…? No, there was no getting around it. "Yes. Did I lie to you about it? Yes. Am I hugely sorry I did both of those things? More than you can imagine."

"You need help, Spence."

"I probably do."

"No, I'm being serious here," said Cathleen. "You need professional help."

"I'll go see someone if that will make you feel better."

"Do you know what's going through my head right now? I'm sitting here wondering — actually seriously contemplating, Spence — whether or not you are a sociopath. Because I can't think of any other explanation for this. I don't see how you maintain this level of deceit. You had a chance to tell me the truth two days ago and you didn't. Only when confronted with *photographic evidence* are you willing to admit that you slept with this person."

"Jesus, Cathleen, I'm not a sociopath," he said. "I fucked up. I wish I hadn't but I did. I'm sorry."

"You fucked up," she said, flatly.

"I love you. You *know* I love you. She doesn't mean any-thing to me. You can tell she's out of her mind. Who would take a picture like that? She is not a normal person."

Silence on the line. "I love you, Cathleen."

More silence.

"I have to get off the phone now," said Cathleen.

"Can we talk later?" said Spence.

"I don't know." And she hung up.

Spence put the phone back in its cradle and sat down on the couch. Just what exactly was he guilty of? He had dated two women at the same time. More precisely: he had long-distance dated one woman who he genuinely cared about (Cathleen), and occasionally albeit repeatedly slept with another woman who happened to live closer by (Crazy Molly). He never *dated* Crazy Molly. That wasn't the word for it. He would bump into Molly at a party, the possibility of sex would rear its tantalizing head, and Spence would think some drunken blend of the fol-lowing two thoughts: this will be the last time / I'd be an idiot to pass this up. That was his crime. And now he'd been caught.

That all this would happen now Spence found truly unfair, because the last time he slept with Molly was going to be the *last time!* He was finished with all that! The span of time between "orgasm" and "guilt and self-loathing" had grown infinitesimally small! Finally he felt like he was get-ting some clarity, finally he was seeing the path forward, he was picturing a life with Cathleen, sweet Cathleen, settling down, growing up, putting his life into some sort of order. Just last week he had given considerable thought to moving

out to Boulder to be with her. He could start mountain bik-
ing again. Their kids could grow up on skis.

   Instead, what had happened was this. Two days earlier, on
the night of what was to be the *last time,* Molly had, in a round
of dead-of-night postcoital snooping, stumbled upon a card
sent to him by Cathleen (Cathleen was the kind of girl who, at
thirty-six, sent men cards, which could explain why she was
taking all this so hard). The next day, Crazy Molly tracked
Cathleen down and called her up and said something along
the lines of "stay away from my boyfriend," and Cathleen
went berserk. She called Spence, sobbing, hysterical, hurling
accusations left and right. And here he made what might have
been a pivotal mistake: he went with a blanket denial. He said
flat out that none of it had happened, he'd never slept with
her, Crazy Molly was crazy, it was right there in her name, he
loved Cathleen, she was the kind of girl he wanted to marry,
hadn't they talked about having three kids together? If he
had had time to develop a strategy, he might have just as eas-
ily gone with the truth, because, really, he didn't think the
truth was so bad. The truth: Spence believed he was falling
in love with Cathleen, but while he was figuring it out he had
engaged in some typically shitty male behavior, although he
did so entirely devoid of malice and without believing that
it could have any negative impact on their growing relationship. And Cathleen — thirty-six and single and living in Boulder, carrier of felted hand-knit purses and wearer of clunky
mountain-time-zone shoes, whose obsessive love for her two
dogs telegraphed a desperate desire for a family — probably
would have given him a second chance.

   Of course, hindsight is twenty-twenty. He went with the
denial, and Cathleen more or less bought it. She lobbed a few

doozies at him along the lines of "I need some sort of concrete evidence that you are committed to this relationship," which Spence handled with the care of someone charged with disposing of nuclear waste. He bought her a ticket to come to New York for five days so they could discuss his level of commitment. Things appeared to go back to normal.

But then, earlier that day, Crazy Molly had emailed Cathleen a few photographs to bolster her case that she was, in fact, Spence's girlfriend. Including, most notably, a picture of herself lying naked in bed next to him while he was fast asleep. Her arm was outstretched, holding the camera up in the air in the manner of a drunken reveler. His eyes were closed and she was grinning like a maniac. Who takes pictures like that? Crazy people, thought Spence. Still. Tough to explain away.

Crazy Molly was known as Crazy Molly not because she took a lot of psychoactive medication, or even because she'd been institutionalized in college, but because she was a crazy sex girl. She was sort of famous for it. That was the only reason Spence went to bed with her in the first place. Sometimes a man needs some crazy sex. And he knew he could never explain this to Cathleen, Cathleen who was by no means a prude, who liked dirty talk in bed as much as the next girl (maybe more), but who did not understand that what they were having was not in fact crazy sex. The truth was this: Cathleen thought *she* was a crazy sex girl. She thought she and Spence were having wild and crazy sex and she was immensely proud of herself for it. And the idea that she was falling short by an order of magnitude would what? Horrify? Disgust? Perplex her? All of the above.

And now Cathleen was tossing around the word *sociopath*. When exactly did women start using that word in dating situations? Spence wondered. Had Oprah done a show on it or something? Because, lately at least, it seemed like it kept coming up.

———————

Amanda and Mark liked to be in bed by ten, so Holly left after the dishes were done. Married people with early bedtimes annoyed her, as did married people who whispered to each other at parties and married people who went on diets at the same time. And married people who said "We're pregnant." She could probably come up with a few more if she gave it a little thought. She made a quick call from the cab, and, when she pulled up in front of her building fifteen minutes later, Lucas was already there, leaning up against one of the doorposts with his hands in his pockets. It was interesting, Holly found herself thinking, that in all the dinnertime talk of her desperation and loneliness and woebegone divorced-girl patheticness, she had somehow failed once again to mention him to Amanda. This was, given the parameters of her friendship with Amanda and the intricacies of her relationship with Lucas, a fairly major omission. The parameters of her friendship with Amanda were that they told each other everything, and the intricacies with Lucas were, he was twenty-two years old and she was sleeping with him.

Holly had met Lucas six weeks earlier, at a baby shower hosted by her friend Betsy, salsa dancing Betsy, Betsy who was notorious for being incapable, in this city of eight million people, of meeting any man not of the hand-down-the-front-of-the-pants variety. Lucas was Betsy's younger brother, and he lived with his parents in the immense Park Avenue apartment Betsy had commandeered for the shower. At the time, of course, Holly didn't realize that Lucas actually lived there, at home, with his parents. She'd figured he'd just stopped by to help out with the coats.

The night before the baby shower, Holly had had sex for the third time with Steve, a forty-three-year-old real estate agent who was on Lexapro for anxiety and who Amanda had taken to calling "the Texan" because Holly happened to mention that he wore cowboy boots on their first date. Holly resisted calling the Texan "the Texan," because she knew that once a man had a nickname the relationship was doomed. None of her friends ever ended up with a man they'd given a nickname, with the sole exception of Fleur, who eloped with a guy the rest of them knew only as "Coke Can." It was incredibly awkward for all involved. Sadly, the Lexapro meant that the Texan was all hat and no cattle in the bedroom. That's not quite the right metaphor. He had the hat and he had the cattle, but no lasso? Or, he had a hat and a bunch of cattle and a lasso and a branding iron and some chaps, but the dinner bell never rang? Whatever. The man couldn't come. Like most men of this sort, he was quite proud of how long he could last, he thought that this was a real selling point, and that any woman would love to engage in multiple lengthy rounds of inconclusive intercourse which ended with her partner slumped at the foot of the bed with his head in his hands. Holly had broken things off earlier the day of the shower. It's not that she didn't like sex, it's just, she liked for there to be an end in sight. Besides, she knew how this particular story played itself out: you wound up with an irritable, frustrated, hostile man who also happened to be an incipient lunatic. The island of Manhattan was full of them.

Holly had had to leave the shower early, and Betsy's brother—Betsy's *baby* brother—showed her to the guest room to get her coat. He helped her into it, and then he put his hands on her shoulders and turned her around and kissed her on the lips. This sort of thing never happens to me, Holly found herself thinking, midkiss. She hadn't spoken two words to this person, and now they were kissing somewhat furiously in a bedroom full of baby-shower-attendees' coats. Maybe this is the party favor, she thought. Maybe this is how they do things on Park Avenue.

Two days after the shower, her telephone rang.

"I have to kiss you again," a voice said.

"Who is this?" said Holly.

"Lucas. I'm the one who kissed you at the baby shower on Saturday."

"Betsy's brother."

"Yes," said Lucas. "Can I come over?"

"I don't think so," said Holly.

"I just want to kiss you."

"Well." She thought about the Texan and his Lexapro penis. "I guess that would be all right." She gave him her address.

"Great. I'll be right over."

"Lucas?"

"Yeah?"

"I just ran out of toilet paper," said Holly.

"Okay…?"

"Can you pick up some on your way over?"

Afterwards, lying in a tangle of sheets, Holly had turned to him and said, "Can I ask you something?"

"Sure."

"How old are you?"

"Twenty-three."

"You're twenty-three?" said Holly. Her eyes wanted to go wide but she kept them under control.

"I'm," he reached over and grabbed a pillow and scrunched it up behind his head, "almost twenty-three."

"Oh my god. You're twenty-two?"

"Technically. But my birthday is coming up. Why?" said Lucas. "How old are you?"

"Old," said Holly. "Old enough to be your mother, if we lived in biblical times or, you know, Appalachia."

"You're not old."

"You have to promise me one thing," said Holly. "Promise me you won't tell your sister we slept together."

"I don't tell Betsy about my personal life."

"Good. You know what? Don't tell anybody. Let's just keep this our little secret," said Holly. "And now I even sound like a child molester."

"That's straight out of the handbook."

"Page eleven," said Holly. "Right after the part where I lure you into the back of my van with a box of kittens."

Now it was six weeks later, and Holly and Lucas had fallen into something of a routine. On nights when Lucas went out with his friends, he would, more often than not, call Holly at ten or eleven and once even at one, and she would usually, but not always, invite him over. Occasionally — twice, actually, not including the night of Amanda-and-Mark — Holly would call him. It was an arrangement. It was no strings attached. It was what Holly wanted.

"Why are we watching this?" said Holly, as she made her way back from the kitchen with a glass of ice water. Lucas was in bed, propped up against the headboard with the remote control in his hand, tuned in to the local news.

"I want to see the weather," he said.

"You can go check it on my computer."

"It's coming right up."

"That's what they always say," said Holly. She crawled back into bed next to him. "They want us to sit here and watch the report on bacteria in hot-dog-vendor water so they say it's coming right up, but really they just move it around to different parts of the broadcast. If I were in charge, some nights I would skip it altogether. Make people crazy."

A woman was raped on her way to work in Jamaica, Queens, this morning. At seven o'clock this morning, DeeDee Reynolds kissed her three children good-bye and headed off to Mount Sinai Hospital where she worked as a nurse's aide. Moments after closing her front door, she was brutally attacked…

"Who is raping at seven a.m.?" said Holly.

"What do you mean?" said Lucas.

"I mean, who's in the mood to rape another person at that time of day?" said Holly. "I can barely put my contact lenses in."

"Whoever he is, he's got a lot of get-up-and-go," said Lucas.

"If only he could channel that into something other than raping people," said Holly.

"You're the perfect woman, you know that?"

"I do," said Holly. "And thank you."

Lucas muted the TV.

"I got a call today from this friend of mine who lives in Austin," he said. "He wants me to go out there and help with this club he's starting. Live music, drinks, local bands, but also the South by Southwest stuff. It sounds like it would be fun, and a good opportunity. His dad has an in with someone and thinks we could get a liquor license without too much trouble."

"You should do it."

"Come with me."

"Move to Austin with you? You're kidding, right?"

"I'm serious," said Lucas. "I think I'm falling in love with you."

"No, you're not. Trust me. Don't even say things like that."

"Why not? It's true. I think you're amazing."

"Hold this," Holly said. She handed him her glass of water and then sat up, folding her legs under herself Indian style. "Did you know they don't let kids say 'Indian style' anymore? At my nephew's school they call it 'crisscross-applesauce.' The teacher says, 'Everybody get in a circle and sit down crisscross-applesauce.'"

Lucas just looked at her.

"Oh my god," Holly said. "Please don't tell me you grew up saying 'crisscross-applesauce.'"

"I'm not eight."

"Right. Good. So." She picked up a pillow and clutched it to her stomach. "Ordinarily, I am the person who falls in love quickly and somewhat inappropriately and then goes on to destroy what is a good thing. That's always been my style. So, you know: I get it. And I feel right now the way I imagine all those guys felt with me. And I have to say, for the first time in my life, I feel something approaching compassion for them." She took a breath. "I just got divorced, you're only twenty-two, I'm not ready for anything serious, and neither are you."

"Okay."

"We should be sensible and just enjoy this for what it is, because it's great, you know, it's fun and casual, and we shouldn't start loading it down with expectations and, you know, stuff like that."

"Yeah. Fine."

"That's all you have to say?"

"What else is there to say?" He rolled over and grabbed his Corona from the nightstand.

Holly looked at him. He did seem fine.

"What?" said Lucas.

"I don't know." She got up and headed for the bathroom. "Whenever I've been on the other end of this conversation, I've always had a lot more to say."

the mighty moppets

Y ou look really gay in that shirt."

"Thank you," said Leonard. He smoothed his hand slowly down his chest. "It was very expensive."

"Is it my imagination," Holly said, "or are you getting gayer and gayer?"

It was not Holly's imagination. Leonard had been, for a long time, a very straight-seeming gay man, but over the past several months, due to a confluence of circumstances and fashion choices, he had been appearing progressively gayer. It was probably, primarily, mostly, the chemical hair straightening. Leonard had spent four hundred dollars to get his hair straightened with the new Brazilian hair-straightening chemical, and now it clung to his head like a wet washcloth and then spiked out at the ends down at the top of his neck, which was huge, due to the steroids he got from a pharmacist who ran an underground steroid ring out of his fourth-floor walk-up on Christopher Street. Leonard had found out about it at his gym.

Leonard was Holly's former, and only recently again current, writing partner. They had worked as a successful sitcom writing team for five years and then they split up so Holly could write her book. They had also slept together, years ago, but now they were like brother and sister. They were, truth be told, like a brother and sister who had slept together. Holly felt she had a claim on Leonard that went beyond the mere prerogatives of friendship, and Leonard felt the kind of queasy and confused tenderness that one would imagine a brother might feel after having had sex with his sister, twice, a very long time ago.

"Can you focus?" said Holly.

"I feel too good to focus."

"Why don't you take one of your pills?"

"I already took one."

Holly looked at him. He was stretched out on the couch and yet still somehow managing to rock his body slowly back and forth. "You swallowed it or you snorted it?"

"I ingested it."

"Through your nose or through your mouth?"

"—"

"Leonard. It's not even noon."

"I was going to swallow it. I was all prepared to swallow it, but then you went to the bathroom and I accidentally pulverized it with your Palm Beach snow globe and inhaled it and now I feel *so good*. Which makes it hard for me to consider it a mistake."

"Your doctor belongs in prison."

"Doctors," Leonard corrected her. "My doctors belong in prison."

Holly put her head in her hands. "I don't want to work this weekend, Leonard. We have to pitch on Monday and we don't have anything and now you're high as a kite."

"I can still work. Look at me: I'm working. I'm focused." Leonard sat up and put his hands on his knees like a benched football player who wants to be put back into the game. "Just tell me what we're doing. What crappy show is this we're writing for again?"

The show was called *The Mighty Moppets,* and it was an embarrassing piece of crap. It was about a junior high school girls' basketball team, and it aired at three thirty in the afternoon, on Nickelodeon. What was next? Writing for a game show? The show was shot in Toronto to take advantage of Canada's tax breaks, but the writers worked in New York so the network could keep a closer eye on them. The staff was composed of writers who were on their way up, writers who were on their way down, and Canadians. Leonard and Holly were on their way down.

"Leonard, you have to care about this script," Holly said. "You have to care about this job. You have to come in here in the morning, on time, sober, with your ADD medication *still in tablet form,* and you have to forget that you've written for better shows and funnier actors and have been paid a lot more money, you have to put your *whole heart* into this job, or we're going to get fired."

Leonard just sat there.

"Do you hear me?" Holly said. "We're going to lose this job. And our career is going to be over, Leonard. This is the bottom rung."

Leonard was still silent.

"What."

Leonard, calmly and with zero affect, said, "The day that I care about this job, the day I wake up in the morning and realize that I care the tiniest shred about this shitty stupid tween cable show whose target audience is an eight-year-old girl who wants to buy My Little Pony, is the day I finally kill myself."

"Leonard."

"I can't care about this job, Holly. It will damage me."

Holly sighed. "Okay. But you have to *act* like you care."

He thought about it. "I will try to act like a person who is pretending to care."

That was the trouble with the ADD medication. It was getting harder and harder for Leonard to refrain from grinding up the pills and snorting them. The pill, when taken as directed, was effective in keeping him focused on the task at hand. He would take one before he played a video game, and then he could play for hours, hours of complete absorption, the absorption of a carefree twelve-year-old boy playing a video game while hopped up on Adderall. It was as close to a pure and clean pleasure as Leonard got. He felt, while doing that, the way he supposed a normal person felt while watching the sun set over the ocean after a six-mile run. The problem was that the same pill, when pulverized with the back of a spoon or a paperweight or a bottle of Grey Goose and then snorted, was better. Different, and better, like watching the sunset over the ocean while high on cocaine. That's where things got tricky.

Leonard's various addictions had escalated in the months he'd been in New York. Two things about Los Angeles conspired to engender an ounce of moderation. First of all, it was a company town. Wherever Leonard went, he saw people he knew, agents he'd like to represent him, writers he'd like to work with, and the part of him that was still ambitious and felt what was left of his career slipping through his fingers knew it was best to avoid being flat-out crazy drunk and high all the time. And second, there was the driving. Leonard owned a 1.3 million dollar house on Mulholland Drive, and the bars he liked to frequent were clustered along Santa Monica Boulevard in West Hollywood, and the only way to get from one location to the other was via Laurel Canyon, two narrow lanes of twists and turns and the occasional treacherous drop through the dry brush and eucalyptus trees into some music producer's black-bottom swimming pool. Oh, Leonard could drive drunk. He had perfected a technique which involved closing his right eye and hunching down in his seat so he could line up the double yellow paint with the left edge of his windshield and the hood ornament of his Mercedes. But the move to New York had meant he didn't have to worry about that anymore, he could drink until he was barely sentient, he could pass out in taxis, he could stumble from curb to front door, front door to elevator, elevator to bed, all in what a reasonable person would consider a state of blackout intoxication. Leonard didn't consider it a blackout, because, well, he got from the bar to his bed, did he not? That didn't happen by magic.

By six o'clock, they had something. Not much, not enough, but something. Leonard was thinking quite seriously about rewarding himself with another ADD pill, but he couldn't figure out how to snort it without Holly registering the dramatic spike in his mood. He couldn't tell if he worked better high or if it was just that, when he was high, he didn't mind working.

"This woman will not stop emailing me," said Holly.

"Spence's girlfriend, you mean?"

"Seriously, I think she might have some sort of problem."

"Did you call her?"

"I did."

"And?"

Holly sighed and shook her head slowly. "That poor, poor, sad, poor girl."

"What did he do to her?"

"I have to give you the whole story."

"I would expect no less," said Leonard.

Holly put her feet up on her desk and crossed her ankles and rested her chin on top of her fingertips in a way that made Leonard think she would have made a good judge, or probation officer, or executioner. "Okay, so, her name is Cathleen," Holly began, "and she lives in Boulder, and she met Spence last summer on a bike trip. They start long-distance dating after the trip, and pretty soon they fall madly in love. He's flying to Colorado every couple of weeks, he's talking about marriage and kids, he's like a dream come true. She thinks they're going to get engaged at any moment. The only real question up in the air is will she move to New York or will Spence move to Boulder. Then, one day, she gets a call out of the blue from this other woman who says that she's been dating Spence since September and that *they're* in love and she wants Cathleen to stay away from her boyfriend. Cathleen can't even believe this is happening. She calls up Spence and confronts him, and he denies everything. He says flat out none of it ever happened, there's not one shred of truth in it, he swears up and down and then up again. He claims this other girl is crazy, and he goes on and on about how much he loves Cathleen. The next day the girl emails Cathleen pictures of her in Spence's apartment, including what I gather was a naked although not pornographic picture of the two of them in bed."

"Nice."

"And she read my book. Now she wants my opinion."

"About Spence?"

Holly nodded. "She's thinks I'm an expert on him or something, which, let's face it," Holly smiled and shrugged a self-deprecating shrug, "I kind of am. The funny part is, she's been using my book as evidence against him, like it's proof he's a serial cheater, but for all his faults, Spence never cheated on me."

"I thought he did," said Leonard.

"No," said Holly. "Never. I just put that in so the book would have a plot. I told her that last night, and she sounded almost disappointed. But she still wants my advice."

"About what?"

"Whether to give it another try, I guess. And the whole time she's telling me this, I'm thinking, why would she even consider him after this? Honestly. Is it *that* bad out there?"

"You tell me."

"I'm not out there," said Holly. "I'm either in here with you or at home having amazing sex with my twenty-two-year-old."

"—"

"What," said Holly.

"Don't say it's amazing sex," said Leonard. "Don't say that to people."

"Why not?"

"Because whenever a woman your age is dating a ridiculously young guy, she always claims that the sex is amazing."

"Yeah? So?"

"It sounds pathetic."

Holly scrunched up her nose. "It does?"

"Trust me on this one."

"Okay. I'll stop," Holly said. "God knows I'm pathetic enough without having to go around advertising the fact." She took her feet off the desk and turned back to her computer screen. She scrolled to the end of the scene they'd been working on and tried to figure out where they'd left off. "Let's finish this so we can go see a movie tonight."

"No movies," said Leonard. "It's Friday. I can't go to the movies on a Friday night."

"How come?"

"It makes me nervous. All those people sitting so close to me."

"Come on."

"I'm serious. I'll have a panic attack."

"Sitting in a crowded movie theater freaks you out, but you have no problem blowing a perfect stranger in a public restroom," said Holly. "Somehow, that doesn't cause you any anxiety."

"I have a complicated psyche."

Leonard did, in fact, have a complicated psyche. He found himself reflecting on this later, from the comfort and relative safety of his bed, at three o'clock in the morning. He was wide awake. He had sobered up enough to be reminded why he did not like to be sober. Certainly not at night, in the dark, by himself. He had a pill for this condition, of course, but he decided not to take it. He had suffered from insomnia all of his life. He viewed it as a fundamental part of his personality, and he didn't think it was wise to medicate it entirely out of existence.

He stared up at the ceiling and wondered, *Where did all my money go?*

This was Leonard's insomnia game. Remembering how rich he had been and trying to figure out exactly what the hell had happened. Just how rich had he been at his richest? At the end of the first quarter of the year 2001, he had a net worth of 2.3 million dollars and an income of 1.5 million a year. His business manager—who in true Hollywood fashion charged fifty thousand dollars a year to open Leonard's mail and pay his bills and prepare his tax returns and invest his money in index funds—would send him an elaborate financial statement every quarter, with Leonard's net worth outlined in a red box in the lower right-hand corner of the last page, which is why he knew the figure with such precision. Two point three million dollars. What the hell had happened to it?

Part of the problem was that his salary had escalated so quickly that he never really thought of it as real. Money is energy and you have to let it flow. You don't let it stagnate in the bank, you let it flow, you let it pass through your hands and out into the world, and it will keep coming back to you. Perhaps not if you let it flow to drug dealers. That might have been the problem with Leonard's adherence to this model of New Age abundance thinking.

It wasn't all drugs, of course. He had given some to charity. Yes, charity. AIDS, poor people, sea turtles. He'd felt so good about himself, writing out those checks. After he signed his second overall deal, he bought part of a rain forest in Uganda and turned it into a nature preserve. Fifty acres of virgin tropical rain forest! Bought by him to be preserved, untouched, in perpetuity! Of course, in his darkest moments, Leonard had given considerable thought to selling it back. Who was he to say that the Africans couldn't destroy their corner of the earth? Hadn't we had free rein to ravage ours? Isn't that what the industrial revolution was all about? Wasn't there something he had read about how the Third World would never be able to catch up if they weren't allowed to exploit their resources to the fullest? Hell, the land might have even appreciated! He had gone so far as to place a call to his business manager a few weeks earlier in order to broach the subject.

"You can't sell it," Lou had told him. "You don't own it."

"I thought I bought it."

"You did buy it. You bought it and you gave it to the Nature Conservancy. It's theirs now."

"Shit."

"Yeah, right, shit. You should have listened to me."

So that money was gone for good. They had given him a plaque with a picture of a duck on it. It had become difficult for him to walk around his house without battling intense feelings of shame, brought on whenever his glance happened to fall on things like the duck plaque or his Dualit toaster, which looked like an Airstream trailer parked on his kitchen counter. The toaster was only four hundred dollars, but a reproach nonetheless, ever since Holly informed him that a toaster is supposed to cost twenty bucks. He also had a lot of custom-made furniture, not to be confused with antiques, which retain some resale value. Part of the problem with his "net worth" was it included things like paintings and furniture and the twenty-thousand-dollar Cartier watch he had bought for a guy named Digger, who was gone now, along with the watch and piles of cash that Digger had managed to alchemize into cocaine and Prada. So Leonard's net worth had been a soft number. Lou had tried to explain it to him. There were "hard" numbers and there were "soft" numbers.

The fifty thousand dollars he paid Lou was apparently a "hard" number. His investments turned out to be soft numbers, due to the market downturn of the early years of the Bush administration, which coincided with his sudden need for liquidity. Damn that Bush! His income turned out to be an exceedingly soft number, in that it went down to zero in the second quarter of 2001 when he decided he didn't want to be a sitcom writer any longer.

Which is what, when it came down to it, had really happened to Leonard's money. *The movie.* He sat up. He switched on the light beside his bed, swallowed a Klonopin, and turned on the TV.

the ancient principle
of *wu-wei*

The restaurant Amanda had suggested for Wednesday's lunch was that horrible specimen, a trendy diner, famous for being hateful, sticky, crowded, and loud, and yet appealing to models. It had an improbably extensive menu, six pages of filmy yellow laminate covered with thick, close-set black print, with lists and lists of all that was on offer, occasionally broken up by inflexible parameters on what time of day each dish could and could not be ordered, whether it was available on the weekends only, or on Tuesdays after four p.m. but not past eleven. It was the kind of menu that, Holly always found herself thinking, brought to mind a little game called "Things you shouldn't order at a diner." Steak Tartare. Ceviche de Pescado. Flounder Kiev.

"I'm here," Holly said as she slid into the booth.

"Thanks for coming," said Amanda.

"I hate this place."

"I know you do. I'm sorry. I couldn't think of where else to meet."

"I still don't know what I'm doing here."

"You're here to have lunch with me and maybe meet a friend of mine if he shows up, which he may not," said Amanda. "Who knows? Maybe you guys will hit it off."

"Explain this to me again," said Holly. "What are you doing with this guy exactly? I thought you and Mark were happy."

"We are happy," said Amanda. "I don't know. You know I love Mark."

"Then I really don't understand this."

"A person doesn't always need to have a big master plan."

"A person doesn't," said Holly. "But you generally have one, and I'm just trying to figure out what it is."

"Can we not talk about it?" said Amanda. "I don't want to think about it right now."

"Fine."

"I don't want to think about anything. Let's try to be in the moment."

"Right. Great," said Holly. She opened her menu and scanned it. *Shellfish Stew Provencale, available on Sundays only, after 1 p.m. only.* "So, how is your sweet baby boy who loves his father and doesn't want to see him only on alternating weekends doing?"

Amanda looked at her.

"What? That's what was happening in this moment. That's what came up for me. I was trying to honor it."

Amanda's face lit up. "Oooh. There he is."

She waved to a guy standing over by the register. He was handsome but scruffy-looking, with short brown hair that stuck up out of his scalp at what Holly deemed to be highly improbable angles, suggestive of hair products and blow-dryers rather than a pillow and mere chance. He walked towards them and slid into the booth next to Amanda.

"Sorry I'm late."

"No, no, it's fine. We just got here. This is my friend Holly," said Amanda. "Holly, this is Jack."

"Nice to meet you," said Jack.

"Nice to meet you, too."

"Oh, before I forget." Jack reached into his messenger bag and pulled out a CD case and handed it to Amanda. "I made you a CD with some of that music we were talking about, and I put on a few other things I thought you might like."

"Thanks," said Amanda.

"You don't have to like it," he said.

"I'm sure I'll love it."

Holly caught Amanda's eye and raised her right eyebrow. Not everyone could do this, isolate a single brow, and at times like this it came in handy.

"I don't know if I told you," Amanda said to Jack, "but Holly is a novelist."

"Good for you."

"No, really, she is," said Amanda. "Her book came out last spring."

"It was published?" said Jack. He looked at Holly with a little more interest. "Would I have heard of it?"

"I don't know," said Holly.

"What was it called?"

Holly felt the stab of mortification she felt each time she had to say the title of her book out loud, a title dreamed up by a genius in the marketing department whose plan, apparently, was to strip Holly of any shred of literary credibility right out of the gate.

"*Hello, Mr. Heartache,*" said Holly.

"Ah," said Jack, nodding his head knowingly. "I see. Was it one of those girl novels? What do they call it, chick lit?"

"It was," said Holly. She smiled a big smile. "I wrote the entire thing in lipstick, actually."

"Holly doesn't like it when people call her book chick lit," Amanda told Jack.

"Hey, I love those things," said Jack. "I'm completely serious. Just give me a book with some shoe shopping and a few bad dates, throw in a nanny, maybe a comical mishap with a bottle of self-tanner, and I can't put it down. I have no idea why. It's possible I have a vagina tucked away somewhere I haven't noticed."

"Holly's book is really good," said Amanda. "It's really, you know, not about shoes or anything like that."

"Just answer one question," Jack said to Holly. "Does she get the guy in the end?"

Holly blinked and paused. "Well, I suppose the heroine gets 'a' guy in the end. In a way. But it wasn't really about 'getting a guy—'"

Jack held up his hand and said, "Say no more."

The waiter returned with three cups of coffee and put them on the table with such clatter and clank, with such sloshing and saucer spillage, he might as well have said, "Given half a chance, I would kill you and your families."

"So, um. How's work?" Amanda asked Jack.

"It's fine."

"Are things still weird with your new boss?"

"A little, but I'm taking a new approach. I'm trying to just let it happen to me," said Jack. "Practice a little *wu-wei*."

"Ah yes," said Amanda. "The ancient principle of *wu-wei*: force nothing."

"What does that mean?" said Holly.

"Honestly, I'm not really sure," said Amanda. "Explain it again, Jack."

"If you don't force anything, if you follow your natural

tendencies, you'll be in harmony with the Tao and everything will unfold as it should. It's feeling and doing what is natural and feels right to you."

"So, what, you just do whatever you want and whatever happens, happens? This is your philosophy of life?" said Holly. "Interesting."

"What," said Jack.

"That's the philosophy of my two-year-old nephew, too. You guys should start your own sect."

"Why? What's your philosophy of life?"

"Off the top of my head?" said Holly. "How about this: do the right thing."

"Don't mind Holly," Amanda said to Jack. "She's lived in Manhattan for fifteen years but she's still got a shred of Bible beater in her."

"How is that being a Bible beater?" said Holly.

"Trust me," said Amanda.

Holly did still have a shred of Bible beater in her. She couldn't help it. She was raised to be one, the way some girls are raised to be southern belles or Olympic gymnasts. It had been just as rigorous, too, the training, and just as hard to shake. She'd spent the bulk of her adult life trying to shake it, and for the most part she had succeeded. She'd done such a good job, in fact, that several of the Christians who knew her back when she was still one of them were now convinced that she was going to end up spending eternity in hell. Of course, these particular people thought just about everybody was going to end up in hell, so Holly tried not to take it too personally, but when your own mother starts sending you letters to that effect, urging you to come back to the bosom of Jesus before it's too late, well — mission accomplished.

"What," said Holly, "are we supposed to be so sophisticated that there is no longer such a thing as right and wrong?"

"I guess the question is, whose definition are you going to use for what is right and what is wrong?" said Jack. "Because actually, one way of looking at things is that being in the Tao is 'right,' even if it is in conflict with conventional morality."

"Jack is a big Buddhist," Amanda said.

"No, I'm not."

"Really? I thought that's what you were," said Amanda. She looked genuinely perplexed.

"Well, I am a Buddhist, but I don't like to call myself one," he said. "People have all sorts of ideas about it, and preconceptions, and so I don't like to go around announcing to people, 'I'm a Buddhist.'"

"I don't get it," said Holly. "I mean, I don't care if you're a Buddhist or you're not a Buddhist, but don't, like, be a big Buddhist and then refuse to call yourself one."

Jack sat back and folded his arms across his chest. "I'm not even sure I know what a 'big Buddhist' is."

"Is he for real?" Holly said to Amanda. She turned to Jack. "I mean it, are you for real? Even if you're only sort of a halfway Buddhist, you should know what being a big Buddhist is."

"I think, it's possible, that language is failing us here," said Jack.

"Language isn't failing *me*," said Holly. "I'm fine with language. I'm just trying to figure this out."

"Let's talk about something else," said Amanda. "Seriously. What are you guys going to have?"

"I think I'm going to get a cheeseburger," said Jack.

Holly took a deep, deliberate breath and then closed her

menu. "Yeah, well, you know what? I screwed up. I'm supposed to be someplace, like," she looked at her watch and scooched out of the booth, "now."

"Don't go," said Amanda.

"No. I'm sorry, I have to. But it was great to meet you, Jack, truly, it was a treat and I hope we get a chance to do this again some time."

"Nice to meet you."

"Call me," Holly said to Amanda.

———————

It should perhaps be noted that this was not Amanda's first brush with infidelity. A few months after Jacob was born, she started strolling him over to a community garden each afternoon as a way to kill a few of the hours that stretched interminably between lunch and dinner. That was one of the things, Amanda found, that nobody really adequately conveyed to you about having a baby: how much of it was just coming up with ever-new ways to kill time. The garden was filled with slow-moving nannies, old women in cardigan sweaters, office workers with sandwiches, and after a few weeks Amanda had a nodding familiarity with a few of the regulars, including a man who turned out to be a full-time stay-at-home dad. His name was Noel, and he wore a beat-up Red Sox hat and a khaki photographer's vest and wire-rim glasses. He filled the pockets in the vest with pacifiers and Cheerios, Handi Wipes and Goldfish crackers. The first time Amanda spoke to him, it was to compliment him on this system, after he managed to come up with a flex Elmo Band-Aid for a stranger's sobbing three-year-old. There followed a friendly conversation about the seemingly endless profusion of stuff these tiny people needed to have on hand at all times, the hours spent digging around in diaper bags, trying to remember where everything was stashed. The next day he was there again, and they ended up on the same bench, faces turned towards the bright afternoon sun. They talked about a film they'd both seen on Showtime the night before which had won the Prix du Jury at Cannes. "It is impossible," Noel had pronounced, "to bore the French."

Over the next few weeks, Amanda and Noel settled into something of a routine. They would sit on a bench and talk, about books they liked, movies they wanted to see, things going on in the neighborhood. It was nice, they both agreed, to talk to another full-time parent who didn't feel the need to drone on endlessly about their kid. Over time, Amanda pieced together what she came to think of as his story. He had worked in reinsurance, which had something to do with selling insurance to insurance companies, one of those soul-sucking corporate jobs that, it sounded to Amanda at least, made an extra effort to be meaningless, and he was using the career time-out provided by his daughter's infancy to find himself. His wife was a managing director at HSBC who worked fourteen-hour days and flew to Hong Kong once a month and FedExed her breast milk home in special temperature-controlled containers she bought from the monkey keeper at the Bronx Zoo. While Noel never laid it out quite so baldly, Amanda got the impression that his wife's job was so much more impressive than his that, at some point, it was less embarrassing for everyone for him to just quit.

Amanda told Mark about Noel over dinner one night early on. Now, Mark was one of those men whose view on full-time child care was summed up in the phrase "I could never do it." He would say this at dinner parties or when out with Amanda's parents, ostensibly as a compliment to Amanda—She's so great! She *can* do it!—but it only managed to convey that he felt the endless, mindless repetition of hands-on parenthood was a job best suited to a person who had a candy corn where their brain was supposed to be. Mark was fascinated by Amanda's Park Boyfriend, as he took to calling Noel, and he liked to amuse himself when he came home from the office by asking her questions about him, about his pathetic career prospects, and how much more money his wife made than he did. How his "novel" was coming along.

It was one of those perfect New York October afternoons, when the explosion of oranges and yellows against the bright blue sky makes you feel like your life is passing through your fingers, that you've felt this autumn-feeling before and you'll probably get to feel it again, but one day you won't anymore, because you'll be dead. Amanda and Noel were on the bench again, talking about sushi places, and at some point he reached over and brushed a stray hair off of her face and touched her cheek with the back of his finger—purposefully, Amanda later decided—and a charge as sure as an electrical spark passed between them. Her entire body flushed, and she froze like a deer caught in the headlights. So this is chemistry, she remembered thinking. He looked her in the eye, a look that had only one possible meaning. She looked back.

Amanda pushed the stroller home in a daze. At six thirty, she shot a syringe full of Children's Benadryl into Jacob's mouth and put him down without so much as a bath or a good-night story. She left a note on the kitchen counter for Mark that said she wasn't feeling well, and could he please take care of his own dinner. Then she crawled into bed and turned out the lights. She didn't want to pick up toys or do the dishes or talk to her mother on the phone. She was still on fire. She played the moment on the bench through her mind over and over again, the feel of Noel's finger on her cheek, the heat that rose between them, the look in his eyes. He had made her an offer, as clearly as if he said the words out loud. All she had to do was accept. She imagined feeling his hands on her body and being kissed, really kissed. All she wanted, she told herself, was to be kissed. She decided she'd shave her legs before she went to the park the next afternoon. *Just in case.* At midnight, Mark crawled into bed beside her and she pretended to be asleep. By four a.m., she had written all the way to the end of the story, the guilt, the irreparable harm she would do to her marriage, to her son, to Noel's daughter, the lives ruined, the trust destroyed, where she would live, what she would do, the sad desperate life of a single mother.

Amanda never took Jacob to that garden again. It took several weeks, but her fever eventually faded, and she comforted herself with the knowledge that she had preserved her life as she knew it. She would see Mark plant a kiss on the top of Jacob's bald head before he left for work and feel her body flooded with relief. But she couldn't help thinking, after her life returned to normal, once the dailiness reasserted its hold, that maybe it wouldn't have done any harm to go a little further, maybe it wouldn't have been so bad to fly a little closer to the flame.

the platonic ideal
of amazingness

Betsy Silverstein was only half Jewish, but with Betsy, half was plenty. She was at a party she didn't want to be at, in a room full of people she didn't want to meet, given by a person she didn't know. It was the kind of party that made you want to kill yourself. At least, it made Betsy want to kill herself. Everybody else seemed to be having a good time. She tried to remember what her therapist told her to do in situations like this. *Don't compare your insides to other people's outsides.* Which was difficult, because that's exactly what Betsy most liked to do.

She stood over by the bookshelves and pretended to be interested in them. Her eyes took in the titles but her brain was humming along a different track, trying to make sense of the scene she found herself in. The first thing you noticed was the light, a garish pink haze which came from the red fluorescent bulbs that outlined the ceiling. It had the disorienting effect of making you feel drunk, or high, even if you were neither. And not in a good way, Betsy thought. In a way that makes you feel lost and crazy and alone. The dining room table was made out of, what, pressed tin? Something very shiny, anyway, and instead of chairs, there were six of those big rubber balls you find at the gym, each perched on a small silver stand. She was drinking vodka out of a juice glass that looked like it belonged in her grandmother's house. It was short and squat, and it had gold filigree that was rubbed out and fading. All of this was calculated: the fluorescent lights and the white carpet, the exercise balls and the flea market glasses, the hay bale wrapped in plastic that served as an otto-man, the old tire swing dangling from the sixteen-foot ceil-ing in the hallway—it was all calculated to hit just the right note of whimsy. We are stylish and quirky and original and we don't take ourselves too seriously.

Betsy looked down at her feet and grimaced. Everybody had to take off their shoes in order to protect the white carpet from the encroaching grime of the city. If you didn't want to take your shoes off, you had to put on white flannel carpet-protecting booties provided by the hostess. The booties looked like lunch sacks with drawstrings around the top. Betsy had opted for them because she needed her heels so her butt would look better and her breasts would stick out. But, stand-ing there, discreetly surveying the room, she had to admit it might have been a mistake. The women had split about sixty-forty in favor of the booties, and the ones in the booties all looked ridiculous. The only woman who looked good was the hostess herself, who wore tiny perfect four-inch party heels that Betsy overheard her claim were "indoor shoes." Betsy felt like throwing something at her.

A familiar face loomed on the horizon. Spence Samuelson. Somebody! He ambled, sock-footed, over to Betsy and kissed her on the cheek.

"Hey, sweetheart. You look amazing," said Spence.

Betsy did look amazing. That was the word for it. To be even more precise, Betsy looked twenty-eight, and the fact that she was thirty-seven made that feat amazing. Betsy had been looking twenty-eight ever since she was twenty-four, although it was getting increasingly difficult of late, more and more extraordinary and astounding things needed to be done to her to keep it that way. Still, at this particular moment in her life, Betsy had achieved a sort of Platonic ideal of amazingness; she was at the pinnacle of her amazingness. At the pinnacle, but perhaps teetering.

"Are we supposed to be developing photographs in here?" said Spence.

"Isn't this horrible?" said Betsy.

"Is it just me, or do you find it strange that this woman is raising a toddler under fluorescent red light?"

"She's got to have lamps somewhere."

"Find one," said Spence.

There was not a lamp in sight. It was difficult to imagine that anybody actually lived in this apartment, let alone a woman with a small child. It was one of those strange urban existences where real life is confined to a smaller and smaller area, in this case, a dank windowless closet-slash-office just off the long hallway which was crammed to overflowing with the detritus of ordinary living. Betsy discovered it while she was looking for the bathroom. It was like opening a door into a parallel universe, a universe where finger paintings were Scotch taped to the walls, where calendars and eyeglass cases and magazines and telephone books and alphabet magnets and memo boards actually existed.

"How are you?" asked Spence.

"I'm good," said Betsy. She flashed a bright smile.

"How's your little brother?"

"Lucas? Lucas is good," said Betsy. "I think he's having a

torrid affair with someone, but in that twenty-two-year-old way."

"What about you? Who are you sleeping with these days?"

"Nobody."

"I don't believe you."

"Believe me," she said, in a tone of voice that was meant to be believed. Betsy hadn't had sex, actual sex-sex, full sex, in two hundred and fifty-three days. She decided on her thirty-seventh birthday that she wouldn't sleep with anyone unless it was in the context of a committed relationship which had some sort of future, and she was only gradually coming to the realization of what happens when a woman her age makes a decision like that: she never has sex ever again.

"How is that possible?" said Spence. "We've got to find you someone."

"Please. I have no pride left."

"Let me think," said Spence.

"I'm willing to go up to sixty," said Betsy. "Sixty-five if he's spry."

"I've got to know somebody."

"What about your friend Ed?" Ed had been Spence's roommate at Brown. He was in the middle of a divorce, no kids, and Betsy figured she could get in on the ground floor.

"I actually mentioned you to him."

"You did?"

"Uh-huh."

"What did he say?"

"Nothing, really."

Betsy looked at his face. Even in the dim haze of the pink fluorescence, she could tell that something was up.

"Shit," said Spence.

"Tell me."

"There's nothing to tell. The guy's a creep."

"What did he say? I really want to know. Honestly."

"I don't know if I should tell you this."

"Tell me," said Betsy. "Trust me. *Tell me.*"

Spence searched her face. She looked like she really wanted to know. "Okay, first of all, you should know that this is complete bullshit and he has no idea what he's talking about, but he told me he doesn't want to be fixed up with you because he still wants to be able to have kids."

Spots started dancing before Betsy's eyes.

"And I told him he was being an idiot, *of course* you can still have kids. You know that! The man is an idiot and has no idea what he's talking about. I have an older sister; I know about this stuff. We had a big fight over it. Seriously. I'm not even sure we're friends anymore. You don't want to go out with that guy anyway. Trust me. We'll find you someone a million times better. What about that guy over there?" He motioned towards a redheaded guy in a suit standing by the Mallomar pyramid.

"Who is he?"

"I have no idea. But I'll go meet him and I'll talk to him and I'll deliver him to you on a silver tray."

"Thanks, but I don't think so."

"He could be your husband. You probably ought to meet him."

"I'm sure," said Betsy. Her head was spinning and her butt was starting to sweat. "I was about to head out anyway."

"I fucked up, right?" said Spence. "Shit. I shouldn't have told you that. I've had five vodka tonics. The guy is an idiot. He doesn't know anything about it. Look at you. You look amazing."

Betsy just smiled.

"And you're sweet and funny and smart. Everybody loves you," said Spence. "*I* love you. Seriously, I think the stars are aligning. My girlfriend from Colorado just dumped me. Come home with me. Heal my broken heart."

"I'm fine. Really."

"You sure?"

"I promise," she said.

"Well, kiss me, beautiful," he said. Betsy offered her cheek. He gave her a real cheek kiss, a kind and lippy one, and held her body hard against his in a way that conveyed both tenderness and pity. She could feel his eyes on her as she walked across the room, which she did with as much dignity as a person wearing three-inch heels encased in floppy white flannel protective booties could muster.

How had this happened to her? Betsy thought for the millionth time, as her cab sped through the rain, up Madison Avenue, making every light. She was starting to hyperventilate. She bent over and put her head between her knees and tried to breathe through her nose. The cab seat smelled revolting. Like a smelling salt, it brought sudden clarity. She was thirty-seven years old, utterly alone, and a man whose wife just dumped him, a man who was *her age exactly,* was refusing to go on a date with her because he wanted to be able to have kids someday. And it wasn't just that. Earlier that day, Betsy had had lunch with Nathan, one of her ex-boyfriends. Nathan had done his part to ruin her life — he had gone on to marry Gail, the woman he started seeing (he claimed) right after (but in truth, two weeks before) he and Betsy broke up — but

Betsy still liked him, and they met for long, flirty, semi-inappropriate lunches every six months or so. She was sitting in a dark booth sipping a glass of red wine when Nathan walked in with an infant strapped to his torso in one of those dopey quilted baby slings. Is he trying to make me want to kill myself? Betsy thought. Instead of two hours of suggestive reminiscing, she had to sit there and try to act interested in Gail's new baby! And she hated Gail!

The cab pulled up to her building, and Betsy went inside. The lobby was much too bright. The doorman was on his stool, paging through the *Daily News*.

"Hey there, Betsy. Big night?"

"I wouldn't call it big. Normal-sized night."

"You are a beautiful woman, don't ever forget that," he said. "Each night I wait for you to come home so I can see if you are still as beautiful as you were the night before."

"You're a charmer," she said as she got into the elevator.

"I do my best."

The elevator doors closed. Betsy slumped against the paneling and stared at the lights above the doors.

Her doorman would fuck her. This was not much to cling to, but when you are thirty-seven, going on thirty-eight, you are dangerously close to a time when even the willingness of a twenty-three-year-old high school dropout who earns nine dollars an hour opening and closing the door for you will be in question. How had this happened to her? She had been so young! For so long! With such bright prospects! She'd gone on five dates with Liev Schreiber! Seven years ago, but still! She had watched as her friends married ordinary men and set off on their ordinary lives. And now she saw. Now she knew. But it was too late.

cancer dog

The dog that caught Holly's eye at the shelter was not particularly cute, at least not conventionally so, which is why, Holly figured, he was still there, lingering on death row while the puppies and the pugs and the Irish setters and the Labradoodles managed to find new homes. But there was something comical about his eyebrows, which were big and black and tufty, and the way he cocked his head to one side, like he was listening very intently to a soft voice in the next room or just about to tell a joke. Later, she would buy him a squeaky rubber cigar chew toy to complete the look, but Chester—that was his name—had enough self-possession to refuse it.

Right after her aborted lunch, the lunch with Amanda and Jack, Holly had popped in to the animal shelter to look at the dogs on a whim. Chester had been curled up in the back of his cage, chin on paws, looking appropriately forlorn given the exigencies of his present circumstances, but when he saw Holly he slowly made it to his feet and walked forward and tentatively licked the three fingers she'd poked through the wire mesh and that was it; she *knew*. Once Holly got it into her head that something was meant to be, the thought was nearly impossible for her to shake, which is one of the reasons it took as long as it did for her marriage to break up. Holly believed in destiny even more than she believed in love.

"Isn't he adorable?"

"I didn't know you were planning to get a dog," said Lucas. He'd stopped over after going to see some friends of his who'd just started their own doo-wop band. He'd invited Holly to join him — these days, Lucas invited Holly pretty much wherever he went — but she'd claimed she was too old to go all the way to Red Hook to listen to three postadolescents bang on washboards while they sang "My Bucket's Got a Hole in It."

"He was kind of an impulse purchase," said Holly. "His name is Chester."

"Chester? Really?" said Lucas. "You sure you want to go with that?"

"That's the name he came with," said Holly. "I don't want to confuse him by changing it."

Lucas knelt down next to the dog bed and scratched Chester behind the ears. Chester just lay there. "Don't take this the wrong way, but he doesn't seem very, um, energetic."

"Yeah, well, he has a brain tumor."

"What?"

"That's why he was in the shelter. His previous owners didn't want to pay for his operation and everything so they just left him there to die," said Holly. "Those people should be shot."

"Yeah, but I don't get it," said Lucas. "You adopted a dog with a brain tumor? On purpose?"

"I didn't know about it at first," said Holly, in a tone of voice that suggested she thought this much should be obvious. "I fell in love with him, and then when I said I wanted to adopt him, the woman who ran the shelter explained what the deal was. I couldn't then say to Chester, I wanted you, but now that I know you aren't perfect I'll have to take a pass, good luck to you, enjoy the gas chamber, I'm going to go pick out a better, tumor-free dog."

"You know, that wouldn't have been the craziest thing to do."

"I couldn't do it."

"So what's going to happen to him?"

"He has to have an operation to take out the tumor. The shelter found a vet who's agreed to provide his services for free. I just have to pay for the drugs and his medications and stuff like that and supervise his recovery."

"That could get pretty intense."

"Dogs get over cancer all the time. It's different than with people. He's not going to die. Are you, Chester? You're not going to die, are you?"

Chester gave a halfhearted thump of his tail.

"See?" said Holly. "He wants to live."

Later, Holly was in the kitchen making Monte Cristos for a little late dinner, and she noticed that Lucas was fiddling around with her cell phone.

"What are you doing?"

"I'm setting up your text messaging," he said.

"Oh, no you're not."

"You're going to love it."

"I am not going to start sending text messages. That is for the young people. The old people, we don't text."

"I'll teach you."

"I don't want to learn. I'm opposed to it. I don't text message, I don't instant message, really, anything that has to do with 'message,' I'm not into," said Holly. "Except answering machine messages. As a culture, we should have stopped at answering machines."

"You didn't want an iPod either, but now you love it."

"The iPod is an exception, because it blocks people out. All these other things let more people in."

"You don't really feel that way."

"Oh, yes I do," said Holly. "I am completely opposed to this proliferation of useless communication. You should hear the things my mother will tell me when she's on her cell phone. On her cell phone while my father is driving the car, that is the worst. She gets me on the phone and just downloads everything that has passed through her brain in the past two days. You throw email in and I want to stick my head in the oven. This is what I finally had to tell my mother: if you're on your cell phone, don't call me. Unless somebody is dying, don't call me from a cell phone. Friends, too, I don't want to chat while you're in line at the dry cleaners."

"Do you want me to stop calling you from my cell?"

"No, that's fine. You just call to tell me what time you're coming over. I appreciate it," said Holly. "That way I have time to run around my apartment and hide anything incriminating, and I can make sure my legs are shaved, and I can, you know, bleach my mustache if I want."

"You don't have a mustache."

"That you know of," said Holly. "I don't have a mustache *that you know of*. Because you always call before you come over."

Chester took that moment to walk into the kitchen. Holly squatted down, and Chester put his paw on her knee. She put her right hand out, and he put his paw in it.

"Look at this," said Holly. "He's shaking hands. Good boy, Chester! Good boy!"

"No, no," Lucas called from the couch. "You can't let him shake. You can't let him put his paws on you."

"Why not?"

"Because it'll make him think he's dominant."

"So?" said Holly. "He has a brain tumor. Maybe thinking he's dominant would make him feel better about his life. Right, Chester? Good boy. You're such a good boy."

"I'm serious. They don't let dogs shake hands anymore," said Lucas. He came over to the pass-through and perched on one of the bar stools and looked down at Chester. "Trust me on this one. No shake, Chester. No shake."

Chester put his paw down and tilted his head up at Lucas.

"Have you ever heard of the alpha roll?" Lucas asked.

"Nope."

"You sort of grab him by the shoulders and flip him onto his back and stare into his eyes until he looks away. It shows him that you're the alpha dog. It'll make him feel more secure. Otherwise, he'll be nervous and feel like he has to be in control all the time."

"Where did you learn all this stuff?"

"I don't know. People know it," said Lucas. He popped a cube of cheese into his mouth. "It's known."

———————

The first time Amanda had an inkling that Jack might have a thing for her, that all of their emailing back and forth might signify something more than a slightly inappropriate friendship, was due to a single word at the end of a very ordinary sentence.

What did you do today, beautiful?

What had she done that day? Jacob's sitter had gone AWOL two weeks before—first claiming a sick daughter, then food poisoning, finally a ruptured disk—and Amanda was too overwhelmed to look for a replacement. Jacob's sitter was actually a nanny, but Amanda subscribed to a sort of reverse snobbery popular among stay-at-home mothers of a certain class who claimed not to have nannies yet nonetheless managed to secure for themselves twenty to forty hours of child-free time each week. Amanda found she could just barely tolerate her life with the help; without it, she felt like she was going under. Jacob had spent the morning methodically pulling books off the bottom two shelves in the living room. Amanda had decided to use it as an opportunity to work on the meaning of the word *no* with him. Two hours of "Jacob? *No*" followed each time he tottered too close to the shelves, and each time it was immediately followed by his maniacal lunge for the books. By the time the morning was over, Amanda was reasonably certain that Jacob had learned that the word *no* meant "propel oneself headlong into a bookshelf." Finally, she gave up. She constructed a barrier by pushing the ottoman and a few of her dining chairs up against the shelves, and, as she stood there, admiring her resourcefulness, she was hit by the realization that this was how her living room would look for the next twelve months. Then it was lunch. Tofu dog medallions and Goldfish crackers. Then nap time, which was the occasion for the first shower in two and a half days. Then she watched *Starting Over*. Then—

It made her want to cry. That was her day. She felt desperate, and she didn't know why, and she couldn't tell anyone, she couldn't even tell Jack the truth, which was that the best part of her day, the thing that made her light up, was getting his emails. And now he was calling her beautiful.

She'd written back:

I didn't do anything today. Honestly, not one thing.

Three minutes later, she was walking down the hallway with a bunch of dirty clothes when she heard the little submarine sound her computer made when an email arrived. She put down the laundry basket and clicked on the little postage stamp on her computer screen.

"It was morning, and lo, now it is evening, and nothing memorable is accomplished."

– HDT

It had taken Amanda a minute to figure out the initials. Yes. Henry David Thoreau. Walden Pond. That was her day, exactly.

——————

"Are you sleeping with anybody besides me?"

Holly considered, briefly, lying, because she feared that Lucas would take the truth the wrong way. She decided instead to go with the whole unvarnished truth and hope that that would put her temporary sexual fidelity to him into its proper perspective. "No, but that doesn't mean anything. Trust me."

"What do you mean?"

"I'm very monogamous. Constitutionally. My brain can only take so much novelty in that department," said Holly. "Plus I'm getting plenty of sex with you. It keeps me from running around and doing all sorts of stupid things with strangers, because I can just do them all with you while I get my head together. I figure I'm saving myself from diseases, and, I don't know, all sorts of random sexual humiliations."

All of a sudden, Lucas grabbed Holly by the shoulders and pulled her off the couch and wrestled her down onto the rug. He flipped her onto her back and held her down while he stared deep into her eyes.

"What's this?" said Holly.

"The alpha-dog roll."

"That's what this is?"

"Yes. I'm alpha-dog rolling you."

"I like it."

The phone chose that moment to ring. Holly reached up and grabbed it off the coffee table and looked at the caller ID. "Do you mind if I take this?" Holly asked Lucas from the floor. "It's Amanda. She'll think it's strange if I don't pick up."

"No problem. I'll watch TV in the bedroom." He planted a kiss on her collarbone and then walked down the hall.

"Okay," said Amanda, skipping the preliminaries, "what was that all about at lunch?"

Holly flashed back on her lunch with Amanda and Jack, the cheeseburger-eating Buddhist.

"I had to get out of there," said Holly. "That guy was driving me nuts."

"What are you talking about?"

"I hate that loosey-goosey pseudospiritual crap. Did you see him? He ordered a cheeseburger. Don't call yourself a Buddhist and order a cheeseburger! It shouldn't be, you know, if it feels good, do it. We don't need a religion for that. It's all around us."

"He just doesn't like to make a big deal out of it, Holly. I shouldn't have even brought it up."

"Yeah, well, I don't think that's what Buddhism is, anyway. I don't think it's about raking your Zen rock garden and trying to seduce married women."

"I think it made him uncomfortable to talk about it like that. You were being pretty confrontational."

"Because I don't like what's going on between you two! I don't think it's a good thing for anybody involved. And it has nothing to do with" — Holly tried to remember the phrase Jack had used — " 'conventional morality.' It's just, some sin trails its own penance."

"Nobody's sinning! He isn't even interested in me," Amanda said. "I'm serious, Holly, nothing's happened."

"Yeah, well, good. I just think you should be careful, that's all," said Holly. "I mean it. That guy's going to go with the flow and your entire life is going to get flushed down the toilet."

Amanda didn't say anything, but Holly knew she was still on the phone because she could hear her breathing.

"Guess what," Holly finally said.

"What?"

"I got a dog."

tweens are the
new teens

I'm thinking about doing the AIDS ride again this year."

This was from Leonard, who was stretched out on his back on the office carpet, where he'd been since he came back from lunch. He hadn't moved an inch all afternoon. Leonard did most of his comedy writing lying down, as if the very concept of it made him physically ill, while Holly sat at the keyboard and argued with him. Usually he favored the couch, but on his particularly dark days, he took to the floor.

"You should," said Holly.

"I think it might help me get back in shape."

"You had fun last time."

"Will you sponsor me?"

"Yes," said Holly. "On one condition."

"What's that?"

"You have to promise to wear a condom when you have sex."

"Just while I'm on the AIDS ride, or all the time?"

"Would you agree to do it all the time?"

"I would," said Leonard, "if you sponsored me for twenty billion dollars."

"What will a hundred bucks get me?"

"I'll wear a condom on the AIDS ride."

"And?"

Leonard sighed a big mock sigh. "And at the big before and after sex parties."

"Deal."

Holly took her checkbook out of her desk drawer and wrote the check. "You know, it's hard for us straight people to give money to AIDS when we keep reading that you guys are back to doing crystal meth and having wild anonymous unprotected sex all the time," she said. "It kind of, I don't know, takes the joy out of it for us."

Leonard reached his hand up and took the check from Holly, examined it, folded it in half, and slid it into his chest pocket, all without moving from the floor. "Well, I'm sorry our epidemic isn't more joyful for you."

"Work on that, will you?"

Leonard stroked his chin thoughtfully. "Perhaps another parade."

Later, on the subway ride home, Leonard had the notion that writers of his ilk often have when they feel their careers aren't what they should be. He wanted to call his agent. He wanted to call his agent and yell at him, but his particular wheel of fortune had turned in such a way as to make even Leonard realize that to do so would be an unwise course of action. Jake Weinstock had been trying unsuccessfully to pawn Leonard off on a junior agent for the past eighteen months. "Call Jessica if you need anything" was how he concluded every two-minute, end-of-day, call-sheet-clearing Bluetooth conversation with Leonard. Well, Leonard didn't just fall off the turnip truck, Leonard knew where this "call Jessica" business led. Oblivion! Not that Jessica was anything but an entirely adequate agent. No indeed. She was an up-and-comer with long shiny young-agent hair and a clipped and smiling air of ruthless efficiency. But that was precisely the problem: her youth, her ambition, her up-and-comerdom. Jessica saw Leonard as someone whose time had come and gone. He was Not Her Problem. If Leonard was anybody's problem, he was Jake Weinstock's problem, and Leonard intended to keep it that way. Leonard had been one of Jake's first clients, back when Jake was a squirrelly nobody driving around Burbank in a brown Corolla, when he was scaring up new clients on show nights, staff writers who had managed to get their first job through nepotism or sheer blind luck, and who hadn't yet found satisfactory representation. Fifteen years ago, nobody would have pegged Jake to become one of the most power-ful TV Lit agents in town. He also was possessed of a strange, well, *loyalty* wasn't a word Leonard liked to use within fifty miles of the Hollywood sign, but that was the only way to explain the fact that Jake Weinstock hadn't dropped him as a client. Loyalty, or Jewish guilt. Because Jake Weinstock was still in at least a few ways a nice Jewish boy from New Jersey, and Leonard had been his first big client, with his first huge overall deal, and if now, years later, Leonard had wasted four years in the prime of his career self-financing a gay-themed independent film and burned countless bridges with his arro-gance and his attitude, with the unconcealed contempt he ladled out to PAs and network executives in equal measure, if he had blown most of his fortune on drugs and clothes and ambitious home-remodeling projects, if he had taken a lucra-tive career and darn near ground it into the dust, well, there was a part of Jake that felt like he owed it to Leonard to still return his calls.

Three months earlier, at the tail end of a bout of depression that had found him spending eighteen hours a day in the fetal position on the floor of his screening room, Leonard had managed to set up a face-to-face meeting with Jake. "I'm ready to go back to TV," Leonard had said, after settling down on Jake's low-slung couch.

Jake had just stared at him. A seven-foot-tall Darth Vader action figure loomed over his left shoulder. It cost eighteen thousand dollars in the Sharper Image Black catalog. A showrunner Jake represented had given it to him as a Hanukkah present.

"This season. I'm ready to go on staff," Leonard went on. "Or write a pilot. I'd even be willing to write a pilot and consult on a show."

"I see."

Leonard folded his hands in his lap and then unfolded them again.

"Do you remember how," Jake began, in a dispassionate tone of voice, "back before Bob Barker retired, every few years one of those *Price Is Right* models, you know, the ones that stick their hands in the air in front of the new cars, would get fired?"

"Yeah?"

"And then she'd go on *Entertainment Tonight* to complain about it, and say it wasn't fair, maybe even accuse poor old Bob of sexual harassment," said Jake. "And how each one was always *completely* surprised by it? Even though, just a few years earlier, it happened to a woman who was just a little bit older than herself?"

"Yes."

Jake just looked at him.

"What are you saying?" said Leonard.

"I'm saying, you have no right to be surprised by this," said Jake. "I can't get you a job, Leonard. Nobody has jobs. You know why? Because there are no jobs for writers at your level." This was agent-speak for "writers your age."

"What do you mean? What are they doing instead?"

"They're selling their houses," said Jake. "They're selling their houses and moving to Vermont and buying apple farms."

"Apple farms?"

Jake nodded. "Where they will spend the next forty years sitting out in the barn, pretending to write screenplays. I hope you saved your money."

"I did," said Leonard.

"Good. Great. You don't know how happy I am to hear that."

"I saved it," said Leonard, "and then I spent it."

"Jesus."

"I put a lot of money into my film," said Leonard. "And now we can't get distribution."

"Do you know why you can't get distribution?" said Jake. "I'll tell you why. Because the studios aren't going to release a film that is composed primarily of close-ups of a model-slash-waiter-slash-hustler you're dying to fuck who happens to be living in your guesthouse."

Leonard had to admit, the close-ups had gotten the best of him.

"Can I be honest with you for a minute, Leonard?"

"Go ahead."

"It was too gay," said Jake. "It was way, way, way too gay."

The movie was pretty gay. It was about a sixteen-year-old

street hustler who falls for a married john and eventually kills himself, although not before destroying his lover's marriage and family. It was, much as Leonard had intended, a striking departure from the mainstream television comedy he'd spent the prime of his career writing, but a departure into exactly *what* seemed to be a matter of debate. The part of the young hustler was played by a guy named Digger who was seventeen and had just moved to LA from a small town in Idaho. Leonard had met Digger in a bar on Sunset, and two days later had moved him into his guesthouse, where Digger had taken to sunbathing in a pair of skintight swim trunks that looked like a cross between a Speedo and a pair of those silky running shorts that were so popular during the eighties, driving poor Leonard into a frenzy.

"And it wasn't funny! You're a *comedy* writer, Leonard. You write *comedy*. You're supposed to make people like me laugh. I felt like I was having a molar extracted while being forced to watch gay porn."

"—"

"You've got to pull back from that," said Jake. "Fine, you did your passion project, you got that out of your system, but you've got to step back into the mainstream if you want to work."

"I thought you said there weren't any jobs."

"There aren't. Under normal circumstances, for you, there wouldn't be. But I'll tell you what I'm willing to do for you. I'm willing to team you back up with Holly."

"I'm finished writing with a partner, Jake," said Leonard. "I do better work on my own."

"That seems to be a matter of opinion," said Jake. "Ever since you and Holly split up your partnership, her 'novel writing' career and your 'film directing' career have taken the same trajectory." Here he made a diving motion with his hand along with a whistly noise that culminated in the sound of a bomb exploding. "You both need jobs, and she's my client. That's the part that's Good for Jake."

"I don't want a partner."

"You don't have a choice. You're only marketable, in this market, as a team. She's younger than you, for one, which is good. Plus, she's a woman. And she keeps you under control. I'm not saying that's true or not true, but it's the word around town. The Word Around Town is that once you split up your partnership, you went off the rails. Hell, maybe you don't need to be kept under control. Maybe your shit's all together. I don't know, and I don't want to know. I just can't have any more Leonard Stories out there."

Leonard was aware of the Leonard Stories. The time he flew to Vegas when he was supposed to be home writing the next week's script and ended up accidentally pawning his laptop for coke after a rent boy stole his wallet. The month he came to work in his pajamas as a protest against Warner Brothers' efforts to cut costs by switching to a cheaper brand of coffee. Perhaps a bit of babysitting wasn't the worst idea.

"Okay," said Leonard. "I'll do it."

"I can't believe I'm doing this. Honestly. I turn down clients all day long. So why am I doing this for you? Why did I stay up last night trying to figure out how to inject some life into your career?"

"I have no idea."

Jake sat back in his chair and closed his eyes. "To stay human."

Leonard couldn't think of what to say to this.

"You're lucky that you're one of the things that I do to stay human," Jake said. His eyes were still closed. "Because there are not a lot of things on that list." His eyes popped open. "That is a short list, let me tell you."

"Well, I appreciate it," said Leonard.

Jake stood up and ushered Leonard to the door. "And I'm not making any promises. I'll see what I can get for you. Let's just say, you're not going to be writing for HBO. This is going to be a beggars-can't-be-choosers situation, and I don't want to hear any complaints, okay?"

Jake walked Leonard out, past the cubicles, past the eager assistants with their desks piled high with scripts, all the way to the elevator bank. This was Jake's signature move, the walkout, and it made up for the fact that no face-to-face meeting with him ever lasted longer than twelve minutes.

"No drugs, Leonard, seriously," Jake said when they reached the elevators. He pushed the down button. "That's what gets you into trouble. It makes people uncomfortable. Promise me."

"No drugs. I promise."

"Except, you know, whatever" — Jake tapped his temple a few times with his index finger — "medication they've got you on, keep that up."

Which is how Leonard and Holly ended up, repartnered after a four-year hiatus, writing about menstruation for a New York–based show that starred four twelve-year-old girls and aired on Nickelodeon. "Tweens are the new teens," Jake had said to Leonard when he called him from the parking lot that is the Friday-night southbound 405 and presented him with the job offer. That, and "Don't fuck this up."

boundaries, they call them

Spence Samuelson's mother Vera came to visit him twice a year. Each of her visits was ten days long, incorporating a week and both adjoining weekends. The weekends were a whirl of activity: four days filled with jaunts out to the Brooklyn Botanical Garden and up to the Cloisters, walking tours of Harlem, sunset cruises on the Circle Line, special exhibits at the Met, orchid shows and Broadway plays and dinners in Chinatown, tea at the Plaza and cocktails at the Carlyle and carriage rides through Central Park, all of it punctuated by Vera commenting to her son, "Isn't this nice? You get to be a tourist in your own town." At the end of each visit, Spence was convinced they had finally done it. They had Done New York. There was nothing left to see or do or explore or eat, and maybe next time wouldn't his mother prefer to go to London with her friend Harriet like Harriet keeps suggesting? Maybe? But then a month or two would pass, and his mother would start coming up with things she absolutely had to do on her next visit, like going back to Ellis Island so she could look up her hairdresser Zosia's Polish relatives, and Spence would fear that it was never going to stop.

Vera was afraid of venturing out onto the streets of New York on her own, rapists taking up a substantial part of the real estate within her cerebral cortex, which meant that she spent the week between the two event-packed weekends holed up in Spence's apartment all day watching cable television and snooping around. He knew she snooped because she would occasionally slip up and say something like, "I saw you got a holiday card from Suzy Weston. She sure has put on weight." And he would point out that that card was inside his desk drawer, and she would say she was looking for a *pencil* so she could do the crossword puzzle, but she's sorry, she won't look for any more pencils when she's in her own son's apartment all day long. Each evening, when he came home from the office, she was perched on the edge of the sofa, dressed up, lipstick freshly applied, waiting to be taken to dinner or a show, but preferably dinner and a show, and a little upset that Spence hadn't taken at least *one* day off work to spend time with his mother. She drove this theme home with a series of seemingly innocuous statements she dropped like handkerchiefs throughout her visit. "Look at all these people! The Met is always so *crowded* on the weekends."

All of it had started innocently enough. Six months after their father died, Spence and his sister Nancy had dreamed up the "week in New York" as a way to cheer up their mother, who had taken to wearing her dead husband's green terrycloth bathrobe for days on end. It was April, and Vera had enjoyed her trip so much she decided to come back in October so she could see the leaves turning in Central Park. And before Spence knew it, there it was. His mother's descending on him was a twice-yearly event, causing Spence to subconsciously dread the two months that it was impossible not to love if you happened to live in New York.

Spence loved his mother. Truly he did. He reminded himself of this fact often in the weeks leading up to her visit.

She drove him crazy, but he loved her. She was a pain in his ass, but he loved her. And she wouldn't be around forever. That was the other thing. Ever since her husband died, Vera had been getting increasingly frail, forgetting to eat, afraid to take a walk around the block if there was snow on the ground or rain in the forecast. At the beginning of each visit, as he watched her trundle out of the baggage claim area at JFK, with her purse clutched to her stomach and her beige raincoat slung over her arm, he'd be hit in the gut with a fear that felt bottomless.

"You have to eat better, Mom," Spence said when they got back to his apartment. She had taken off her cardigan and was arranging it on a hanger in his closet, and her shoulders looked tiny and rounded.

"I eat as much as I feel like eating."

"You're losing weight."

"I don't like to eat dinner alone."

"Why don't you go over to Nancy's?"

"She doesn't want me there."

"Of course she does."

"No, she doesn't."

"Mom, don't be ridiculous. Go have dinner with Nancy and the kids. They love having you over."

"One evening a week, that's all I'm allowed."

"What?" Spence said. He put a small stack of clean towels on his bed. "What are you talking about?"

"And I have to be out the door by eight thirty."

"Nancy actually said that?"

"Boundaries, they call them. Apparently she read a book about them in her church group. She and Mac go to a church that preaches you shouldn't have too many dinners with your aging parents."

"I don't believe you, Mom."

Vera retrieved a pink plastic vanity case from inside her suitcase. "But I just keep my mouth shut. It's her house, she can make whatever rules she wants." She flipped open the vanity case and proceeded to arrange an impressive collection of creams and unguents across the top of Spence's dresser. "I don't know what would make a person want to go to a church like that, but who am I to say?"

Spence called his sister when he got to the office on Monday morning. He was brimming with righteous indignation. He had just spent an entire weekend with his mother, he had spent Saturday afternoon shuffling down aisles filled with chocolate waterfalls and chocolate pyramids and chocolate chess sets at the New York City Chocolate Show, he had spent Sunday at a matinee showing of *The Boys Are Back!,* a fifties-style musical that involved a lot of tossing of hats around to no apparent end, while apparently his sister, who lived out in Chesterfield, not ten minutes away from their mother, was limiting contact to one dinner a week! It was preposterous!

"Listen to me, Spence. You have her for one week, two times a year. I have her the other, oh, fifty weeks of the year. So please do not tell me that the purpose of this call is to inform me that I'm not seeing enough of our mother."

"Just let her stop by for dinner when she wants. Just put down an extra plate. She doesn't like to eat alone."

"She's over here *all the time,*" said Nancy. "If I didn't limit the dinners, she'd be here every night."

"Would that be so horrible?"

"Okay. You're not getting it," said Nancy. Spence could hear the telltale clanks of a dishwasher being unloaded with some degree of violence. "The woman calls me three times a day. Three times a *day*, Spence. And if I don't pick up at home, and I don't pick up my cell, she drives over to see if I'm dead. And not because she's worried I'm actually dead, Spence. Because she wants to *train* me, like a *dog*."

"I think you might be overstating things."

"Oh, am I? Last week, she drove over and brought the boys each a big candy bar, and she gave Megan a coloring book. When Megan got upset, Mom told her that she should stop eating sweets because she was getting fat. Megan's *eight*, Spence. And when I yelled at her, she told me she was trying to be *helpful*, to help Megan not get fat, because there is nothing harder than being a fat teenage girl. If you lived ten minutes away from her, you'd need boundaries too. You'd need a shotgun."

So. That hadn't gone so well. But Nancy and Mom had never gotten along. Spence could remember endless screaming matches between them when he was growing up. They had terrified him. After Nancy graduated from DePauw, the two hadn't spoken to each other for eighteen months due to his mother's rather too-pointed remarks about a black boyfriend, something about her being unwilling to ever dandle a Negro grandchild on her knee. So in a way, this was progress. In a way, Spence reminded himself after he hung up the phone and wandered down the hall to get some coffee, *in a way*, things were better than they'd ever been.

Spence was asleep on his couch, cheek pressed to sticky black overstuffed leather, when his phone rang. His mother had commandeered his bedroom, which is why he had spent yet another night on the couch.

"Hello?"

Spence heard a sniffle, and then a small "It's me."

"Cathleen," said Spence. He swung his feet to the floor and sat up. He hadn't heard from her in weeks, ever since the Crazy Molly photographs arrived in her in-box and she accused him of being a sociopath. He had called her several times, but she'd never picked up, and he'd figured things were probably over.

"What time is it there?" he asked.

"It's two hours earlier than it is where you are, Spence, the way it always is. Six thirty. I couldn't sleep."

"I'm glad you called."

"I've been awake crying all night. I'm just, my head is spinning, Spence. None of this makes any sense to me. I don't understand any of it. I need an explanation."

"I know, I know, I'm sorry. I feel horrible," said Spence. He could hear his mother shuffling around in the other room, and he lowered his voice. "Um, would it be possible, I mean, can we talk about this later in the week? Like tomorrow night, even? I mean, you know, like a big serious talk? Right now is, well, my mother is in town."

"So? I mean it, Spence. So? Your mother is in town. We're in the middle of a *huge* thing here. I think your mother can wait."

Spence wasn't so sure, but he dutifully rolled off the couch and walked down the hall and locked himself in the bathroom with the cordless phone pressed to his ear. He turned on the exhaust fan to white-noise out his end of the conversation so Vera would have trouble listening in. Then he sat down on the toilet seat and braced himself.

"Okay," said Spence. "I'm here."

"I wasn't going to tell you this, but I feel like I should, if we're going to have any chance whatsoever."

"Tell me," said Spence.

"I talked to your old girlfriend Holly."

It took a second for this to register. "You *what?*"

"I called her up the other day."

"Holly *Frick?*"

"Yeah. We had a long conversation."

"Why would you call Holly?"

"I wanted to hear her opinion about all this."

"About what?"

"About your behavior. I read her book last weekend and I thought she might have some insight."

"Why would you think that?"

Cathleen did that thing she sometimes did, where she talked to Spence like he was a four-year-old. "Spencer, you do realize Holly's novel is about you, don't you?"

"It's about her ex-husband. Alex something or other. They met after we broke up."

"Have you read it?"

"I couldn't have less interest in reading anything."

There was a long, loaded pause from Boulder. "You might want to get your hands on a copy."

Before Spence had a chance to respond, he heard a huge crash. "What the?" Spence said. "Hold on a second." He threw the phone down on the bath mat without waiting for a response and hurried into the kitchen. Vera Samuelson had a slippered foot on a dining chair and an arthritic knee on the kitchen counter. An old metal baking sheet was lying in the middle of the kitchen floor, along with Spence's martini shaker and a small box of birthday candles. The cabinet above the refrigerator was open, and she was poking around inside of it with a tarnished silver-plate punch ladle she had sent back with Spence one Christmas to use when he "entertained."

"Mom, get down from there."

"Just tell me where you keep that nice griddle I gave you."

"I'll get it for you, just get down," he said.

She put her hands on his shoulders, and he grasped her by the hips and eased her down. She felt spongy and fleshy and brittle and bony, all at the same time.

"Don't climb up on things, Mom. You'll break a hip."

"I didn't want to bother you. It sounded like an important call."

"Just ask me, please, and I'll come get it down for you."

Spence looked for the griddle in the cupboard over the fridge, and then in the one over the microwave. He finally found it in the cabinet under the sink, hidden inside a rusty wok left behind by the previous tenant.

"Did I tell you that Annabel Rogers broke her hip?"

"She did?" Spence had no idea who Annabel Rogers was, nor did he care, but such things didn't matter for the bulk of his mother's stories.

"She slipped on a grape in the grocery store," she said. "Three weeks later she was dead."

"You're making my point for me, Mom. That's why I don't want you climbing up on things."

"Do you know what you need? You need a step stool."

"I don't need a step stool."

"I'll buy you one," she said. "My treat. Just take me to the store. You can pick out one that you like."

"I don't need a step stool, Mom. I'm six-two. I can reach everything I need to reach."

"For my visits, I would like a step stool," she said. "So I don't break my hip making pancakes for my son while he is busy all morning talking to people on the telephone."

The telephone! Shit! Spence hurried down the hall to the bathroom and picked up the phone off the bath mat.

"Uh, Cathleen? I'm sorry about that, my mother needed me to —"

"Fuck off, Spence." He could hear her slam the phone down. He sat on the toilet seat and listened as the dial tone unspooled through the air.

Later, after the pancakes were eaten and the dishes were done, Spence spotted his mother heading down the hall toward the bedroom with his tarnished punch ladle in hand.

"I'm taking this back with me," Vera said when she saw him watching her. "It doesn't look like you're getting much use out of it."

froot loops

Amanda liked to shop with others; Holly liked to shop alone. When out with Amanda, Holly tended to come home with overpriced trendy items bought from boutiques with draconian exchange policies, clothes that lived out the rest of their natural lives in the back of her closet, tags dangling accusatorily. Over time, she had come to accept this as the price of friendship.

Which is why Holly allowed herself to be dragged along Bleecker Street—the fancy part, *bien sûr*—and into yet another scary and intimidating shop on a bright Saturday that April. Friendship. The clothes hung limply from chrome hangers on chrome bars suspended from the ceiling by chrome chains. If you so much as exhaled near the merchandise, everything jangled. The store was a perpetual wind chime. The clothes hanging from the hangers weren't actually for trying on, not really, not unless you were a size double zero, zero, or two—everybody else was shamed into asking one of the salesgirls for a larger size. The girl would then vanish through a door at the back of the store and—while this was speculation on Holly's part, she liked to think it was true—get into a special elevator that plunged deep into the bowels of the earth where they kept the pants in sizes like four and six and eight. There was a size ten down there somewhere, but nobody had dared to ask for it in years.

"I can't shop in here. Everything is tiny. Let's go to Banana Republic."

"No more Banana Republic. I'm serious, Holly. You dress like a twenty-three-year-old paralegal who works in midtown and thinks the solution to any fashion dilemma is a pair of black pants," said Amanda. "We need to get you some jeans."

"What's wrong with my jeans?" said Holly.

"Just trust me. You need better jeans."

A salesgirl came over as if on cue. "Can I help you find something?"

"We're looking for some jeans for my friend," Amanda said. "Something hipper than what she's wearing."

"But not too hip," Holly told the salesgirl. "I'm not a hip person. I just want to look reasonably normal."

"I'll go grab a few for you to try on."

"Hold on a sec," Holly said to her. "Okay. Listen to me. I don't want to go back into that dressing room and take off my boots and my pants and start putting on jeans only to discover that the ones you brought me are all too tight, and then when I ask for the next size up, be informed that they're the biggest size you carry. I can't take that today. Seriously, I'll blow my head off. So look at me, look at my ass, look at my gut, take it all in, and then tell me honestly if you anticipate we're going to have a problem."

The salesgirl nodded her head and pursed her lips while she examined Holly's rear end through half-shuttered eyes. "I think? We'll be okay."

"Okay, forget it, thanks, but that's too much uncertainty for me."

"No, no, we'll be fine," the salesgirl said, and headed off towards the stacks of denim.

"You're out of your mind, you know," Amanda said.

"I'm just trying to avoid an episode of unnecessary humiliation," said Holly. She pulled a hanger off the rack which was holding a piece of filmy zebra-print material that looked like a handkerchief with long beaded strings dangling from the corners. "What is this? Is this supposed to be a top?"

"I want to find something to wear to Babbo. Mark's taking me there Saturday night for our anniversary."

"I forgot your anniversary was this month."

"Seven years."

"I was thinking the other day, Alex and I would have been married five years this past December."

"If he hadn't cheated on you and walked out on you and then divorced you, you mean."

Holly held a sweater up to her shoulders to see how deep the V-neck went. "You make it sound so final."

"Try that on," said Amanda. "I'm just trying to keep you from doing that thing you always do, Holly, clinging to something after it's clearly over, feeling like nothing else will ever match up to it. You did that when we graduated from college. You kept saying, 'It's never going to be like this again.' Over and over. 'It's never going to be like this ever again.'"

"But I was right. It never *was* like that again. And I just like to be aware of it when it's happening, that's all. I like to soak things in."

"Whatever. You and Alex were miserable. You had one good year and four horrible ones. Maybe you should have soaked more of that in."

Amanda liked to remind Holly how unhappy she was when she was with Alex. It was one of her favorite things to do. She'd say it again and again, seemingly as a way to cheer Holly up—You think your life's bad now? At least you're not still with Alex!—but it was starting to seem to Holly like Amanda thought the whole thing was actually some sort of character flaw, this willingness she had shown to remain in an unhappy relationship, and that if she'd had so much as a single glowing ember of vitality she would have hightailed it out of there and beat Alex to the punch. The more Holly thought about it, standing there, in the middle of the shop, trying to appear interested in the clothes on the rack without being the proximate cause of too much clangor, the more unfair this felt. Why does anyone stay in an unhappy relationship? Because people do. They do it all the time. And the truth is, when you're in it, when you're up to your neck in the everyday part of life with another human being, sometimes you don't exactly *notice* how bad things really are. It's not always as apparent as it would seem. Unhappiness, when it involves another person, can be like that line from *The Sun Also Rises* about going bankrupt, how it happens two ways: gradually, and then suddenly. That's what it had been like for Holly, at least, and when Alex walked out on her, she was still in the "gradually" part.

It's not that Holly thought she'd never get divorced—she knew it was at least a possibility, if only based on statistics—it's just, she always figured other things would happen first: they'd have a baby, buy an apartment, argue a bit about couches and in-laws and who forgot to put the recycling out, have another baby, make the reluctant move to Connecticut, start going to bed at different times and stop buying cards when they gave each other birthday presents and start scheduling sex and stop smiling when the other one walked through the front door, all the while tossing minor slights and disappointments and failures to communicate into what would become a well-stocked reservoir of resentment, take a stab at couples counseling, go on a grim beach vacation without the kids, trudge through a final year or two of loaded silences broken up by the occasional screaming fight and no sex whatsoever—and *then* they'd get a divorce. That's how it was supposed to work. And if Holly had gone through all of that, well, at least she would've had a heads-up. At least she wouldn't have been so, so—surprised. She never got the chance to fall out of love with Alex, to do it properly, slowly and thoroughly, and the result was he was like a phantom limb. Gone but still there. And like a true phantom limb, the preponderance of feelings associated with him were painful.

"So, I guess that all blew over," said Holly, once they had made it into the changing room and started to take off their clothes. That was another thing about shopping with Amanda—she liked to share a changing room. Holly had long ago given up trying to fight it.

"What?"

"The stuff with that guy. What's-his-name. Jack."

Amanda pulled a beige knit top over her head and looked in the mirror without saying anything.

"What. What aren't you telling me?"

"Nothing," Amanda said. She did a little debutante slouch and examined her reflection. "What do you think of this for Babbo?"

"Amanda."

"—"

"*Amanda*."

"I promised myself I wasn't going to tell anyone."

"Okay, now you really have to tell me."

She let out a big breath, like air escaping from a balloon. "Jack and I had sex."

"*What?!* When?"

Amanda smiled, and then she started to giggle, to laugh, really, and her entire face lit up with what looked suspiciously like joy.

"Just now. Last week. It's only happened twice," said Amanda.

"Twice you did this?"

"And one time we made out at a bar."

"You made out in a bar? Are you nuts? People could see you. Somebody could recognize you."

"I know. I felt bad about that. So we decided, well, we met at his apartment just to talk about what happened, and then, you know—"

"I knew this was going to happen," said Holly. "I'm always right. I hate being right."

There was a knock on the changing-room door, and the salesgirl popped her head in. She was holding a small stack of denim and had an exquisitely pained look on her face. "Will a twenty-seven waist work for you?" she said.

"I'm afraid not," Holly said.

"They run big."

"Not that big," Holly said with fake cheer. She closed the door and turned to Amanda. "See? I'm always right."

"I cannot stop thinking about it, Holly. I'm completely obsessed. It's like this movie I keep playing over and over and over in my head."

"You know, it's not fair to compare illicit sex to married sex. They're completely different animals. It's like comparing apples to oranges," said Holly. "It's like comparing an apple to an animal, actually. To a leopard. I mean it. They're that different."

"He makes me crazy."

Holly shook her head slowly. "I can't believe you're telling me this. Really, I'm stunned. You haven't mentioned him in weeks."

"Yeah, well, you didn't like him very much when we had lunch that time. I think I just felt strange."

"So you just stop talking about him? That's crazy. I liked him fine. As far as lovers go, I mean, he seemed fine."

"Yeah, well, I don't know," said Amanda. "It was a weird lunch. And things had been heating up, and I guess I was kind of embarrassed."

"I thought you said the sex part just happened last week."

"It did," said Amanda, "but we've been having phone sex for a while."

"Are you serious? Phone sex?" Holly's voice got loud and Amanda shushed her. "You guys actually do that?" she whispered.

"All the time."

"No. No! *Really?*"

"We're like rabbits," said Amanda. She pulled the beige top off over her head. "We're like rabbits with phones."

"What, you mean, while you're at home? Inside the apartment?"

Amanda nodded and put her shirt back on. "I can't help myself. I'm being a horrible mother." She started buttoning up her buttons. "Jacob is scooting around on the floor, and he's crying, and I'm throwing Froot Loops at him to shut him up because I'm on the phone with Jack, who's asking me what my pussy is like. And I just toss a few more Froot Loops on the floor and proceed to tell him."

"Yowza."

"And Jacob's not even supposed to be eating sugar."

"Yeah, you know, that's not good."

"I know it's not good. I told you, I've lost my mind."

"What are you going to do if Mark finds out?"

"Mark is not going to find out."

"Yeah, you know, that might not be entirely in your control."

"Trust me. I'm being extremely careful," said Amanda. "Plus, you know Mark. He'd never dream that I'd cheat on him. He has some sort of crazy overinflated self-esteem that makes the thought impossible to enter his mind. Besides, we haven't had a single fight since this started. He's convinced it's the Paxil. I've been really attentive to him when he's around, I'm really present, because I'm telling so many lies I have to focus to keep them all straight."

"I'm not sure that counts as being 'present.'"

"Maybe not in the strict Zen sense. But let me tell you, I am *in the room*."

Amanda and Holly were old friends, and they were best friends, but they were not, it is perhaps the time to point out, old best friends. For the first fifteen years of their acquaintanceship, they were just that: acquaintances. They met freshman year in college, housed on different floors of the same dorm, a strange, womblike brick edifice tucked away on the edge of campus with a private dining hall and an ingrown social ecosystem. They both moved to Manhattan upon graduation, and something about the combination of the hothouse dorm experience and the impersonal big city meant they felt they had more in common than they actually did, and they became New York friends, the kind that keep in a loose and forgiving kind of touch but only manage to lay eyes on each other two or three times a year. Their lives, throughout their twenties, intersected at odd and occasionally interesting places, a joint stint as bridesmaids at a wedding in St. Lucia, even three weeks as roommates when Amanda got caught between leases, but mostly it was confined to drinks together every once in a while, each time with a promise that they would do it more often. Mostly, they functioned as yardsticks for one another, an easy way to see if they were falling short, if they were keeping up, if their lives were on track. And their lives had progressed more or less in lockstep up until a year earlier, when Amanda gave birth to Jacob, and Holly's husband Alex walked out on her. These two monumental life disruptions took place within the span of three weeks, and while it might seem that that would be enough to thrust them out of each other's orbit forever, what ended up happening was exactly the opposite.

Holly had always been an open book, emotionally speaking, and she was never more so than in the months after Alex's surprise departure. She told Amanda everything. Of course, Holly told *everybody* everything, but after a few months the only listener left standing, at least the only one who wasn't being paid by the hour, was Amanda. Sometime in her third trimester, Amanda's thinking had turned dull and fuzzy, like someone had wrapped her brain in thick cotton batting, and once Jacob was born, it only got worse. She got to the point where following the plot of an episode of *Law & Order* was too taxing, but that was what was so good about Holly's situation: it didn't *have* a plot. It was just this strange, murky mess, like a bright green pond, and the two of them spent endless hours together wading around in it, pulling things up out of the muck to discuss and then tossing them back in, only to reach down and pick up the same thing the next day and talk about it all over again. It helped that Jacob was a sleeper, one of those rare, almost mythical babies that sleeps like a cursed character out of a fairy tale. It also helped that Amanda was in a low-grade state of shock herself. She was either bored with motherhood, or deeply, profoundly disappointed by it, she couldn't tell which, she didn't *want* to know which, and so she filled the empty corners of her cotton-battened mind with Holly's problems as a convenient way of avoiding her own.

By the time Holly went to dinner at Mark and Amanda's—the evening of the Paxil and the slipper socks, the one with the kitchen conversation in which the idea of Jack was first broached—Amanda and Holly were talking on the phone once or twice a day, seeing each other most weeks, and yet each of them had a secret they were keeping to themselves, a secret they feared would elicit the other's judgment or scorn. Holly's secret was Lucas, and Amanda's was Jack.

The afternoon light was just beginning to fade as Holly got off the C train and trudged up the stairs of the Eighty-sixth Street subway station and turned onto Central Park West. *Amanda is having an affair.* Holly could hardly believe it. Part of her felt like she was entering into a new stage of life, a grown-up world where married women take lovers—Take lovers! Who says things like that? But that's what Amanda had done!—and she should just get used to it. The other part of her, the part that still felt like a seventh grader, thought this: how is it that Amanda has a husband and a baby and a lover and I can't even find a halfway decent boyfriend my own age?

She turned onto her street and looked up. Was that? No… was it? She hadn't seen him in, how many years? Six? More than that, even? Still, it was clearly him. He had a very distinctive way of standing, a certain combination of height and posture with something cocky about the slope of his shoulders, and even after all these years, she could spot him from half a block away. He was standing directly in front of her building and he did not look happy. She slowed up and was just about to turn around when he caught sight of her and started striding towards her.

"Have you been talking to my girlfriend on the phone?" said Spence.

"Excuse me?" Holly said.

"Damn it, Holly. Have you been saying stuff to Cathleen about me?"

"I have no idea what you're talking about," said Holly. She started walking towards her building and Spence trailed along beside her.

"Cathleen. My girlfriend. She told me the two of you have been talking on the phone and comparing notes."

Holly stopped walking and looked at his face. "She said that?"

"Last night."

"If she told you that, then I guess, yes, I do remember that a woman by the name of Cathleen did contact me and we had a brief conversation."

"Jesus, Holly, stay out of my business."

"Fine."

"I'm serious about this."

Holly opened the front door of her apartment building and then turned to face him.

"I don't want to be in your business, Spence. But this woman called me and she was very upset and I thought it would be cruel to hang up on her. I'm tired. I've had a very long day. It was nice seeing you again, but, you know, good-bye."

She went inside and shut the door.

race for the cure

Betsy Silverstein was sitting at her desk, staring at her Rolodex. She had decided a while back to start using a Rolodex as a way of asserting her individuality, a little dash of retro hipness that she found aesthetically pleasing, the *thwap thwap thwap* of the flipping cards so much more soothing than the various electronic alternatives. Earlier that day, though, one of the new girls walked past Betsy's desk and said, "Oh my god, you use a *Rolodex?!*" and started laughing. Betsy tried to explain the spirit in which it was acquired — that she wasn't old enough to actually have had a Rolodex *back when people had Rolodexes* — but she wasn't convinced she'd gotten through. And now she was staring at it, suddenly afraid that it was sitting on top of her desk like a jar of hand cream for people with age spots or a sixty-four-ounce tub of Metamucil.

"Oh my god. You're still here?"

Betsy looked up and saw her former co-worker Trish Barton — platinum hair, prominent clavicles — dangling shopping bags from her wrists and striding towards her.

"Of course I'm still here," said Betsy. She put on her brightest smile. "I love it here."

In that "you're still here" lay the central problem of Betsy's career. A few years after she graduated from Hamilton, Betsy had taken a job as a junior publicist at a boutique agency and, by doing so, started down a career path that had one of two possible outcomes. You either morphed into a power player—somebody who barked orders into phones and alternately threatened and cajoled people, who traded in favors and gossip and free passes and gift baskets, and who, generally, by age thirty-two was well on the road to being a fifty-year-old publicist—or you got engaged. You planned your wedding from your desk while pretending to work, you got pregnant, and, in your fourth month, you decided it was all too much and confessed to your co-workers that the money you brought home was so, well, *insignificant* compared to your husband's income, and you quit. They threw you a lunch, with cocktails that bled into happy hour, and then you went off and started your life. There really wasn't room in the industry for someone like Betsy, meaning a woman who was no longer hot and yet had failed to use the years of her deteriorating charms to become truly phenomenal at her job. So much of it depended on flirting and parties, on extracting promises from journalists who showed up at events for no reason other than the blind hope that they might get to have sex with that cute publicist who called all the time and *really seemed to like him an awful lot*. If not sex, at least she would *talk* to him. But Betsy had shot past ingenue and was closing in on object of pity. Men no longer wanted to forgo a night on their couch just for a chance to talk to her at an ill-conceived cocktail party held inside a BMW showroom to launch a perfume that smelled like Fruit Roll-Ups. And at the same time, she couldn't get an Olsen to the meatpacking district on a Wednesday night—it was a cliché, an Olsen in the meatpacking district, don't think she didn't know this—try as she might. What good was she?

"I feel like I'm in a time warp," said Trish. "You look *exactly* the same as you did when I worked here. That was six years ago!"

"You look the same too," said Betsy.

"No, I don't," said Trish. She did a little I've-given-up gesture with her perfectly manicured hands. "I look two babies older."

The next morning was a Saturday, and Betsy woke up at five, got dressed, and took a cab to Columbus Circle and headed into the park. Unpacking the bananas for the Race for the Cure turned out to be even more annoying than it sounded. She had to take them out of the cardboard boxes and arrange them on the table, making sure the red Dole sticker was faceup on each one, and then she was to affix a little pink ribbon sticker next to the Dole sticker in an artful, anti-breast-cancer-y sort of way. All of this had to be done just so, because Dole was a sponsor of the event, and at some point in the morning a team from Dole corporate would casually saunter by the banana table on their way to the VIP tent and, well, history had borne out that the Dole people were very particular about their stickers. A monkey could do this, Betsy thought, as she opened the first box and looked inside. Well, not a monkey, a monkey would eat the bananas, but this…this was clearly a message.

The previous afternoon, shortly after Trish Barton trailed out of the office and left to catch the train back to Westchester, Betsy's boss, whose name was Roz, had summoned her.

"I've been meaning to talk to you about your plans" was how she put it.

"My plans?" said Betsy.

"Your career plans. You've been here for quite a long time, and I'm curious about what you see yourself doing five years from now. Two years from now, even."

"Well, I like what I do. I like my job. I'd like to keep…doing my job. I'm not sure what my life will look like five years from now, or two years from now, but that's more or less my plan."

Roz laughed her laugh, a machine gun fired into a sack of gravel. "I'm sure you'll be sick of this place before two more years go by."

"I guess that's possible."

"I'm going to be honest with you, Betsy. There is not a lot of opportunity for advancement in this place. There's only room for one queen bee. And most of the junior publicists I hire, well, you've seen them, they come and they go. Most of them are gone by the time they're thirty. And maybe that's for the best. Maybe that helps keep everybody excited and fresh and motivated."

"I'm excited, Roz. I'm motivated."

"Fresh" hung out there in the ether, unspoken.

Roz leaned forward, conspiratorially. "I'll tell you something I wouldn't tell most of the girls around here. I view the job of junior publicist as more of an internship. A chance for you young girls to learn, and then to go off and take what you've learned someplace else, someplace where you can make real money. I don't know how you manage to survive on what I pay you."

This was a lie. Roz knew exactly how Betsy survived. Betsy's daddy paid her bills. And the truth was it made Roz mad, Roz, who grew up in Nebraska, whose parents ran an auto parts shop, who'd made it on her own with no help whatsoever, without so much as a single birthday check bigger than twenty-five dollars. She'd spent the first twenty years of her adult life wearing outfits scrabbled together from shirts she bought at flea markets and cheap black skirts worn long after they'd gone gray, living with roommates in shitholes in Brooklyn decades before it was remotely cool, riding buses, bringing her lunch to work, each day a mighty struggle against the metropolis that a few extra dollars would have eased immeasurably. She could count the number of times she took a cab before she turned thirty on one hand! And finally she had made it, she had crawled to the top of her particular heap, she had packed on sixty pounds along the way, she'd smoked four billion Parliament Lights, she'd missed out on a husband, she'd forgotten to have a baby, and still little miss thirty-eight-thousand-dollars-a-year aging junior publicist Betsy Silverstein carried a more expensive purse than she did. Betsy would never admit it, never admit that something didn't quite *add up,* that year after year after year she came in wearing stylish clothes, and took cabs home, and bought tickets for benefits, and lived in the West Seventies. Alone! In a two-bedroom apartment! Not that she wanted anyone to know this. She was extremely furtive about all of it. Sometimes Roz just wanted her to come clean, to say exactly how much money she had and exactly where it came from, was it in a trust, did she get a check every month, did she own her apartment, was it in her name, did she have to work, *did she have to work,* DID SHE HAVE TO WORK?

"I've never complained about my salary."

"I realize that," said Roz. She settled back into the mesh of her Aeron chair and her torso assumed the dimensions of a refrigerator box. "Still. I think it's time we make some transition plans for you. Start working on a timetable."

"I'm not sure I understand what you're saying, Roz. Are you saying I'm too old to do this job?"

Roz could smell the lawsuit. Not that Betsy would ever do such a thing—it wasn't her style—but Roz did not get where she was by leaving those kinds of doors propped open. "Of course not. There's no such thing as 'too old' around here. Look at me. I'm a goddamn dinosaur."

"Because I don't need to run the world. I'm not that kind of person. I just want to do my job well, and I think I do that."

"Yes. Well." Roz's gears started turning. She suspected that she'd been outfoxed. "If that's the case, just so you know, I'm going to have to start treating you the way I treat the other junior publicists. Because it's not fair to them if you keep getting all the best assignments. They won't learn anything that way."

"I understand."

"Good."

Which is how Betsy ended up on banana duty. The two new girls—blond, suspiciously tan, and virtually indistinguishable—were manning the VIP tent. Betsy knew she wasn't missing much, just, you know, Kim Cattrall downing mimosas, Mariska Hargitay feeling pleased with herself. And the truth is, after she got past the initial humiliation, Betsy discovered that organizing the bananas was sort of soothing. The yellow was so yellow, and the little red stickers were so perfect and red. She felt like she was channeling her latent OCD into something constructive. There were a few dozen people milling around in the early-morning light, setting up Gatorade stations, unpacking T-shirts and pink baseball caps. A bunch of volunteers were gathered around a stocky Hispanic woman who held a clipboard and periodically blew a whistle she kept on a lanyard around her neck. Betsy tuned it all out, lulled by her task, her world the air, the dawn, the mist, the rows and rows of yellow fruit.

"Can I have one?" a voice said, snapping her out of her reverie.

Betsy was only supposed to give the bananas to the runners, and this guy was clearly not a runner. Still, why not? "Sure."

"Thanks," he said. He picked up a banana and began to peel it. "Can I start one for you?"

"No thanks."

"Are you sure? I'm really good at it. Look." He showed her his half-peeled banana. "Almost no smushing of the banana top."

"I don't eat bananas," said Betsy.

"You don't eat bananas?"

"No."

"What kind of person doesn't eat bananas? Bananas are the best."

"I know, but—" said Betsy. She looked at him. "Never mind."

"What were you going to say?"

"Nothing."

"Come on."

"I was going to say, they're kind of fattening."

"*Bananas?*"

"For a fruit, I mean. Fattening for a fruit."

"I'm, well, the truth is I'm stunned. I'm floored." He took an enormous bite of the banana and started chewing it. "I mean it. Mystery solved."

"What do you mean?"

He swallowed. "All this time, I thought the reason I weighed three hundred pounds was because of things like pizza and beer and ice cream, Krispy Kremes and Papaya Dogs, my morning McGriddle, the fact that sometimes I eat two dinners in one night just because there's nothing good on TV, and finally, a skinny person tells me the truth. It's the bananas."

Betsy smiled. She liked being called skinny, even if it was by someone who was enormously fat.

"That's it. No more bananas *pour moi. Pas des bananas!*"

"You look good."

"Don't start lying to me right off the bat. If we're going to have any chance whatsoever, Miss Betsy Silverstein, let us just agree that I am a lot of things, I have a lot of truly compelling and unique qualities, but I do not…look…good."

"How do you know my name?" said Betsy. She was more than a little alarmed.

"You go to my gym."

"You go to my gym?" said Betsy. This guy did not look like he went to anybody's gym.

"I am employed by your gym. I sell memberships. In fact, I sold you your membership, which is why I know your name. Although apparently I did not make much of an impression."

"I'm sorry—"

"Lonnie," he said helpfully.

"Right. Lonnie. I remember you."

"No you don't. But don't worry about it. The best salesmen are like me," he said. "Completely unmemorable."

"So," she said, "are you here to do the ten K?"

"Am I Racing for the Cure, you mean? I'm afraid not. I like to limit myself to racing for things I have an outside chance of contracting. Testicular cancer, enlarged prostate, pattern baldness. Nope, I'm working today." He motioned to a sad-looking card table about thirty feet away, festooned in red and yellow crepe paper with a big glass fishbowl on top. "Perhaps you'd like to put in your business card. I'm in charge of the raffle, and if you play your cards right, I might be able to tilt things a little in your favor, if you get my drift."

"What's the prize?"

"Well, we're raffling off a chance to have a person such as myself call you at home during dinner and try to get you to sign a contract for a three-year gym membership that you'll make use of, if statistics are anything to go by, and I think they are, a total of seven point four times and yet will continue to haunt you, month after month, year after year, as the eighty-eight dollars is tacked on to your credit card bill, a legally binding agreement that you will not be able to extricate yourself from even if you move to a different state, due to our largely illusory partnership with substandard gyms the world over. No. Wait. That's not it." He scratched his head and looked up at the sky. "I think, uh, maybe a pony?"

the academy of
overexamined relationships

When Holly stepped outside her building on Monday morning, she was surprised to see Spence there, standing exactly where she'd left him two days before, only this time he was wearing a suit and tie and brandishing what appeared to be a remaindered copy of her book.

"What are you, stalking me now?" said Holly.

"I just finished reading your book."

Now, Holly hadn't set out to perform a character assassination on Spence when she sat down to write a novel, not really. It's amazing how little malice there was in something that, when viewed from the outside, and in retrospect, seems nearly wholly malicious. For Holly, the story was always in the details, and the details, it turned out, were not interchangeable. At first, she'd tried to make Spence unrecognizable to himself and to everybody else by altering the various particulars of his life, by turning him from a tall, blond, Ivy-educated attorney who grew up in St. Louis with a bossy older sister and a nightmare of a mother, to a short dentist with curly black hair who grew up as an only child in Albuquerque. It was when Holly sat down to write about the time Spence had taken her home for Christmas that she realized the flaw in this plan. She didn't know the first thing about Albuquerque. Was it even cold there in December? What sort of clothes would her heroine have packed, had she needed to pack them? And the more she thought about it, the more complicated this business of fictionalization became, especially considering she had a perfectly good Christmas in St. Louis with Spence's family right there in her back pocket, complete with a Boxing Day screaming match starring his sister and his mother that she'd witnessed in stunned silence from the comfort of the family couch, which was velour and the precise hue of a Sun-Maid golden raisin. *Write what you know.* And so that's what she had done.

"You waited long enough," said Holly, while she fished around in her purse, making sure her keys were inside. They were. "What did you think?"

"I think I'm going to kill you! That's what I think!"

"I don't want to have this conversation right now. I'm late for work." Holly set off in the direction of the subway, and Spence trailed along beside her.

"Jesus, Holly, you didn't even attempt to disguise me."

"I have no idea what you're talking about."

"Palmer? The guy in your book? The one who's exactly like me?"

"It was a novel, Spence. Fiction? I made it up."

"Bullshit, Holly. That is bullshit and you know it."

Holly quickly considered her options.

"Okay, so, it's possible I used some parts of my life in my book. That's what writers do. I'm not going to apologize for it."

"It's a complete and total character assassination."

"I really don't see that."

"Oh, you don't see that?" said Spence. "You said, what,

that I'm withholding? And that I'm cold and psychologically defective and I hate women?"

"I said some nice things about you, too."

"Name one."

"I said you had silky hair."

"Jesus, Holly. I mean it. Jesus!"

"And anyway, don't you think you're a little hostile sometimes, Spence? I mean, don't you think you have a little latent hostility towards people of the female persuasion?"

"Because of my mother, right? Because I secretly deep down hate my mother. That's your theory, am I correct?"

Holly just shrugged her shoulders and kept on walking.

"It's complete bullshit, Holly, the whole thing."

"Listen, you sit down and try to write a book sometime. Sometimes you have to exaggerate things a little to make them interesting. You can't write a book about an average relationship in which nothing much ever happens that sort of just peters out after four years because one of the people in it can't commit."

"I could commit. My god, Holly, I proposed! I asked you to marry me! What more did you want?"

Holly stopped walking and took a deep breath and looked him square in the face. "You threw the ring at me, Spence. You said, and I remember your words exactly, 'Here's your goddamn ring.'"

"Because you were driving me crazy! I couldn't take it anymore!"

"I don't want to have this fight again," said Holly, and she started off down the sidewalk at a healthy clip. "And I'm not going to apologize for my book. I have nothing to apologize for. You were an asshole when we were together. And I'm sorry you were an asshole, but I'm not sorry I wrote about it. And anyway, who cares? I'm serious, Spence, who cares?! The book came out a year ago. Nobody outside of my immediate family read it, and they pretty much all hated you already."

"Well, it's completely fucked things up between me and Cathleen."

"Spencer. Come on." An expression crossed her face that he hadn't seen in years, but he remembered it like it was yesterday. "You slept with another woman. Then you lied to Cathleen when she confronted you about it. Then the other woman emailed pictures of the two of you together to her. Naked pictures, Spence."

"Jesus," said Spence. "She told you all that?"

"I'm afraid so."

"I feel like I'm in the middle of my worst nightmare."

"Well...?"

"Well, what?"

"I was going to say, maybe you can learn something from all this."

"I don't want to learn things from you," said Spence. "I'm no longer enrolled in the Holly Frick Academy of Overexamined Relationships."

"Fine. I don't care what you do. Just do me a favor and stop showing up in front of my building. I've got to go," said Holly, and she disappeared down the stairs into the subway.

———

Jesus, Spence thought. Things were rocky enough with Cathleen at the moment—those pictures! Impossible to get around!—without Holly inserting her nosy, shit-stirring yenta self into the mix. The thought of the two of them, talking on the phone about him, conferring, comparing notes. It was…not fair. That's all there was to it. It was not fair! There was something almost primally upsetting to Spence about this, because he liked to keep the parts of his life separate, he liked to keep his various relationships from overlapping and contaminating each other. He knew that not everybody lived this way, with all of this compartmentalization, this specialization, but it was the only way Spence felt comfortable. This wasn't because of dishonesty, not primarily, not entirely: he just felt better if the people he knew did not have independent contact with one another. Only problems could ensue.

He had spent Sunday night sprawled out on his couch, reading Holly's book in a state of escalating disbelief. From what he could tell, she had taken all of the various cockamamy theories she'd been spouting her entire life about love and sex and relationships and strung them together with unflattering portraits of her family and friends and a cartoonish skewering of him and somehow convinced someone to publish it. No wonder Americans had stopped reading books. He remembered hearing that Holly had published a novel when it first came out, and he'd decided right then and there that he would never read it. He felt instinctively that this was the worst thing you could do to a writer, just, you know, *not read* their book. Maybe read the first three pages and then quit. Standing up in a bookstore, so you never actually bought one. That had been his plan, and he had stuck to it for well over a year, until Cathleen got her hands on a copy and began treating it like it was some sort of legal document, like it was an accurate, entirely factual account of the four years of his life he'd spent involved with Holly Frick.

"This is just like the time you lied about what went on at Derek's bachelor party," Cathleen had said to him on the phone the week before. Spence had no idea what she was talking about. Derek's bachelor party? He didn't even know a Derek! Then a lightbulb went off: he knew an Eric, and Eric had indeed had a bachelor party, and there had been two strippers who had been persuaded to stage an impromptu girl-on-girl sex show on the floor of the hotel suite for an extra six hundred bucks, and *of course* he had lied about it to Holly, and *of course* she had somehow found out about it, but that was aeons ago! Spence was somewhat prepared to shore up the lies he ended up telling in a given relationship, but now he was being confronted with lies he'd told years ago, to a completely different woman, the finer points of which he couldn't even *remember* — it was too much. It was really too much.

And Cathleen. The woman was like a detective. He'd thought, when all this began, that he could ride out the storm the way he had in his past relationships, he figured it would all blow over in a matter of weeks, but Cathleen was tenacious, tracking down Holly, chattering away with Crazy Molly, slowly building her case against him. For someone who was so obsessed with fidelity, she was putting in an awful lot of time with a man who, if one were to be objective about the facts at hand, was less than entirely devoted to it as a bedrock principle in his romantic relationships. He had explained everything to her, more than once, and each time his explanation had taken a few baby steps closer to the truth, until finally he had turned a corner and had decided to go with total, or as near total as possible, honesty. This decision was largely due to the existence of Crazy Molly's digital photo collection, which turned out to be date-stamped and quite extensive.

Technology! The very things that made it possible to carry on an affair—cell phones, beepers, email—were just the ones that tripped you up in the end! And when Spence heard the news that Crazy Molly had had a cell phone tucked away in the pocket of her sweater when she showed up at his front door looking for "closure" and proceeded to confront him with a rather encyclopedic oral history of their "relationship," as she kept calling it, and that Cathleen was sitting on her couch in Boulder, phone pressed to her ear, listening to the entire conversation—well, it boggled the mind! This, two weeks after the emailing of the incriminating naked-sleeping date-stamped digital photo! How could a man combat that type of thing? A guy in his office had gone away for the weekend, ostensibly on a business trip, leaving his wife at home with their two children. A week later, the guy's wife opened up the travel Scrabble and found scorecards scribbled on scratch paper with her husband's name alongside someone named Janelle. Now, that was a low-tech unmasking! That was old school! You never heard about things like that anymore. Nowadays it was all about keystroke monitors and secret pay-as-you-go cell phones being discovered in glove compartments, redial buttons pressed at odd hours, learning how to flag your partner's emails as unread, passwords, and secret passwords, and supersecret passwords—questions about why you changed your password, questions about why you *know* that I changed my password—couples all over the country were doing it! And at the same time, it was precisely these new vectors of private communication, these little ways for people to whisper to each other, these ways to maintain private relationships that were quite often appropriate until they weren't anymore, that enabled these illicit affairs to get going in the first place. It was interesting, Spence thought. Someone really ought to look into it.

Spence had met Cathleen in an incredibly low-tech, almost old-fashioned way, on a mountain-biking trip outside of Moab, Utah. The catalog classified the trip as "rustic," which, it turned out, meant they ate rice and beans every night and had to shit in a bucket, after a heartfelt lecture by a scruffy guide about the length of time it takes human fecal matter to decompose in the desert. There were seven single women on the trip, each clocking in somewhere north of age thirty-four, each possessed of a unique yet subtle tinge of desperation. Cathleen stood out, however, because it seemed like she was really there because she wanted to bike through the desert and look at the stars and go to the bathroom in a bucket.

Nothing major happened on the trip, but the final night, after they failed to conquer Slickrock, the two of them drank Mormon-strength margaritas at an open-air bar with cactus centerpieces and an overdone lizard motif and Spence found himself thinking…maybe. She was short and intriguingly curvy, with masses of wild curly auburn hair that had been tied up in a ponytail until that last night, after they'd had a chance to take a proper shower at a Holiday Inn. She was a landscape architect, specializing in Xeriscape design, which she explained as a philosophy developed in the seventies that emphasized using indigenous plants and water-conscious planning and eschewing the great American lawn. Spence got a glimpse of her spirit when he said, "You mean those freaks who grow weeds in their front yard?" She owned her own house, a 1920s craftsman bungalow which she was restoring with painstaking historical accuracy, and her weekends were spent stripping paint and scouring flea markets for antique light fixtures and spare tiles. She had two big yellow dogs, both rescues (of course), and a lot of her life revolved around getting home in time to walk them before they crapped on the oak floors she'd spent a month of her life refinishing. Everything about her shouted "I can take care of myself," which Spence found appealing, because he couldn't quite imagine taking care of anybody but himself.

She was always processing things, seeing things from both sides, making connections and interpretations, and explaining him to him. She was so into therapy, it was like she did the work for both of them. For example, one time, early on in their relationship, Spence was supposed to call her at ten o'clock (midnight his time), and he didn't. The next day, Cathleen sent him an email that read: "What I hear you saying through your actions is that you don't want to be expected to call me at a predetermined hour. That is fine, but you should know that one consequence may be that we won't get to talk as much as we're used to, due to the time difference. You know I refuse to carry a cell phone on principle." All in all, Spence had to admit to himself as he read it over the following morning, it was an extremely reasonable response. Because he *did* resent being expected to call at a certain hour, and the consequence was in fact a consequence (since he looked forward to their nearly nightly telephone calls), but it was nice having it all laid out there so clearly. So many little things that would have become problems, that would have metastasized into fights in his previous relationships were simply ironed out by her reasonableness. It was like she had evolved to a point where she could carry on a relationship with him all by herself. Spence found this refreshing. He had grown tired of dating high-strung women who burst into tears and threw things at him. With Cathleen, there was a lot of "What I hear you saying is that…" and "When you do that, it makes me feel…"

And now it turned out, she was just like the rest of them. Now he had a screaming, weeping, full-blown hysteric on his hands. No more "Let me see if I understand what's at stake for you…" Not so much as a single "When you sleep with other women, it makes me feel like I'm not important to you.…" Just, you know, *Fuck off, Spence*. Well, at least he was back in familiar territory. At least he'd been here before.

the big buddhist

The last time Holly went to the Strand, she emerged two hours later with one of those Taschen folios entitled *Alchemy & Mysticism,* two of May Sarton's later journals, a six-dollar replacement for the copy of *The Corrections* she'd accidentally dropped in the bathtub, and a shrink-wrapped edition of *The French Laundry Cookbook.* The bag was so heavy, she had to take a cab home. That night, she realized the only actual *reading* material she'd bought were the journals, and, after a few pages of *At Seventy* — storm-flattened daffodils, a nasty bout of diverticulitis, a dead raccoon — she found she couldn't continue. Holly had made the mistake of leaving a copy of *Journal of a Solitude* on the toilet tank back when she was still married to Alex, and later, when he saw her reading it in bed, he'd said, "What's May bitching about now?" It was like the time her sister suggested she read Emily Dickinson to the tune of *Gilligan's Island.* Once certain thoughts got into your head, you couldn't get rid of them.

So, on this particular Sunday afternoon, before she had so much as walked through the bookstore's front doors, Holly had made a few rules for herself: (1) she could only buy books she actually intended to read; (2) they had to be light enough that she could take the subway home; and (3) she couldn't spend more than thirty bucks. She was poking around in the literary biographies, and already dangerously close to her limit, when she heard an unfamiliar voice.

"I know you."

"Yeah," said Holly. "Hello."

"Amanda's friend."

"Holly," she said.

"Right. I'm Jack."

"I remember," said Holly. "The big Buddhist."

He smiled. "That's right."

"Nice to see you," said Holly. She gave a sharp little nod of her head and then turned back to the bookshelf and studied the spines. After a few moments, Jack pulled a slightly battered copy of *Robert Frost: The Early Years* off the shelf and said to her, "Have you read this, by any chance?"

"No."

"You know who Robert Frost is, right?"

Holly looked at him the way you would look at someone who asked you if you knew who Robert Frost was, and then proceeded to recite, tonelessly, "'Two roads diverged in a wood, and I, I took the one less traveled by'—"

"'And that has made all the difference.' Exactly. This is kind of a funny story. Do you want to hear it?"

Holly shrugged a lukewarm "why not?"

"Okay, so, Robert Frost was always thought of, you know, as this humble, honest, salt-of-the-earth kind of person. The quintessential farmer-poet. Everybody in the country loved him. Not just his poems—they loved *him*. So this guy right here," Jack pointed to the cover of the book he was holding, "Lawrance Thompson, becomes Frost's official biographer. He sets out to write an exhaustive, three-volume biography, and as he gets to know Frost and edits his letters and talks to his friends and his family, he slowly grows to hate him. And I mean, he really *hates* him. He decides that Robert Frost is truly a despicable human being. So, as you read along, each of the volumes gets meaner and meaner. Here." Jack flipped to the back of the book. "Look at the headings in the index. 'Rage.' 'Revenge.'" He turned a few more pages. "'Jealousy.' 'Cowardice.' In one of the later volumes, there's even a long list of entries under 'Badness.'"

"Interesting," said Holly, a little formally. "I did not know any of that."

"Just trying to make bookstore chitchat with a famous author."

"Yeah, well, they keep my book in the pink section, so the girls don't get confused."

"I'm sorry if I offended you at lunch that day. Amanda explained it a bit after you left."

"No, no, it's fine. I'm used to it by now."

"Tell me something about your book," said Jack. "Was it a success?"

"Not remotely."

"Really? Amanda told me you got some really nice reviews."

"I sold four hundred and twenty-three copies in hardback," said Holly. "As of last Thursday."

"You know the number exactly?" said Jack. "I didn't think they told authors that."

"They don't," said Holly. "A friend of mine has the code to BookScan. We were planning to open a bottle of champagne when it hit five hundred, but that is looking increasingly unlikely."

"At least you have a good attitude about it," said Jack.

"Not really," she said. "This is mostly for show."

"Are you writing another one?"

"Another novel?" said Holly. "No way. I've got my problems, but my masochism has its limits."

"What are you working on instead?"

"Right now, I'm writing for a TV show. Writing for television is apparently right at the edge of the limit of my masochism," she said. She turned back to the shelves and started looking at the books again. "What about you, are you looking for anything in particular?"

"No," said Jack. "I'm going away on a retreat next weekend, and I wanted to get something to read on the train."

"A retreat?"

"With my Buddhist group."

Holly reached up and retrieved Quentin Bell's biography of Virginia Woolf off a high shelf. "What is that, like, meditation, bunk beds, whole grains, that sort of thing?"

"Pretty much."

Holly gave him a look.

"What?"

"I just think it's kind of interesting, that's all."

"What's interesting?"

"It's really none of my business."

"Tell me anyway."

"Okay. I just think it's kind of interesting, how you apparently take all that stuff so seriously that you go away for weekends to meditate and you buy the books and you probably have all sorts of weird purple cushions lying around your apartment, but you still," Holly searched for the phrase, "*carry on* with Amanda."

Jack looked at her like he had no idea what she was talking about.

"Oh, I know all about it, my friend. The sex," said Holly. "The dirty talking."

"She told you that?"

"Don't blame her. People tell me everything," said Holly. "It's almost a curse."

"Okay, well, let me start with, I don't separate the carnal from the spiritual," said Jack. "I don't have that split somehow."

Holly rolled her eyes.

"And I don't own any purple cushions."

"All I'm saying is, you have no idea what you're doing, what you're involved in, what the stakes are for everybody involved, and it's not enough to say 'whatever happens, happens' and 'I'm just a leaf in the stream' because, at the very minimum, what you are doing is profoundly unethical."

"Okay, first of all, you might be right, and I will think about it."

"Thank you."

"I just wanted to stipulate that up front."

"It is thus stipulated."

"But I'd like to point out that I didn't go looking for this. I'm as surprised by it as anyone." Jack put the Frost biography back on the shelf where he found it. "You know, I've got to run across the street to Paragon to get some long underwear. Do you want to keep talking?"

If the Strand was all brains, then Paragon was all body. It was packed to overflowing with the fit, the sporting, the adventurous, the outdoorsy—people who, Holly felt, really had no business living in New York City, and if they had any sense at all they would immediately pack up and move to someplace like Bozeman so they could be with their own kind. Jack weaved past the golfers and the skiers and the swimmers and the backpackers and descended a handful of steps into the clothing section while Holly trailed along behind him. After a bit of searching, he settled on a set of black synthetic long johns that, on the model in the photo at least, looked vaguely like a wet suit. They came in a cardboard cylinder that was covered with images of red chili peppers, as if to drive home the level of heat the product was capable of delivering. "You're going to be too hot in those," a salesguy said helpfully when he noticed Jack reading the text on the back of the canister. He had three days' worth of stubble on his jaw and looked like he scaled mountains before breakfast. "I'm going to be outside a lot, and I want to stay warm," Jack explained to him. "Dude, you're not going to be warm, you're going to be *hot*. Trust me, you're not gonna like it. Get these instead," the guy said, tossing Jack a clear plastic bag containing a set of regulation long underwear in a silk and cotton blend. "So these are less hot than these?" Jack asked. "They're *warm*. They're perfect. They're what you want." "I hear you, but you know, I think I like hot. That's the kind of long underwear I'm interested in buying. If I didn't want to be hot," said Jack, "I'd just be buying regular underwear." "Dude. Trust me"—the salesguy lowered his voice conspiratorially—"we really only sell those to girls." Jack stood there, with a package of long underwear in each hand, and for a moment it looked like he was going to put the chili cylinder back on the revolving display. "I hear you," he said finally, "and I appreciate your concern, but I'm going to have to trust my instincts on this one. But thank you. I mean it." "Suit yourself," the guy said, and then he sauntered off in the direction of the powder jackets, visibly disgusted.

"Good thing that wasn't embarrassing," Jack said to Holly when they got out onto the sidewalk. "Glad I asked you to come along to witness that."

"He really didn't want you to buy those," said Holly. "And now, I must admit, I'm genuinely curious to see how it turns out."

"I'll let you know."

"Do that."

"I've seen this sort of thing with other girlfriends of mine," Holly said. She and Jack had made their way down Broadway and then crossed over to Washington Square. They were sitting on a park bench, eating soft pretzels and watching a pair of skateboarders who were apparently competing to see who would end up in the emergency room first. "They meet a guy at the kiddie pool and three weeks later they're ready to run away with him. Then something happens to pull them back to their life and their family and they take a few deep breaths and then that's it. It's over. They're back inside their life and a month later they're fine and happy."

"They're happy?"

"Maybe not happy-happy," said Holly, "but they're happy enough."

Holly was focused on her food or, more precisely, on the balancing thereof, mustard on pretzel on waxed paper on knees, can of Diet Coke carefully placed and replaced a few inches to the right of her hip on one of the narrow green planks of the park bench. Jack watched her for a moment, a little amused.

"So, what about you? Why did you and your husband split up?" said Jack.

"Why did I get a divorce, you mean?"

"Yeah."

"Basically?" she said. "My husband decided to start dating again."

"What do you mean?" said Jack. "He had an affair?"

"It wasn't really an affair. It's not like there was 'another woman.' He just started staying out with his friends a lot, going out drinking on the weekends, and then strange women would call the house and ask for him."

"Really?"

"Yeah. It would be like, I'd pick up the phone, and some girl I'd never heard of before would ask if Alex was home. Like I was his roommate or something. He didn't even try to hide it."

"So what did you do?"

"I pretended it wasn't happening for longer than was, you know, in retrospect, entirely dignified."

Jack smiled at this.

"Finally one night, he was brushing his teeth, and I said something casual, like, should I be worried about this?" said Holly. She carefully pinched a few inches off her pretzel and put it in her mouth. "And he said, 'Probably.' Things went downhill pretty quickly from there."

"He sounds like a real jerk."

"Yeah, well, they all sound like jerks after it's over. But for a while there we were best friends, and he always made me laugh, and we had the world's most interesting conversations, and there's a part of me, that if you told me I had to be trapped on a desert island for ten years and could pick one person to be trapped with, I'd pick him," said Holly. "Of course, I'd be his only option, sexually speaking. Things would be much easier."

"When did you split up?"

"It was a year ago this past January," said Holly. "It's funny. I've had all this time to think about it, to try to make some sense out of it, but I think, in the end, he was just one of those people who couldn't handle being married. He just couldn't do it. Which is sad, because I loved it. I loved him."

"I'm sorry."

"It's okay. You're supposed to love the person you marry. I'm getting over it."

"Have you started dating again?"

"I wouldn't call it dating, exactly," said Holly. "I'm having sex with a twenty-two-year-old."

"Really? Twenty-two? I'm impressed."

"Yeah," said Holly. "He's adorable. He's really the perfect man, and I'm sure he'll make some girl just about to graduate from junior high school very happy someday."

"Who knows? That sort of thing can work out. I think sometimes these ideas we have can get in the way of our happiness."

"Maybe." One of the skateboarders launched himself directly at a fire hydrant, flipped over, and landed on his back on a pile of dirt. "It can get kind of strange, though. He's always saying things like 'Your towels are so nice.' And 'Your sheets are so soft,'" said Holly. "The other night, I brought him a big bowl of spaghetti carbonara in bed, and he said, 'These are just like my mother's dishes.'"

"He said that?"

She nodded. "And he's so young, so untherapized, so un-Manhattanized, he's not even slightly freaked out by that. It's merely a point of information."

"I'm just impressed that you serve spaghetti carbonara to men in bed."

"It's possible I'm overcompensating," said Holly. "Should we be worried about that idiot?" The skateboarder was lying in the dirt, motionless, emitting a series of strange, high-pitched yelps. His friend was on his knees on the sidewalk ten feet away, clutching his sides in hysterics.

"I say we give him a few minutes, and then see if he can move his legs," said Jack. "I want you to know, I realize that this thing with Amanda is a mess."

"Yeah?"

"I do."

"Well, what about the obvious? Dating someone who isn't married? There are a million great single women in this city—"

"And none of them can find a decent guy to date, right? Isn't that how it goes?"

"Isn't that how what goes?"

"The whole New York City myth," said Jack. "The idea that the city is simply packed with fabulous single women in their thirties who just can't find a halfway decent man to go out with."

"Well? Isn't it true?"

"Not in my experience."

"What do you mean?"

"Who do you think I've been going out with all these years? That parade of 'fabulous' New York women."

"Yeah, so, what's wrong with them?"

"In my experience?" said Jack. He emptied a mustard packet onto the last limb of his pretzel while he formed his thoughts. "They're guarded, elusive, terrified of intimacy, and incapable of sustaining any interest."

"That's because they live here. You spend fifteen years as a single woman in Manhattan, it's going to screw you up a little."

The skateboarder had made it over onto all fours and was struggling to catch his breath.

"You know what I want?" said Jack. "I want somebody who's warm."

Holly took a swig of her Diet Coke. "Move to Kansas."

"I'm serious," said Jack. "I want a warm woman. Is that too much to ask for?"

"No, see, but I don't think that's all you want," said Holly. "I think you want a woman who's stylish and articulate and funny and smart, who has a real career, who keeps up with her New York City grooming routine and goes to the gym and has a flat stomach and who also happens to be an incredibly warm and nurturing individual. And maybe all that doesn't fit together so well."

"Amanda's not like that."

"No, she's not," Holly admitted.

"That's the weird part of all this," he said. "She makes me think I want a wife."

Holly just looked at him for a second. "You know, women become wives when they get married," she finally said. "You don't need to start out with somebody else's. You can make your own."

"Fair point."

The sun was sinking between two buildings across the square. Holly looked down at her watch. "I didn't realize it was so late. I should get going."

"Really?"

"Yeah."

"It was nice to bump into you."

"It was fun," said Holly. "Thanks for the miniature Robert Frost lecture, and the front-row seat for the underwear thing."

They stood up. Jack walked her out of the park, under the arch, which was already lit up and gleaming in the fading light. They stood together at the foot of Fifth Avenue, waiting for a taxi.

"There's a thing next weekend that I wanted to go to," said Jack. "A party for this artist I know, at a gallery in Chelsea. Amanda can't go with me, for obvious reasons, so, I don't know, I was just thinking, maybe you'd want to come along."

"You want to go with me?"

"That's what I was thinking."

"Yeah, you know, I don't think that's such a good idea," said Holly. "Things have just been crazy for me lately, my dog is sick, I've got this script due, and I promised myself I was going to use this month to really get myself together, to figure out my life —"

"It's just a cocktail party, Holly. Not three weeks in Barbados."

"I know, but, still." She looked down at her shoes. "I'm going to have to pass."

"Maybe another time."

"Another time."

imaginary problems

When Leonard moved to New York to take a job on *The Mighty Moppets*, he installed a house sitter at his home in Los Angeles and rented an apartment in the Archive Building in the West Village for six thousand dollars a month, bringing his monthly nut up near fifteen grand, perhaps somewhat imprudently. Two months into his new lease, the woman who lived in the apartment directly above his ran a bath and proceeded to pass out on her kitchen floor, causing her tub to overflow down into his apartment, staining the ceiling over his bed a rusty brown. Leonard had put in a call to his business manager, Lou, with the complaint, and Lou had gotten on the phone from LA and arranged for Leonard to move into a vacant apartment two floors down. Lou had hired the movers, a person to pack and unpack Leonard's stuff, another one to set up his electronics, as well as a person to supervise the move, to transfer the contents of his fridge, to remove the half-used roll of toilet paper from the dispenser next to Leonard's old toilet and reinstall it next to the new one. All of this was done so seamlessly, with so little inconvenience to Leonard, that he left for work on a Thursday morning from one apartment and returned home ten hours later to an identical apartment two floors down. That Leonard was no longer rich enough to live like this, to pay strangers to insulate him from the cares and inconveniences of daily life—that didn't seem to register, and Lou, who perhaps had a moral if not a fiduciary duty to drive this point home, had fifty thousand reasons to maintain the status quo.

And yet, even with all of this care, even with all of this expensive professional attention to detail, still, somehow, the cable installation had been overlooked, and when Leonard got home on Thursday night he discovered his TV didn't work. He told Holly he was going to check himself into a suite at the Gansevoort over the weekend, and Holly, ever sensible, refused to let this happen. Which is why they were spending the day in Leonard's new yet identical apartment, late on a Friday afternoon, awaiting the cable guy and trying to come up with ideas for stories.

"What if Angela thinks her parents are getting a divorce," Holly said, "because they've been acting weird and whispering all the time and talking to strange people on the phone, so she goes to her friends and they give her all sorts of support and understanding and advice, but at the end of the episode, it turns out, her parents were really just planning a surprise birthday party for her."

Leonard was lying on his couch with his eyes closed and his hands folded on top of his chest. "Angela's the black one, right?"

"*Leonard.*"

He opened one eye. "The Chinese one?"

The Mighty Moppets featured a white girl, a black girl, an Asian girl, and a Muslim girl who were best friends and played basketball for Boston's fictional Immaculata Junior High. Even though the show was set in the present day, the nuns at Immaculata still wore full-length black-and-white habits because the producers thought it looked funnier. In an effort to skewer stereotypes, the African American character was fabulously wealthy, the Chinese girl was the coolest girl in school, the Muslim one was a smoldering sexpot, and the white girl was left with no discernible personality whatsoever. It was a disaster, an after-school special littered with hacky smash cuts to nuns eating hot dogs and nuns squeezing cucumbers while shooting the camera sheepish, guilty looks.

"She's the black one," Holly said. Then she sighed. "Angela's the black one and Mimi is the Chinese one and Taylor is the white one and Nuala is the Muslim one."

Leonard got a puzzled look on his face. "Why is a Muslim going to a Catholic school?"

"This is the first time that thought has occurred to you?" said Holly. "We've been writing for this show for the past two months, and today is the day you finally begin to ponder why a Muslim girl is attending a Catholic junior high?"

"Apparently I haven't been paying very close attention."

Holly slumped over and banged her head against the table a few times.

"Nuala won a soccer scholarship," she said. "In episode two, her parents meet with the nuns, and they come to an understanding and make a few jokes about headscarves and nuns' habits. How we're all the same underneath. Cue credits."

Leonard looked puzzled again. "They give soccer scholarships to Catholic junior high schools?"

Holly shook her head slowly. "Don't start pulling threads."

———————

Holly's mother Fiona called her once a week, usually on Friday afternoons, before she left for her mah-jongg game but after she came home from MOPS. Holly wasn't one hundred percent sure what MOPS was, except that it involved church and small children and gave her mother a chance to rail against *all these crazy parents these days indulging their kids with made-up peanut aller-gies and nonsense about choking hazards and things that can fit through toilet-paper tubes*. If it were up to Fiona, she'd lock the MOPS tod-dlers in the church basement with a big batch of peanut but-ter cookies and a sack full of marbles and see who managed to make it out alive. Still, volunteering made her feel good.

"That was a very stupid thing to do, Holly," Fiona said, after Holly told her about adopting Chester. Ever since Holly announced she and Alex were getting divorced, Fiona felt she had permission to air her thoughts with brutal frankness, since Holly had made such a mess of her life during the years Fiona had kept her opinions to herself. "That poor dog is going to die and you are not in the position emotionally to handle it."

"He's not going to die. The vet says he's got a really good chance."

"What on earth made you think that adopting a dog with a *brain tumor* was a smart thing to do?"

"I never said it was smart," said Holly. "I just wanted to, so I did."

"You wanted to."

"Yes, Mom. I wanted to."

There was a long, transcontinental pause. "I've never done anything I wanted to in my entire life."

This was the other side of Holly's postdivorce relationship with her mother, little cloudbursts of shattering honesty that seemed to come out of nowhere and always left Holly feeling a little floored. One time, while they were driving to the mall, her mother said to her, apropos of nothing, "You know, I think I could have been happy married to a woman."

"Come on, Mom, that's not true," Holly said into the phone.

"I've done things I wanted to do," Fiona said. "But it's never been sufficient motivation, all by itself. I've never done something that I shouldn't do, that would be stupid to do, simply because I *wanted* to do it."

"Yeah, well, I think that's sad."

"Maybe, but it's kept me out of *a lot* of trouble."

"What's wrong with trouble?" Holly said. She thought about sleeping with Lucas, and adopting Chester, and even, for a quick second, about the afternoon she spent talking to Jack, and the suspicion she had, that if he weren't involved with Amanda, she might really like him. "I'm going to try to have more real problems and fewer imaginary ones. Like it says in that poem hanging next to the toilet."

Holly's mother thought about it for a moment, and then she said, "I'd rather have a hundred imaginary problems than one real one."

———————

When Holly came back from the bathroom, Leonard was absentmindedly scratching his right forearm. As she watched him, the scratching moved up, to his upper arm, and then to his neck.

"You're scratching again?"

"Looks like."

"I thought your doctor gave you something for it."

"He did, but it started up again."

"How come?"

"Stress about the move."

"It's all done," said Holly. "You're moved. What's to stress out about?"

"You know," said Leonard. He gestured broadly. "*This.*"

Holly looked around. The furniture was arranged exactly the way it had been in the apartment upstairs, the art was hanging on the walls, and there was not a cardboard box in sight. "I honestly have no idea what you're talking about."

"Waiting for the cable guy."

Holly just looked at him. "This is what normal people do, Leonard. When they move, they wait around for the cable guy. They don't pay someone fifty bucks an hour to do their waiting around for them, and they don't check themselves into a luxury hotel if the guy doesn't show up."

But that was just it. "Normal people" was the problem. "Normal people" was what worried him. Leonard didn't want to contemplate life as a normal person, as a person who managed his own affairs, who flew coach, who thought twice before picking up the check on a three-hundred-dollar dinner. And this business of waiting around for the cable guy was reminding him of how far and how fast he was sinking.

Earlier that week, he'd had a peculiar interaction with their boss, an extremely unpleasant woman named Marta Brooks. Marta was the genius behind *The Mighty Moppets,* the woman on whose shoulders the creative blame rested as well as the one who would reap the majority of the spoils should the show become the next *Hannah Montana* or *Dora the Explorer*. Marta's creative formula came down to two oft-repeated sentences: "Where's the edge?" and "Give me more heart." On Tuesday afternoon, Leonard found himself in the elevator alone with her, a situation he normally worked quite hard to avoid, but seeking to make conversation, he'd asked her how the numbers were. "I don't care about the numbers," Marta had replied. Leonard said he was just curious, having spent so much time in prime time, to get an idea of the size of their audience. "I don't even look at the numbers," Marta had said. "All I care about is if the network is happy."

That just piqued Leonard's curiosity. What kind of television producer didn't care about the numbers? The numbers were what television was about. Even if *The Mighty Moppets* was designed to sell My Little Ponies to eight-year-olds, it mattered how many eight-year-olds were tuning in each week. He'd spent the early days of his career sitting at the feet of Gary David Goldberg—a man who amassed his nine-figure personal fortune back when it was possible to garner a forty share on a Wednesday night with a show starring a very small black boy, or a girl who was really a robot, or an opinionated handpuppet who hailed from outer space—and Leonard had come away with a healthy respect for the economic equation that is network television. After lunch, he got on the phone with his agent's assistant and had her email the previous week's ratings, a five-page document with hundreds and hundreds of cable television shows and time periods, a dense grid of demographic breakdowns complete with clearances and trends, and when he ran one finger in a straight line across from *The Mighty Moppets* and another finger down from national household share, they ended up colliding at a tiny gray box that contained the number .008.

It was the second zero that threw him.

Point zero zero eight? Point zero *zero* eight?!

Leonard was old enough to have witnessed the great glissade into single-digit ratings that the proliferation of cable channels had brought about in the nineties; he had worked on sitcoms where a 6.9 share was considered a cause for celebration; but he had never in his wildest nightmares imagined that he would enter the realm of double zeros.

"Imagine taking all of your problems and putting them into a matchbox," Holly said. "I'm serious. This will be good for you. Imagine putting your problems — this cable-guy thing, your career, the phantom itching, I don't know, whatever problems you think you've got — in a matchbox."

"Okay," said Leonard. "They're in there."

"Then you go put the matchbox in a big huge pile with everybody else's problems. And then you have to go take a matchbox out of the pile, and those are your new problems. The question is, do you take back your own matchbox, or do you take someone else's?"

"I would take anybody's," said Leonard.

"Come on. You could end up with cancer, or an autistic child. Think of what people go through. You could end up paralyzed."

"*Anybody's.*"

two feathers

When Holly brought Chester home from the shelter, the woman in charge had handed her a business card for a nearby animal hospital and told her she should ask for Two Feathers.

"What do I need the feathers for?" Holly had asked her.

"I'm sorry?"

For a moment, Holly felt the crushing weight of all she had so blithely agreed to take on. She pictured months of pureeing raw meat, wrapping pills in cheese, swabbing up after bouts of canine incontinence. She flashed on all the dogs she'd seen in various states of disrepair, with big white cones around their necks, the ones scooting along down the sidewalk with their withered hind legs tucked into little carts — and now, out of the blue, here was something unexpected, something involving feathers.

"What am I supposed to do with the feathers?" Holly said.

"What are you supposed to do with the *feathers?*" The woman started to laugh. "He's a *person*. His *name* is Two Feathers. He's Native American."

"Oh."

"He's the vet who volunteered to help."

* * *

Two Feathers turned out to be mesmerizingly good-looking, but in a slightly off-putting, asexual way, like Keanu Reeves or Hilary Swank. He met Holly in the lobby of the animal hospital and led her back down a long hallway to a surprisingly spacious, cluttered office. He had to hunt around a bit for Chester's medical records, so Holly sat down across from his desk in a gray molded plastic chair and tried not to get caught staring at him. His hair was pulled back in a low ponytail, and it was so black and gleaming it almost looked blue. His eyes were so deep and black they also almost looked blue. His teeth were so blindingly white they looked, Holly found herself thinking, almost blue. She felt all at once pale and blotchy and flawed, an evil pudding person sent over from England to steal his continent and kill his buffalo.

"Can I ask you a question?" said Holly.

"Of course."

"Is it true that Native Americans get their names by the first thing their father sees after they're born?"

"That's one way it happens, yes."

"And your dad saw two feathers?"

"So he tells me."

"That's cool," said Holly.

"I guess so."

Two Feathers used his heels to propel his wheelie desk chair over to a low gray filing cabinet.

"I guess you're lucky he didn't see something like, I don't know, an answering machine. Or a plasma TV."

"—"

"What I mean is, good thing it was so nature-y. Not that that's a word," said Holly. She was quiet for a moment and then added, "But I think it works in this context."

Two Feathers wheeled back behind his desk and opened up Chester's file.

"Is it all right if I ask the questions for a bit?"

"Of course."

Two Feathers went down a checklist covering Chester's general state of health—had she noticed any lethargy or strange behavior, walking in circles, had she witnessed any more seizures, was he eating well, how was he sleeping—and then he brought Holly up to speed on the results of Chester's earlier diagnostic tests.

"Chester has a meningioma," said Two Feathers. "A cancer of the meninges, which is the tissue that covers the brain and protects it. You've heard of meningitis, right?" He looked at Holly, and she nodded. "It's not a lymphoma, which is good, because it means he won't need chemotherapy. This is the kind of thing that grows but doesn't generally spread."

He went through the protocols, what she could expect, and he gave her a stack of pamphlets and recommended a book called *When Your Dog Has Cancer*. They would start in with surgery, and then follow up with radiation treatments.

"You have to understand, Chester doesn't know he has cancer," said Two Feathers. "You'll find that you can derive a great deal of comfort from remembering that fact, but it also means that the caretaker is the one who bears the brunt of the diagnosis, psychologically speaking."

"I never thought about it that way," said Holly. "I mean, I guess one of the worst parts about having cancer would be *knowing* you have cancer."

"Dogs don't have that burden, which means they avoid a great deal of suffering."

"That's good," said Holly.

Finally, he put the clipboard down and looked at her.

"Do you have any other pets?" said Two Feathers. "Or are you fostering any animals for a shelter, anything like that?"

"No. Is that a problem?"

"I'm just trying to get the whole picture."

"Ah," said Holly. "You mean, am I the crazy dog lady who runs around saving animals from execution or something. Is that what you're thinking?"

"Not exactly that," he said.

"Because I'm not. Chester was an impulse rescue. Not that I regret it. But this is a one-time deal for me."

"Okay," said Two Feathers. "Can I ask, do you live alone?"

Holly nodded yes.

"Do you have any external support system in place, family nearby or a boyfriend or something, to help with Chester's care, or to support you if things don't go as well as we'd hope?"

Holly blinked at him. "You're asking me if I have a boyfriend?" she said. "My dog has a brain tumor, and you're asking me if I have a boyfriend?"

"I'm sorry. It's just an unusual situation, that's all. I'm just trying to get a sense of your emotional resources."

Holly folded her arms in front of her chest. "I've got plenty."

————————

One unfortunate side effect of Leonard's career as a writer was that it called for long stretches of solitary time in front of his computer, which happened to be the portal to several of his most enduring vices. He'd spent the eight months it took to write *Shark Attack* holed up in the spare bedroom he used as an office, shades drawn, in a state of what can only be called pornographic saturation. He kept thinking he would eventually grow tired of seeing pictures of strangers' penises and assholes and butt cheeks and whatnot, but apparently that was not the case. Whenever he hit a rough spot in his script, he'd figure, *What the hell, maybe I'll just take a little peek,* and before he knew it, there he'd be, at it again.

The problem was this: writing made Leonard feel anxious and ashamed. He felt, while sitting in front of his computer screen, watching the words stack up in ways that were always somehow less than he'd hoped, pressed up against his inadequacies, forced to face his creative limitations, tormented by the awareness that this was the best he could do. And he didn't like those feelings. They were difficult for him to tolerate. So, much of his life became a matter of introducing another feeling into his system, a feeling that would temporarily override the other stuff. In his optimistic moments he thought of it as merely a matter of getting the energy flowing, unblocking his chi, injecting a little yang into all the ethereal mental yin he spent the day marinating in, but then, say, after throwing down for the third time and turning back to the document glowing reproachfully from his screen, he would find himself wondering: Is this how Dostoyevsky did it?

He would happen upon a chunky housewife offering her rump and dimpled haunches to the camera, a wicked smile on her lipsticked face (and as much as he didn't want to see it, stumbling on things like that happened more frequently than one might expect), and he'd think: People are crazy. People are crazy! That's all the Internet proved. And he felt a little camaraderie there, like a member of a strange underground community, the concept of "normal" expanding exponentially in the digital haze of cyberspace, until the thought of, say, a monogamous heterosexual couple engaged in thrice-weekly rounds of vanilla sex seemed distinctly abnormal. So there was that.

But then there was the other level, the one that made him feel incredibly alone. He would click through images quickly, dispassionately, like a curator reviewing slides for an art gallery, looking for something to grab him, some combination of body hair and musculature, penis and pose, face and smile, wardrobe or background, something that would trigger *something* in him, a memory, a fantasy, something old, something new, the whole time aware that it was getting harder and harder to get the right synapses to fire, to topple over the first in what was becoming an increasingly long and unreliably arranged line of dominoes.

It wasn't just pornography. Leonard had had an expensive six-week episode involving his MasterCard and an off-shore outfit specializing in no-limit Texas hold 'em — the "no limit" part, in retrospect, should have tipped him off that this was not a wise hobby — and, earlier that month, he'd purchased thirty Xanax from a pharmacy located in St. Kitts. This was, in its own way, an act of sheer and utter perversity, because Leonard had unlimited access to proper Xanax, thanks to his psychopharmacologist, who was notoriously loose with the triplicates. Still, he was curious, and the next morning a FedEx package arrived, containing a Ziploc baggie with thirty pills inside, each an unpromising shade of gray. The word *Xanax* was handwritten on a white label stuck to the bag. Leonard had a flight that afternoon to LA, connecting through Houston, and he popped two of the pills in the cab on the way to JFK. He woke up two days later in a hotel room in Marina del Rey with absolutely no memory of how he got there. It took him over an hour to locate his rental car, which was, according to the keys in his pocket, a white Dodge Neon. Later, when Holly asked him why on earth he'd taken *two*, Leonard said, "I don't know. They seemed so small."

A while back, though, Leonard had found something new. It was called LukesPlace, and was, according to *Time* magazine, a new kind of "commons." There were many things to like about LukesPlace—you could find a futon somebody was willing to give away for free or an Italian tutor for fifteen bucks an hour, you could sublet your apartment or find a place to volunteer, you could join a club or find a dog, you could find a person to walk your dog—but that is not what Leonard liked about it. The thing Leonard liked about LukesPlace was that you didn't have to be altogether on your game and yet you could still have sex with perfect strangers. They even had a special section devoted to it, right below men seeking women, and women seeking men: play. It sounded so innocent, play. And yet, once you clicked on it, you entered into a world of almost mind-blowing excess, variety, and explicitness, a veritable supermarket of flesh. By the time somebody actually showed up on your doorstep, they had whipped themselves up into such a seething froth of desire that they were willing to overlook a little softness at the belly, a little ass sag, a little jowl pudge that would have sent them sprinting in the other direction if they encountered it in a bar. It was a boon, really, and it arrived just when Leonard needed it.

———

"Spence told me he had a fling with some woman in Italy while you were together," Cathleen said to Holly, "but he said you knew about it."

Cathleen had phoned from Boulder again. She'd sent an email earlier that day saying she had a few more things she wanted to run by Holly, just a few loose ends that needed tying up, and Holly, perhaps unwisely, perhaps against the better parts of her nature, perhaps in service of the side of herself that was, in fact, a nosy, shit-stirring yenta, had once again picked up the phone. It had become a three-way conversation, in that Cathleen was reporting what Holly had told her back to Spence, and Spence was offering his rebuttal to Cathleen, and then Cathleen was bringing it back to Holly and dropping it on her doorstep like a well-chewed bone.

The first time they'd talked, Holly had told Cathleen something very few people actually knew, something that Holly liked to keep to herself: although she wrote an oh-so-thinly-veiled autobiographical novel about a nice girl who was virtually indistinguishable from herself and a lying, cheating, unfaithful bastard who was clearly based on her ex-live-in-boyfriend, the truth was that Spence Samuelson had, in point of fact, never cheated on her. The feelings were true, but not the facts. She'd needed something to get the ball rolling in the first chapter, and that was the not-entirely-original-yet-suitably-dramatic device she'd come up with. Holly then happened to mention that she'd had an inkling that something might have happened on a trip Spence took to Italy with his friend Cliff Bissinger near the end of their relationship, but she never did find out for sure. Well, Cathleen had gotten on the phone with Spence and inquired about his trip to Italy, and she'd prodded and probed and asked a few leading questions, and Spence had ended up telling her the truth as he remembered it, which differed in several fundamental ways from Holly's recollection of the same events, the primary one being, he'd spent the week in question not riding his bike with his buddy Cliff through the Tuscan countryside, but having sex with an exquisite forty-one-year-old Italian divorcée he'd met on the flight over.

"I did not know about it," Holly finally said, with forced levity.

"You didn't?"

"Until this moment," said Holly. "I suspected it. But I didn't *know* it. And you know what? Turns out, it makes a difference."

"I'm sorry."

"That shithead."

"I shouldn't have said anything."

"No, it was a long time ago," said Holly. "Still…I *knew* it. Deep down, I knew it. I should have trusted my instincts. I never trust my instincts."

"He said it wasn't a big deal, the Italy thing, and that he told you and you were fine with it."

Spence's trip to Italy! Holly remembered it like it was yesterday. He had come home one night and announced that Cliff had invited the two of them to go to Europe on a bike trip. The plan was to cover about seventy miles a day, over gently rolling Tuscan terrain, with steep climbs to hilltop towns at the end of each day, where they'd sleep in budget accommodations because Cliff had lost his job and didn't have much money. Holly gave the matter some serious thought and then said to Spence, her live-in-almost-fiancé: Enjoy yourself! Wear a helmet!

Spence had phoned Holly from Italy just once, the day before he was due back, a quick call with his flight information and a few vague references to sore quads and cheap wine, sunsets and peasants and cheese. When he got home — *You wouldn't believe how difficult it was to make a call from Italy, those pay phones, with a hundred different kinds of calling cards, and weird coins, it was so confusing!* — and Holly discovered he'd only taken eight photos all week, three of which were of Cliff posing with an enormous air-cured sausage inside the Milan airport duty-free shop, a few bells went off, but Holly elected to ignore them. She did not want to be That Woman. And now, all these years later, in this weird, roundabout way, finally, the truth.

"And, for the record," Holly said into the phone, "he did not tell me about it. And if he had, I would not have been fine with it."

"I didn't think you would," said Cathleen.

"It's strange," said Holly. "I don't care, particularly, and yet I still have this overwhelming urge to pound in his skull with a baseball bat."

"He also said I should ask you the story of how you guys got engaged."

"Spence said that?"

"He said I should ask for the truth and not the 'official version.'"

"He didn't tell you himself?"

"He said I should ask you."

"Oh, jeez, well, first of all, this is not a story that reflects well on me," said Holly. "I am well aware of that fact."

"That's okay."

"But we'd been together for *four* years. We'd lived together for two of them. I'd seen a ring in the window of a jewelry store near our apartment, and one night when we were walking home from the movies I casually pointed it out to Spence, and he got all weird and hostile and said he couldn't deal with all this *pressure,* so I dropped it. Fine. Then I happened to walk by a few days later and I looked in the window and the ring was gone and for some reason it made me incredibly upset. I mean, it was my perfect ring, it was an antique, and it looked like a tiny daisy made out of ice, and it wasn't too expensive, and for some reason seeing it gone made it perfectly clear to me that Spence was never going to marry me, he had no intention of ever doing it, and if I had an ounce of self-respect I would get out before I wasted any more of my time. When he came home from work, I was on the couch crying, and I said that maybe we should just end things if he didn't feel like he could make a real commitment. He went into the bedroom and slammed the door, and I kept sobbing, and a few minutes later he came out and stood in the doorway and chucked the ring at me from across the room."

"No way."

"That was the proposal. The ring bounced off my shoulder and rolled under the coffee table."

"That's horrible."

"That's not even the worst part."

"There's a worse part?"

"I got down on my hands and knees and picked the ring up off the floor and slipped it on my finger and said 'yes.' Or 'thank you.' I can't remember exactly what I said, but that was it. We were engaged."

"Are you serious?"

"I'm afraid so," said Holly. "I broke it off a few weeks later, after telling everybody I'd ever met and buying forty pounds' worth of bridal magazines and putting a very substantial down payment on a silky sheath wedding dress unhealthily influenced by the late Carolyn Bessette. Spence moved out. That was it."

"That's quite a story."

"I hope he at least admitted that I was the one who finally broke things off."

"He did," Cathleen said, although her voice sort of hung in the air somehow, indicating there was more to it than that.

"What. What did he say about it?"

"He made it sound like he sort of," and here was another strange pause, "wanted you to."

"He did? Why?"

"Are you sure you want to hear this?"

"I am."

"Are you sure?"

"No, no, tell me," said Holly. "I'm finding this fascinating."

"Okay, well, he said you were great and smart and the funniest woman he'd ever dated, but when it came down to it, he didn't think that, you know, for a lifelong relationship," Cathleen took a deep, whistly breath, "he didn't think he was attracted enough to you physically."

"Aagh," said Holly. "That is so humiliating."

"He was lying to me, Holly," said Cathleen. "I've seen the picture on the back of your book. You're beautiful."

Referencing this particular picture did not comfort Holly, because if there was one thing Holly knew, it was that she was not remotely as attractive as her book photo. This was not a function of airbrushing or Photoshop or trick lighting or deceptive camera angles — it was simply a miracle. Like the visage of the Virgin Mary appearing inside a corn tortilla. The day Holly showed Leonard the proof, he looked down at the picture and then looked up at her, then looked down at the picture and looked back up at her, and finally said, "How did they make you look like this?"

"I don't look like that," Holly said to Cathleen. "Trust me."

"He was just trying to come up with an excuse for himself."

"This is, wow." Holly flopped down on her bed and stared up at the ceiling. "All this time I've been feeling guilty about writing that book, worrying that I might have hurt his feelings or embarrassed him somehow, and now through this completely random series of events, I find out that he was fucking around behind my back and, oh, by the way, he wasn't all that attracted to me physically," said Holly. "Now I wish I'd written he had a penis the size of a Jujube or something."

It was Italy, for chrissake.

Her name was Francesca Porcini, and she still made semi-regular appearances in his fantasies, god bless her. Even now, years later, when he needed a little help getting over the finish line, Spence would conjure her up and have her walk into the room wearing that white lacy strappy top thing and smile at him and then cross her arms in front of her and loop her thumbs through the material and pull the whole frothy confection over her head. *Francesca*. And in Hollyworld — that's what Spence used to call the imaginary place in Holly's head where all of her demands and expectations and rules were adhered to with unwavering vigilance—he would have been denied that moment. He would have missed out on one of the top-ten experiences *of his life.* And try as he might, he couldn't see how his spending six days in bed with Francesca Porcini in her tiny house wedged into the side of a cliff just outside Positano in the spring of 1996 had done Holly Frick the least bit of harm. He'd missed his chance to see Capri, he never got around to renting a moped, and he even had to skip Pompeii (and ever since junior high, he'd wanted to see those frozen dice players in person)—but Holly, it seemed to him, came out of the whole thing completely unscathed. It had taken her all these years to even find out about it, and she wouldn't have found out about it *ever* if she hadn't written that stupid book about him and started yammering on the phone with Cathleen every night. He wasn't going to start feeling bad about it now. No siree. It was way too late for that.

s – e – x

The nice thing about dating a novelist is, they come with a manual. At least, Holly Frick did. And ever since her book came out, Holly found she had a relatively foolproof way of gauging whether or not a man was into her. If he read her book and liked it, there was a good chance that he liked her. If he didn't read it, or couldn't get through it, or took an embarrassingly long time to finish it, he just wasn't that interested. The whole thing saved her a lot of time.

So when, a few days after their chance encounter at the Strand, Jack sent her an email telling her how much he enjoyed reading her novel, a little bell went off someplace in Holly's brain. That's all it was, a little bell, and it was way back behind all the other stuff — the stuff about Jack sleeping with Amanda, the stuff about Lucas being twenty-two, the stuff about Alex, her ex-husband, and her suspicion that she might still be in love with him — and even though she didn't admit it to herself, Holly did hear it ring.

———

Spence left the office late on Wednesday, and it wasn't until he got home that he realized he didn't want to be there, alone, in his apartment, even if it was nearly ten o'clock at night. He put on a pair of jeans and a different shirt, brushed his teeth, locked his door, and then left.

Spence's apartment building had eight elevators, and during rush hour they were filled to capacity, stopping on floor after floor, inhaling and disgorging passengers with a startling efficiency that was nonetheless annoying. The complex was inhabited by the sort of intense, driven young professionals who could afford to pay at least twenty-four hundred dollars for a studio and who were willing to give up quaint neighborhood bistros and bookstores and trees in order to live a ten-minute walk from their offices. Young professionals, lawyers, Wall Street asshole types. People who worked until four in the morning and were expected to be back at their desk by eight. You could see it on the women especially, the two a.m. elevator ride under the unforgiving overhead light, that haggard look of femininity trapped on the hamster wheel of ambition. Not that Spence paid much attention to the people who lived in his building. Once, he got home from work late and found himself alone in the elevator with a bald man in a dripping raincoat. "What floor can I hit for you?" Spence had asked. The guy looked at him with thinly veiled disgust and said, "I'm your *next-door neighbor.*"

That was New York for you. Some people wanted to make it into a small town and they got angry if you resisted their efforts. But Spence didn't *want* to know his next-door neighbor, he didn't want to make chitchat with bald men in his elevator at ten o'clock at night, and if he wanted to live in a small town, he'd move back to St. Louis.

The revolving door at the front of his building spit him out onto the sidewalk. He looked down the street, trying to think of someplace he could get a drink that wouldn't involve a fifteen-dollar cab ride. His neighborhood lacked charm. On a muggy night like tonight it seemed all sidewalks and gutters. Indian restaurants with bright orange awnings, Duane Reades, a bank on every corner. How he could be surrounded on all sides by commerce and yet not be able to buy a decent shirt was beyond him. It was not the area of town designed for brunches, or for window shopping, or for toddlers, or for cool people, or for gay men, or for rich people, or for tourists, which is why he was so surprised to meet the Scottish girl at the Irish pub he finally wandered into, just around the corner.

She was from Aberdeen, and she had bright yellow hair and a bucktoothed smile, and she worked as a laundress on an oil rig out in the middle of the North Sea. Her accent was nearly impenetrable. The shortest vowels he'd ever heard. Eh eh eh eh ah ah ah. Like a teppanyaki chef had chopped off the tails of all of her words. Spence bought her a drink, and also one for her friend, and for the price of a few pints of Guinness he was treated to two hours of tales of Life on a North Sea Oil Rig. It felt nice, Spence found himself thinking, to be *entertained* by a woman's conversation for once, even if he had to sort of cock his ear in a certain manner to put together recognizable words through her accent.

The only downside to her job, apparently, was that she had to take an hour-long helicopter ride over the freezing North Sea to get to and from work. The ride was treacherous, and choppers were known to go down, and if yours did, you had to unstrap your safety harness and escape from the helicopter while it filled with ice-cold water, and hope help arrived before you lost consciousness. Once every four years you had to retake the safety course, a three-day ordeal that culminated in a drill in which they strap you into the shell of an old helicopter and blindfold you and then plunge the whole thing into the deep end of a freezing cold swimming pool and expect you to extricate yourself before you drown. And sometimes entire rigs explode. That was another downside. And should your rig explode, you must maintain the presence of mind to climb down the platform, not jump off of it, because if you jump off of it, you die the second you hit the water. But apparently that's hard to remember while standing atop an exploding oil rig. Basically, Spence realized, this chick risked dying a grim death in the frozen North Sea because doing so enabled her to go on lots of holidays. It was as simple as that. You weren't going to find a girl around here with that sort of attitude, not in the circles Spence ran in, not with these women with their careers and their ambition and their none-too-subtle sniffing around to find out how much money you made and if you owned your own apartment. She put, perhaps, a hair too much value on fun, but Spence found it refreshing.

He had reached the point in the evening where he was regretting that he had not bothered to commit her name to memory, right about the time she rested her hand on his upper thigh. When her compatriot excused herself to use the bathroom, Spence invited the blonde back to his place, and she insisted that her friend come along, too. Just how much fun were these young ladies looking to have? Spence found himself wondering while he settled up the tab. He tried, on the elevator ride up to his apartment, to playfully drape his arms over both girls' shoulders, but they just laughed at him, like he'd done something funny. He laughed too. When they got to his door, everybody was still laughing.

"Cool place," the brunette said. "Did you just move in?"

Spence looked at his apartment with fresh eyes. It didn't look like he'd just moved in—he had furniture, there were no boxes—but it did seem...cold. What was it? The parquet floors? When he rented the place, he'd somehow gotten it into his head that parquet floors were upscale—perhaps it was the way the real estate agent had said the word, the Frenchiness of it—but over the three years he'd lived there he'd come to suspect that there might be something vaguely tacky about them. Let's just say, Spence did not encounter parquet floors in the more sophisticated venues he frequented around town. A rug would probably improve things, but he didn't trust himself to pick one out without help. He took a date rug-shopping one Saturday morning a while back, and she'd tried to convince him to spend fourteen thousand dollars on one. "That's how much rugs cost," she'd said. She'd made him go to a store called ABC Carpet & Home, a place which Spence quickly discovered was, despite the tacky New Jersey strip-mall name, where baronesses went when they wanted throw pillows.

The girls walked over to the windows and looked out at the city and oohed and aahed in thick Scottish accents. It was a beautiful view, truly, the sparkling lights of the city, cars streaming slowly down below, all of it eerily silent because they were so high up. The windows were what sold him on the place, windows from floor to ceiling, one entire wall of the living room and one entire wall of the bedroom, the sheer expanse of glass broken up by nothing but large rectangles of black rubbery frames and putty-colored hotel-room-style air-conditioning units. Still, the windows. They went all the way to the floor, which meant that if you walked right up to them you felt a sort of vertiginous sickness in the belly. He liked to have sex with women, standing up, from behind, while they braced their forearms against the glass and stared out at the city below. Lights on if she would let him.

The brunette plopped herself down on the couch and indicated that that's where she would be sleeping. While Spence got sheets and blankets and pillows for her, the little buck-toothed blonde climbed into his bed. When he walked past the open door with the linens she grinned a big grin and then flashed him a quick view of her tits, which were small, a tad saggy, and extremely wide set. Like monkey boobs. Women are nuts! Spence found himself thinking as he continued down the hall with the sheets. Still, he went with it.

After it was over, she rolled away from him and went to sleep, and Spence found himself staring up at the ceiling, wide awake, like a girl. He'd called Cathleen twice that day and she hadn't called back. He'd called her the day before, too, at a time when he knew she'd be home, and she hadn't picked up. He found it puzzling. After all that—talking to Crazy Molly, tracking down Holly, interrogating him for hours. Seriously, the woman had been relentless. Like a raccoon trying to get into a garbage can. And then, one day, all of a sudden, nothing. Not a peep.

When Holly arrived at the pediatrician's office, Amanda was already there, sitting in a chair in the corner with Jacob plopped on her lap like a sack of all-purpose flour. Holly was always a bit shocked by how much things had changed since she was a kid, but never more so than in Jacob's Upper East

Side pediatrician's office. It used to be *Highlights* magazine, searching for the ladle up in the tree, but this place was like a Chuck E. Cheese's, with electronic toys scattered everywhere, beeping and flashing. There was a fifty-inch plasma TV on one wall, blaring a show about a talking train in what seemed to Holly to be frighteningly high definition, and several toddlers were standing in front of it, mouths open, nearly catatonic.

"Thanks for coming," said Amanda.

"No problem," said Holly. "Hi, Jacob!" Jacob's blobby blond head stared past Holly in the direction of the talking train.

"You are so great to show up here for this," said Amanda.

"I love to hold babies while strangers inflict pain on them. It's a way to endear myself to the next generation."

"I can't watch him get hurt," said Amanda. "And I don't want him to catch my neurotic needle thing. Mark was supposed to meet me here, but at the last minute something more important than preventing his son from contracting polio came up."

Holly looked around the room. There were two women breast-feeding newborns over by the magazine rack, one with a beatific look on her face, the other wincing in pain. A forty-something woman in a blue suit was focused on her BlackBerry while an au pair played peekaboo with what was undoubtedly the woman's miracle baby.

"Can I ask you something?" said Holly. She lowered her voice a bit and went on. "How is it that all these women have babies and I don't? I don't understand it. What happened to my life? I'm completely baffled by it. Where did I go wrong?"

"Do you really want to know the answer to that question?"

Holly thought about it for a second. "No."

"Because I'll tell you."

"I know you would. Just not today," said Holly. "Today's not a good day for it."

After Jacob got his shot—a look of surprise, a pregnant beat of confused silence, then a piercing scream that brought Amanda in from the hallway to scoop him out of Holly's arms—Amanda decided to walk Holly home across the park so Jacob could meet Chester. Holly pushed Jacob in the stroller while Amanda walked alongside.

"Jack mentioned that he saw you the other day," said Amanda.

"Yeah, we bumped into each other at the Strand."

"So?"

"So, what?"

"What did you think?"

Holly pressed forward a few steps in silence and then said, "He seems like he's not as bad as I thought."

"I knew you'd like him if you gave him a chance."

There were several slow-moving German tourists up ahead, aggressively skinny and wearing weird pants. Holly found that certain weeks seemed to bring out the Germans. Then, for months, you noticed nothing but Japanese. Then a quick burst of Scandinavians, well-scrubbed and toting around blond three-year-olds.

"He's funny, isn't he?" Amanda said, once they'd cleared the Germans.

"Like I said. He seemed nice."

"He's really intelligent," said Amanda. "I mean it. He's scary smart. I think he's the smartest person I know."

"Yeah, I worry about people when you *notice* that they're smart," said Holly.

"What do you mean?"

"I just think something might be going on with that," said Holly. "I mean, we're smart, but you wouldn't know it to listen to us talk."

Jacob started to make a strange mewling sound, a cross between a whimper and a full-blown cry, so Holly stopped the stroller and Amanda picked him up.

"Are you guys still doing all that?" Holly felt strange talking about this with Jacob on Amanda's hip, so she just emphasized certain words by opening her eyes extrawide to get her point across. "I mean, is all that craziness still going on between you two?"

"There's still some craziness."

Holly didn't say anything.

"What am I doing?" Amanda said. "I mean, you saw, he's a great guy, and maybe if things were different, I don't know. But this is not a good situation."

"I don't get it," said Holly. "Is it just s-e-x?"

"Jacob's sixteen months old, Holly. You don't have to spell in front of him. And I'm not sure what it is," said Amanda. "I mean, it's mostly sex."

Holly wrinkled her nose inquiringly. "It's that good?"

"I'm not saying it's the best sex I've ever had," said Amanda, "but it's the best sex I can *remember.*"

They started walking again, making their way slowly around the great lawn. A rather heated softball game was under way, between a handful of grown men in red shirts and another bunch in white ones, all of whom, it seemed to Holly, should have been at work.

"I was thinking about it last night," said Amanda. "I didn't go looking for this. I'm not the kind of person who does this sort of thing. So, you know, maybe this is just my path."

Holly pushed the empty stroller along in silence for a moment. "Is it possible," she finally said, "to be off your path?"

"What do you mean?" said Amanda.

"Just that. Can a person walk off their path?"

"I think it's just a shorthand people use about being true to yourself."

"But no, see, it's not," said Holly. "Because then there would be a path, but you could walk off it by *not* being true to yourself. It would have to be, 'I was off my path for most of the nineties, but then my father died and I went through some tough stuff and I got back on my path.' But that's not the way people use it. It's *all* your path. That bit about the nineties? 'That was just my path!' And if it's all your path, I don't see how 'staying on your path' is such a great accomplishment, since it is impossible, ipso facto, to be off of it."

"Ipso facto?"

"You know what I mean."

"Oh, I forgot to tell you," said Amanda. She and Holly were inside the world's slowest elevator. Holly lived only five flights up, but stepping into her elevator was like entering a parallel universe where time slowed to a crawl. When the doors finally opened, it felt like you should be on the other side of town. "I watched that show you write for the other day."

"You saw *The Mighty Moppets?*"

"Yeah," said Amanda. "It's really awful."

"I told you it was bad."

"It was on after this puppet thing Jacob's sitter had on for him, and I felt guilty about changing the channel once I realized it was your show."

"Thanks. I think. Or something."

"It's weird. Mark and I went to a dinner party on Saturday, and one of the women there was this big Young Adult book agent at William Morris. She said she'd represent me if I ever decided to write a Young Adult novel."

"Really? Just because she sat next to you at a dinner party?"

"I told her a few ideas I had and she thought they were really good. Her husband works in Mark's group."

The elevator doors opened, and the three of them made their way down the hall.

"What about your photography?" Holly said. She parked Jacob's stroller in the communal hallway outside her door and put her key in the lock. "You told me that was going really well."

"It's too static. I feel like I need to tell a story."

"Didn't you just buy a new camera?"

"I'll still use the camera, Holly. I just feel like doing something different."

Holly swung open her door.

"Ignore the smell," said Holly.

"It's revolting," said Amanda.

"I made a batch of meat Jell-O before I left and it kind of stinks up the place. Do you want to say hello to the puppy dog, Jacob?"

Chester was lying on the couch staring blankly at the television, which was turned on but with the sound muted. His head was wrapped in gauze, and his legs were sticking out stiffly over the edge of the cushions in a way that suggested a cartoonish case of rigor mortis. Jacob took one look at him and burst into tears.

"My god, Holly, what's wrong with your dog?"

"He has brain cancer," said Holly. "I told you that."

"Yeah, but I didn't think it'd be so obvious."

"He just got back from the hospital again yesterday," said Holly. "What did you expect?"

"He can barely move."

"He's just sleepy, that's all, aren't you, Chester?" Holly crouched down by the couch and pet Chester's neck, behind the bandages. "He might be a little dehydrated. That's why I made the meat Jell-O. The book said it tastes good so he'll get more fluids in him."

Amanda was bouncing Jacob up and down on her hip furiously while looking down at Chester with undisguised alarm. "Are you sure you know what you're doing?"

"What do you mean?"

"Well, don't you think, it's *possible*"—and here Amanda paused, like she was thinking twice about forging on, like she was talking to a stranger she had found walking down Eighth Avenue wearing nothing but a Santa hat and a pair of striped sweat socks—"that you've got some sort of messiah complex, and maybe it's time to face that and stop torturing this poor animal."

Holly looked up. "It's not a messiah complex if I can actually save him."

"You're right. It's not a complex," said Amanda. "You'll be his actual messiah."

"Maybe," said Holly. She knew she sounded crazy but she

couldn't help herself. "Maybe! There are worse things for a person to try to be."

Jacob would not stop crying, and Amanda kept bouncing him up and down on her hip as she backed away from the couch and headed for the door.

"You know, this city is filled with crazy ladies, and I'll bet most of them started out pretty close to normal. You don't just end up with an apartment filled with stacks of yellowy newspapers and stray animals who go pee inside your shoes. It has to start sometime. I'm serious, Holly. It doesn't happen overnight."

the secret to happiness

Betsy was kneeling in front of her couch, going down on her date, and her mind had begun to wander. She found herself wishing she were alone, in bed, watching the eleven o'clock rebroadcast of *Project Runway*. Her jaw ached. Well, that was an exaggeration, it didn't ache yet, but her knees were definitely throbbing. She felt like an aging scullery maid. *That's why they call it a job,* she reminded herself. Still, this was taking an awfully long time. If this guy was on some kind of medication he failed to mention, honestly, she was going to throttle him. And yet. She pressed on like a trooper. A trooper in the army of fellatio. She felt the way she always felt when she found herself in this position, like she was proving how good she was at it, like there was some sort of prize at the end, like it was a bizarre scholarship competition or an audition for a part in a Broadway musical. Look at me — I'm *the best.* She wasn't one of those girls who didn't try, who just hung out around down there like a delinquent in front of the 7-Eleven, with no purpose, no endgame, no plan. Not Betsy. When she was twenty-four, her then-boyfriend likened her technique to a housewife working on a really tough stain. He wanted her to be more erotic. He wanted her to *enjoy* it more. What's not to enjoy? thought Betsy, but she took the criticism to heart and managed to convince every boyfriend since that her favorite thing in the entire world was sucking on his genitals, which had at least one truly unfortunate consequence, in that it meant she found herself doing it *all the time*.

Well, she liked to think of them as "boyfriends," but the truth, the truth on this particular evening at least, was that this was a second date. A second date! First dates, Betsy had a strict policy, which is that she wouldn't even bequeath a goodnight kiss, and she had another strict policy, which is that she wouldn't have full sex until it was in the context of a committed relationship, but in between, there was this gray area. So here she was, on her knees, in the gray area yet again. It seemed to Betsy that, sometime late in the nineties, fellatio had made a leap into the group of semicasual groping activities housed under the rubric of "making out," while the reciprocal act remained a signifier of a promising and escalating relationship, something just shy of leaving a toothbrush in someone else's medicine cabinet. And as much as Betsy loved Bill Clinton, she couldn't help blaming this one on him.

Okay, Betsy thought. That's it, buddy. The time allotted for your complimentary blowjob has elapsed. She pulled her head up and was greeted by a stuttering series of no's.

"Keep going. God, please, keep going."

Keep going. Fuck you, keep going.

"You're amazing," the guy said.

Betsy kept going.

Betsy did battle with many neurotic fears, but perhaps the oldest and most deep-seated was that she wasn't all that good at sex. When she was fifteen, her parents had packed her off to spend six weeks at Camp Sh'lamim in the Berkshires. Camp

Sh'lamim was one of those liberal East Coast Jewish summer camps founded in the early seventies ostensibly to promote cultural and spiritual values among the reformed Jewish community, but really to facilitate sexual experimentation among the chosen by placing as few obstacles in the way as possible. It was there that Betsy misplaced her virginity—she always contended it wasn't actually lost until a few years later—in a canoe, outside the boathouse, while she was supposed to be at the notoriously ill-attended late-night campfire sing-along. His name was Brendan Cohen, and Betsy became convinced she was in love with him one night after he managed to insert several fingers and part of a thumb inside her while they were making out, standing up, pressed flush against an oak tree. Betsy's virginity misplacement went like this: Brendan just about got it all the way in, and then quickly took it out again, and then said maybe they should go. On the way back to the campfire, Betsy asked if everything was okay and Brendan said he wasn't sure and then Betsy said what do you mean and Brendan said, *I don't think you were doing it right.* Which created a sex complex of lasting power.

While this fear of Betsy's wasn't altogether rational—She was only fifteen! She was in a canoe!—the truth is, it wasn't entirely irrational either. Betsy had received remarkably little positive reinforcement in that department in the years since Brendan Cohen's devastating critique. And she had had complaints. Nothing major, really, but just enough to make her suspect that what Brendan had said might be true. It didn't help that she drew to herself the screwy, the neurotic, the artistic, the heavily medicated, and if she actually did ever have sex with her doorman she could probably rid herself of this hang-up in an afternoon. But she was convinced that the

reason she didn't have a husband, or even a boyfriend, was
that she wasn't *something* enough in bed. She didn't even know
what the "something" she wasn't enough of, was. Which
led her to overcompensate. Which elicited reactions. Which
made her even more convinced that she was doing something
different — and not necessarily *better* — than everybody else.

———————

Leonard was pacing around his living room, waiting for the
bell to ring so he could buzz NYBoy23 up to his lair. Leonard couldn't help thinking about the photo he had posted on
his LukesPlace listing, wondering just how far he had strayed
from reality. The picture was of a guy with Leonard's build
and coloring, if a guy with Leonard's build and coloring had
been going to the gym with some regularity and recently
spent a week or so lying in the sun on a nude beach. A very,
very slight amount of fictional self-representation was toler-
ated on the Internet, and Leonard felt it was entirely possible that this time he had gone too far. He wasn't sure he'd
be able to take it if, say, NYBoy23 took one look at him and
then slowly backed away from the door, offering up excuses.
This had happened once before, and it took days for him to
recover. Leonard examined himself in the big mirror he'd
hung over his sofa. He sucked in his gut. Much better. *Much*
better, in fact. Can you get an entire blowjob while sucking in
your stomach, Leonard wondered? Was that even possible?

He felt a spasm of guilt. In no spiritual tradition the
world has ever known was he about to do the right thing.
Well, perhaps hedonism. Did that count as a spiritual tradition? Leonard wasn't sure. But he wasn't hurting anybody,

he reminded himself. He and NYBoy23 were two consenting adults, albeit with a twenty-year age difference, but still. Both of whom had high-speed Internet access in common and the ability to upload photos onto public-access Web sites, if nothing else.

———————

The fat guy from the gym had asked Betsy out again earlier that afternoon. The guy she'd met in the park that time, Lonnie. He was actually kind of funny, and she was perfectly willing to consider him a friend, maybe not the kind of friend you had a drink with, but the kind of friend you said hi to when you walked past their desk on your way to the Cybex machine, but this thing he kept doing, this asking her out — the truth is, she was starting to get a little offended. Did he actually think she would say yes? It was stuff like this — fat people asking her out, the stump-fingered orthodontist who didn't even call to ask for a second date — that made her question how she looked to the world, just how pronounced a vibe of desperation she was emitting.

"A *contractor?*" Betsy said to her sister Christine when the idea was presented to her over the matzo ball soup that Passover. Despite the unfortunate goyish tinge to her first name, Christine had proved to be the glue that held the Jewish center of Betsy's family of origin. Their mother had been raised Catholic, and their father, other than banning Christmas trees and encouraging in his offspring a vague cultural identification with oppressed peoples everywhere, had long ago stopped caring. But after Christine married Leo, she'd assumed the mantle of suburban Jewish matriarch, and she imposed strict emotional penalties on Betsy and Lucas and sundry extended family members who refused to make the journey up to her well-appointed Scarsdale home for the High Holidays.

"A contractor?" Betsy said again. "From *Long Island?*"

"The Hamptons are on Long Island," Lucas had pointed out.

"Is he from the Hamptons?" Betsy asked Christine.

"No, he's from Great Neck," said Christine. "But that's a good part of Long Island."

"What happened to his last relationship?"

"They found her body in the crawl space below his garage," said Leo. "But my sister assures me he was cleared of all charges."

"Great, Leo. That's very helpful," said Betsy. "How old is he?"

"Fifty-four," said Christine.

Betsy blinked. "Tell me you're joking."

"I've got news for you, sweetie," said Christine. "You're almost thirty-eight."

Betsy's heart started pounding so hard she could feel it in her fingertips. "I don't want to go on a blind date with a fifty-four-year-old contractor from Long Island. I'm sorry, I just don't."

"Leo's sister says he's a very nice guy and quite good-looking."

"If he's so nice, and so good-looking, and so available, then trust me, there's something *really* wrong with him."

"People," Christine said, poking around for kiwis in the communal bowl of fruit salad, "could say the same thing about you."

Later, after Betsy and Lucas got on the train to go back to

the city, Leo turned to his wife and said, "Your sister needs to get over herself."

For a long time, Betsy needed to get over herself, that is true. But now she was over herself. She had spent the past two years being over herself, dating men that made her skin crawl, always saying yes to at least two dates, always letting them kiss her if they wanted to at the end of the second date, to find out if there was some sexual chemistry she wasn't seeing due to the blinding glare emanating from the rest of their short-comings. Two years of that. She had kissed men she didn't want to kiss, and refused to sleep with ones she was desperately attracted to, ones she met at parties and then kissed on street corners in the rain, men who pleaded with her to go home with them, and then, when she demurred, never called.

It was in keeping with that philosophy that, twelve days after the idea was first presented to her, Betsy found herself sitting across the table from Alan Murry, her sister's sister-in-law's contractor. Alan had put on a black T-shirt and a sports jacket and a pair of pants that had once belonged to a suit and had driven an hour in bad traffic into Manhattan to take her out to dinner. He was a nice enough human being, Betsy supposed, he even made her laugh once, telling a story about his college roommate which involved a Pringles can and a very angry squirrel, but she couldn't turn off the voice in her head that droned on all evening: What happened to my life? Where did I go wrong? *Is this really what it's come to?*

"Do you consider yourself a happy person?" Alan asked her, after the waiter cleared away their dinner plates.

"What do you mean?"

"Pretty much just what I said," he said. "Do you consider yourself a happy person?"

"I don't know. I'm as happy as most people, I guess." Betsy smiled brightly, and then took it down a few watts. "I have my days. Why do you ask?"

"My uncle always said this to me. He said to me, 'Alan? Marry a happy woman.'" He leaned back in his chair and folded his arms in front of his chest. "You know, that the secret to being happy in a marriage is to marry someone who was already happy. That that was the part nobody told you. And I thought it was sort of crazy, but the older I get, the more I see that my friends who married happy women are happy, and the ones who didn't have all sorts of problems."

"You can't blame that on the wives," said Betsy, "if these men have problems."

"Yeah, but I think what he meant was, it's hard to make an unhappy woman happy."

"It's not your *job* to make another person happy." Betsy had read enough self-help books to trot this one out with a substantial degree of certainty. "A person isn't *responsible* for the happiness of the other person in the relationship."

"Maybe," said Alan, "but a house can only be as happy as the least happy person in it."

Betsy felt herself getting angry. "I'm not even sure what that means, 'a happy woman.'"

"You know how sometimes a baby comes into the world, and it has a good temperament, and it kind of rolls through life and bad things happen to it like they happen to everybody, but its baseline is way up here—" Alan stuck his left hand a few inches above his head with his fingers rigid and parallel to the floor. "I think that's what he meant. He's dead now, or I'd ask him to be more specific."

"Well, I mean, I think that's a little simplistic," said Betsy.

"All kinds of people are sort of fundamentally happy but I don't know why you would want to be married to them. Life is complex and difficult and painful and if you're smart you're probably not going to walk around grinning like an idiot all the time."

"You're saying happy women are too dumb to be miserable."

"Yes. Maybe. I don't know," said Betsy. She tugged at the hem of her skirt. "I don't like this whole conversation. You know how you can say a word over and over and over again until it loses its meaning? That's how I feel right now about the word *happy*."

"I'm sorry for bringing it up."

"Don't worry about it."

"I wasn't going to," he said. "Are you in the mood for dessert?"

Why Betsy would be thinking of that—last week's happiness conversation—at this particular moment, while servicing a promising ear, nose, and throat doctor who had taken her to Blue Hill for their first date and Pastis for their second, she did not know, except that she had to think about *something*. The task at hand was, quite frankly, not that absorbing. The date with Alan the Long Island contractor had ended uneventfully enough—a kiss on the cheek, a mutual assurance that they'd had a nice time—and then the report came back to Betsy through Christine via Leo's sister out in Great Neck that Alan thought Betsy seemed sad. Christine treated this like it was a valuable piece of intelligence from the dating front, like it was something Betsy could do something about, akin to changing her hair color or wearing more revealing clothing. Well, Betsy had pointed out, she *was* sad! That was exactly the word that applied to her!

And the thought that insufficient happiness would

somehow disqualify her for a relationship seemed like the most unfair of all possible reasons for rejection. What was she supposed to be so happy about? What, exactly? Her career had never been a shining orb she rotated around, and it was starting to seem like, well, she had miscalculated. She'd decided long ago that she wasn't going to attempt to Have It All and here's what she ended up with instead: nothing. She should have tried to become Maureen Dowd or something.

Finally, she thought.

She swallowed and smiled and sent the good doctor on his way.

———

Leonard had given up sucking in his stomach and was trying his best to relax and enjoy his blowjob. The deal the two had hammered out online had been for mutual blowjobs, to be administered sequentially rather than simultaneously, no drugs, no surprises, no real names. NYBoy23 had an interesting technique, in which he punctuated every dozen or so bobs of the head with a single lingering, long, deep one, which was good except for the fact that each time he did it, his nose ended up smashed into Leonard's overhanging belly. *I am so fucking fat!* Leonard thought each time it happened. Then the guy's head would start to bob again and Leonard would do his best to return to the moment, but it wasn't easy. *What is wrong with you? Seriously, what is your problem? Can't you even enjoy this, one of life's most basic pleasures, this hot young guy is down there with his hot mouth sucking on your big huge hot—* and then the nose again—*Holy shit, you are one fat fuck!*

It took him a long time to come.

how *are* you?

Saturday morning, Holly went with Lucas to the Brooks Brothers on Fifth Avenue to exchange a blazer that his grandmother had bought him for graduation. His grandmother had given him an identical blazer six years earlier, when he graduated from Collegiate, and it was still hanging in his closet, tags on, zipped up in its Brooks Brothers' garment bag, which is why he felt it was okay to return the new one.

"Guess what?" said Lucas.

"What?" said Holly.

"I got accepted to Columbia Law."

"Good for you."

"I'm kind of surprised. I didn't think I'd get in."

"What about Austin?" said Holly. "Starting that club with your friend out there. I thought you were pretty serious about that."

"I was. I am. I don't know," said Lucas. "My dad wants me to go to law school first. I'm kind of on the fence."

"See, that's great, because I can help you. I can knock you off the fence into the right pasture, which is very clear to me, and that is the pasture of not becoming a lawyer."

"Why do you say that?"

"This is one area where the difference in our ages gives me a perspective that you don't have," said Holly. "Every person I know who went to law school is miserable. Not just unhappy, not just unfulfilled — *miserable*."

Holly paused a second to let that sink in, and then she pulled a blue and white striped shirt off the rack and handed it to Lucas. "This would look good on you."

"Thanks," he said.

"And if you *do* go to law school, you should know that you'll spend the rest of your life trying to figure out a way to stop practicing law," said Holly. "It's true. That's one of the things they don't tell you when you're twenty-two, because if they did, the world would run out of lawyers and everybody would be forced to get along."

"I don't want to be a lawyer," said Lucas. "I just think it might give me time to figure out what to do with my life."

"No, see, that's where they get you. Right there. That sort of thinking. If I do nothing else in your young life, if I serve no other purpose, let it be my legacy that I dissuaded you from going to law school. Someday I'll be nothing but a faint memory, but you'll never stop thanking me for this."

"Why are you so sure you'll be a faint memory?"

"You're right," said Holly. "I'll be a vivid, erotically charged memory that you'll call upon when you're forced to bang your wife for the gazillionth time."

"Maybe you'll *be* my wife," said Lucas. "And I'll be banging *you* for the gazillionth time."

Holly stood on tiptoe and pressed a kiss onto Lucas's forehead. "As long as you're not a lawyer."

A loud, nasally voice rang out across the store. "Holly. Frick."

Holly pulled away from Lucas and saw a short, squat woman with a dirty blond bob standing next to a round table covered in a profusion of neckties. "Susan."

"I thought that was you," said Susan, and she headed over. "I haven't seen you in ages. How are you?" Susan leaned on the *are* in the "how are you," and thereby managed to telegraph the fact that she was up to speed with Holly's whole story — her recent divorce, rumors of her ex-husband's infidelity, the fact that she would, in all likelihood, end up dying childless and alone.

"I'm good, I'm great," said Holly. "This is my, um. This is Lucas."

"Hello, Lucas. I'm Susan Berger, one of Holly's oldest friends in the world."

"Nice to meet you."

"God, don't you hate this place?" said Susan. "Every time I'm in here, I'm like, why am I here? Why are you two here?"

"My grandmother got me a blazer for graduation," said Lucas. "I thought I'd try to exchange it for something that makes me look a little less like George Will."

"A graduation blazer," Susan said. She looked at Holly and raised an eyebrow. "So congratulations are in order."

"He took some time off," said Holly. "You know, while he was in college. He didn't go straight through."

"I spent a little time in Europe after my sophomore year," said Lucas.

"Two years," said Holly. "He spent two years in Paris. He's fluent in French."

"That sounds absolutely wonderful," said Susan. "Oh, to be young."

"I know," said Holly. "I love Paris."

"How did this happen to us, Holly? Weren't we just in college? Wasn't that yesterday?" said Susan. "Last month I went to my *twenty-year* high school reunion. The men were all puffy and bald and I kept running into the bathroom and examining my face and thinking, is it possible that I am that old?"

"You're not old," said Holly.

"I'm not young," said Susan.

"Well," said Holly, "you are older than me."

Susan glanced at Lucas and then said, with a big smile, "Not by much."

Lucas put his hand on Holly's shoulder and said, "If you ladies will excuse me, I'm going to go see if I can find five hundred bucks' worth of boxer shorts."

Lucas headed off towards the back of the store. Susan made a big point of watching him go, turning around and doing sort of a mock swoon while putting a hand to her chest as if to still her beating heart.

"Oh my god, Holly, he is absolutely adorable."

"You think so?"

"I am so jealous," said Susan. "What's that joke? That seventeen goes into thirty-five much easier than the other way around?"

"He's not seventeen, he's twenty-two—"

"Who cares if he is?! Enjoy yourself. You deserve it after all you've been through," said Susan. "Speaking of which, guess who I bumped into last week."

"Who?"

"Your ex-husband."

"You saw Alex?"

"He was at Bloomingdale's. I don't know why I set foot in there, the place is a zoo."

"How is he?"

"Fine. He seemed fine. He was buying socks," said Susan. "Are you two still in touch?"

"We are."

Susan's shoulders slumped an inch or two with apparent relief. "Oh, good. So you know."

"Probably. I probably know it," said Holly. "What am I supposed to know?"

The shoulders went up again. "Nothing."

"Susan."

"I don't know if I should be the one to tell you this."

"Tell me," Holly said. Her skin felt prickly and hot.

"He's getting remarried."

Holly blinked and tried her best to smile. "You're joking."

"That's what he told me."

"I don't believe it."

Susan nodded yes. "Next *month*. They're doing it at the Magnolia Plantation. She's very southern."

"Next month? Really? Wow." Holly put her hand on a clothes rack to steady herself and almost pulled it to the floor.

"I know."

"Well, I mean, good for him," said Holly. "But still. Wow."

"I met her, too. Briefly. She seemed"—and here Susan looked up into the air, trying to summon precisely the right phrase—"uniquely designed to make him happy. And I don't mean that as a compliment to either of them."

———

Spence woke up late on Saturday morning, naked and sweaty and alone, with his torso wrapped in a clingy dank sheet. He'd gone to a party the night before and brought back a girl who'd said to him, at two a.m., on her way out the door: "By the way, your toenails are disgusting." And what do you know? They were. Long, thick, yellowy — they looked vaguely prehistoric. And yet, up until that moment, he hadn't even noticed. The fact had to be pointed out to him by a twenty-four-year-old coat-check girl who gave a toothy blowjob. It wasn't the same as not registering the dirt behind the toilet — this was his own body! As Spence got older, he found that grooming was calling for a level of focus and precision and commitment that he was not altogether prepared to give it. Every time he looked in the mirror, if he really looked, if he looked hard, he'd see that something was demanding to be trimmed or shaved or plucked or tamed or, and this had happened more than once, removed in a dermatologist's office under local anesthesia. One night, while watching TV on the couch, pleasantly yet deceptively saki drunk, he pulled focus and noticed a three-quarter-inch renegade eyebrow hair curling down like a barb of steel wool, threatening to pierce his left eyeball. He went to the bathroom and for some saki-related reason thought it was a good idea to use his toenail clippers to trim it and ended up taking out a large chunk of real estate from the middle of his left brow. From that day forward, keeping his eyebrows trimmed was just yet another thing to stay on top of. Ears too. And the nose. Good god, the nose. It seemed to Spence that life had become a relentless parade of things like that, things to keep on top of, things to do and then to do yet again before it seemed conceivable that it could be necessary to do so. Every year, when tax time rolled around, he felt surprised. Didn't I just do this? Shouldn't this be *done?* And all the dates scattered throughout the year that his mother expected him to remember and commemorate appropriately, her birthday and wedding anniversary, the day his grandmother died, his father's birthday, the day his father died. *This is never going to stop.*

And yet he had no real responsibilities. At least that's what his sister always told him. Wait until you have kids. Then you'll know what it's like to have responsibilities. And all he had to do was spend an afternoon with his niece and his nephews to see the sad truth about having kids: once you did, it never stopped. He still got holiday cards from a few old college friends, and he found himself staring at the pictures of their kids—boys with pale faces and skinny necks, girls who looked like cocktail waitresses but couldn't be much older than eleven—and thinking, *They grow up so fast.* Even when they aren't yours, when all you see of them is a snapshot each year when the holidays roll around, they grow up fast.

Spence had flown down to Sanibel Island the previous summer to spend the Fourth of July with his sister Nancy and her family. He'd made an impulsive promise at Christmastime, when the summer felt *very* far away, and Nancy had held him to it. He bought a ticket on a plane that left JFK at four o'clock on July third and returned on the morning of the fifth, and, early on the morning of the fourth, he awoke to the enthusiastic door-pounding of his niece and twin nephews. He dutifully hauled floaties and buckets and towels and chairs and umbrellas down to the sand and set up camp in the thick Florida heat.

The beach was packed with vacationing families, little clusters of towels and coolers, and Spence was quickly hit with the overwhelming, inexplicable exhaustion he always felt when he spent time around little kids, the strange lethargy of the childless. After less than forty-five minutes of sand castle construction, he found himself looking forward to going back to his hotel room and turning on the television and drinking a beer from the minibar. As the day wore on, this vision took on the luster of a sort of Shangri-la, the cool dark quiet of the air-conditioned room, flipping channels in his boxer shorts, perhaps even popping open an eight-dollar canister of cashews. Just about the time he was about to tell Nancy he wasn't feeling well, that the sun was getting to him, that he'd probably have to skip dinner at whatever crayons-and-paper-placemat joint she had in mind and just have a bowl of soup delivered up to his room, he noticed a man, maybe in his late forties, who was sitting by himself in one of those green slingy fold-up chairs about a hundred yards down the beach, staring out into the ocean. He had a mini-cooler at his feet, and a paperback that he didn't seem to want to read, and he was wearing a baseball cap and a pair of rust-colored swim trunks. Spence couldn't stop looking at him. *Nobody* was alone on that particular beach, on that particular national holiday. It would take *work* to end up like that, Spence found himself thinking. Even now, almost a year later, when he thought about the man in the green chair, he found it inexplicably chilling.

Cathleen had cut off all contact with him. That's exactly the way she'd put it, too. He'd left several more messages on her machine and emailed her repeatedly with no response, until he finally broke down and sent her flowers at work. The next day he received an email that said, "I've decided that it is healthiest for me to cut off all contact with you and I ask that you respect my decision." Even that was different from what he was accustomed to. Spence was used to women who never wanted to speak to him ever again, but they tended to express it with considerably less dignity and self-possession. Cathleen was different. More different, it was turning out, than he'd thought.

――――――

Holly said good-bye to Lucas in front of Brooks Brothers and took a cab straight home. She got out her grandmother's afghan and retired to the couch. The afghan was truly ugly, stupendously so, a late-seventies combo of putty brown, avocado green, and mustard-colored acrylic yarn, which is why it spent most of its time hidden in a plastic zipper bag under Holly's bed. Still, there were times when nothing else would do.

The TV was on, and by the time the sun went down, it had been on for seven hours straight. There had been *Celebrity Fit Club*. There had been a documentary on the hostage rescue at Entebbe, interspersed with commercial break–sized bursts of a *Bridezillas* marathon. There had even been a *Real World/Road Rules Challenge* wrap-up show, which is usually where Holly drew the line. At the moment, the Barefoot Contessa was melting a truly alarming amount of butter in the bottom of a shiny saucepan. No wonder the woman couldn't tuck in her shirt, Holly found herself thinking. Still, she did look happy. Jolly.

The phone rang, just as an enormous wedge of Roquefort was about to get involved. Holly muted the television and picked up the phone in a single fluid motion, all without lifting her head from the cushion or disturbing Chester, who was asleep in a mild postradiation fog across her legs.

"Guess who I just got off the phone with?" said Amanda.

"I have no idea," said Holly.

"Susan Berger. She said she bumped into you this afternoon at Brooks Brothers and you were with a guy who was twelve years old."

"It's none of her business."

"Is it true?"

"It's my own business."

"How come I haven't heard about this guy, Holly?"

"Did Susan tell you Alex is getting remarried?"

Amanda sighed into the receiver. "She might have."

"Well, isn't that what we should be talking about right now? Isn't that why you should be calling me up?" said Holly. "To see how I'm handling this new piece of information?"

"How are you handling it?"

"Not well."

"Holly," said Amanda, her voice dripping with her proprietary blend of disgust and Alex fatigue.

"I'm sorry, I just can't believe he's getting married."

"You had to know it was going to happen eventually," said Amanda.

"See, no, that's the thing. I didn't know. I didn't think it was *ever* going to happen."

"That's crazy."

"Why is it crazy? The man hated being married. He said it was like trying to live with a noose around his neck. Or a plastic bag over his head. Something sweet like that. How can he be getting married again so soon?"

"Most men get remarried within eighteen months of their divorce," said Amanda. "It's true. It's too good of a system for them. They get divorced and they sit in their depressing apartments with no pictures on the walls and no curtains on the windows and nothing but tiny little packets of soy sauce and spicy mustard in the egg holder inside the refrigerator and they all have the same epiphany. They liked having a wife. They just didn't like having *their* wife."

The Contessa was silently spooning the buttery cheesy creamy sauce over a pound of macaroni and then proceeded to pour the resulting mixture into a red, heart-shaped casserole dish. Holly couldn't help thinking that the combination of this particular recipe with this particular crockery brought to mind not romance but a cardiac event. "Did Susan say anything about Alex's fiancée?"

"Not really," said Amanda. "Just that she's southern and she doesn't seem very smart."

"But she's pretty, right?"

"I didn't ask."

"I bet she's beautiful."

"What makes you say that?"

"Because men don't rush off to marry dumb ugly women."

"You've got to let this go, Holly. It's time. I know you're not going to believe me, but Alex getting remarried is the best thing that could happen to you right now."

"Why is that?"

"Because it takes him off the table. Maybe we can finally stop talking about Alex. Seriously, Holly, let's talk about something else for a while. Tell me about this guy Susan saw you with."

"I don't want to tell you about him if you're going to get all weird on me."

"I'll try not to," said Amanda.

Holly didn't say anything.

"I won't get weird," said Amanda. "I promise. Who is he?"

"Okay. Remember my sort-of-friend Betsy?"

"No."

"The publicist. She wore that kind of see-through top to my Christmas party last year?"

"Oh yeah," said Amanda. "The desperate, skinny one."

"He's her brother. His name is Lucas. I met him at a baby shower she was hosting at her parents' apartment."

"How old is he?"

"Young."

"How young?"

"Twenty-two."

"Gulp," said Amanda. "Okay. What does he do?"

"He just graduated from Columbia," said Holly. "And he got into law school. He's figuring things out."

"Are you serious about him?"

"Of course not," said Holly. "I mean, he's great, he's really sweet and we have fun and he's adorable, but he's too young. I know that."

"I'm going to tell you something as your friend, and I want you to listen to me," said Amanda. "Are you listening?"

"More or less."

"You make bad choices," said Amanda. The phone line hummed for a moment, and then she continued. "Alex was a bad choice. Staying with him was a bad choice. Mooning over him a year after your divorce is a bad choice. And what you're doing with this guy is a bad choice. You need to be meeting *available* men your own age who want to get married and start a family."

"It's not that easy, Amanda. You have no idea what it's like out there. The world isn't exactly crawling with men who want that stuff."

"Well, what about Jack?"

"Jack?" This came from so far out of left field that, for a moment, Holly had no idea who Amanda was talking about. "You mean your Jack?"

"He's not my Jack anymore. I told you, that's over," said Amanda. Amanda had told Holly she and Jack had stopped seeing each other, but Holly hadn't really believed her. She figured it was just Amanda's way of keeping her head from exploding with moral indignation and general alarm, and Holly appreciated it, even if it was a lie. But this? This was new.

"It is? Still?" said Holly. "I mean, it's over-over?"

"It's over-over. You were right about it. It was a silly, momentary bit of insanity, and I'm just lucky we had the sense to stop it before anything really bad happened."

"And you never said anything to Mark?"

"That would have been an incredibly selfish thing for me to do," said Amanda. "I think, now that I look back on it, that the whole thing was a delayed reaction to having Jacob. You know, to this feeling that my life wasn't my own anymore. My therapist said it was just my life force, you know, springing up again."

"Doctor Rothman said that?"

"Yes. And he said it was a good thing, that my spirit was rallying, but that I had the choice to be conscious about whether I wanted to get out of my marriage or not."

It never ceased to amaze Holly, how therapists managed to spin things. And the longer you lived in a place like Manhattan, where everyone you knew not only had a shrink but also talked quite freely about just what went on in their sessions, the more you suspected that this was the truth: that the aim of psychotherapy was to make it possible for a person to do whatever they wanted to do, with whomever they wanted to do it, when and where and however the hell they felt like it, while reaping no negative emotional consequences whatsoever.

"Anyway, he's single," said Amanda. "Jack, I mean. And he's looking for something serious. You should call him up."

"Are you joking? I couldn't do that."

"Why not?"

"Because this whole conversation is completely crazy, that's why."

"Why is it crazy?" said Amanda. "I'm not going to leave my husband. I can't be taking single guys off the table for my friends. Besides, he likes you. He told me he did."

"When did he say that?"

"After he bumped into you at the bookstore that time."

"He did not."

"He did."

"What were his actual words?"

"He said he thought you were cute and funny and smart and he couldn't understand why you weren't involved with anybody."

"Yeah, no, it would be too weird."

"Well, don't not do it on my account," said Amanda. "I'm completely serious. Everything happens for a reason. Maybe you're the reason. Who knows, maybe you two will live happily ever after."

"Yeah, well, I'd have to call him first, and I can't see myself doing that any time in the next millennium, but it's a nice thought. It's very generous of you. Thank you."

"You're welcome."

Holly thought about it for a second. "It's kind of like that time you offered to give me your grandmother's antique pearwood wardrobe as long as I figured out a way to haul it off."

she says you made a face

Holly took a cab to the restaurant Jack had picked out for their date, a place on the Upper East Side called JoJo. When the cab pulled up in front of an elegant old townhouse, she realized, with a sinking feeling, that she was conspicuously underdressed. Holly often felt underdressed — underdressing, it could be said, was the linchpin in what passed for her personal style — but this time she feared she might have taken it a bit too far. She had on a pair of dark jeans — reasonably cool jeans, at least, that she'd bought with some arm-twisting by Amanda — and a black semisexy-but-not-quite-a-boob-top top, and her uncomfortable and yet still somehow sensible going-out boots, meaning, in short, that she was Making an Effort, but the restaurant, from the outside at least, demanded something more.

The maître d' took her coat and led her up a sweeping staircase to the parlor floor, which was dark and romantic, with lots of candles and heavy silk curtains and little velvet pillows. It was almost, Holly found herself thinking, as if Jack had gone out of his way to pick the most datey venue he could find, to counteract the fact that Holly had been the one to call him up and ask him out. She appreciated it, even if she did find it a little confusing. The truth was, she found this whole situation confusing.

Jack was there, waiting for her at the table, and he smiled and stood up when he saw her walk in.

"I'm sorry. I should have." Holly glanced down at her outfit and then gestured to the room. "I didn't realize it would be so, um, chandelier-y."

A week earlier, Holly had, in what can only be called a completely out-of-character move, picked up the phone and dialed Jack's phone number. The only way she could explain it, really, was that she always regretted not figuring out some way to cart away that pearwood wardrobe. When she got his machine, her body flooded with relief.

"Hi," she said. "This is Holly. Frick. Amanda's friend. We met, um—actually, if you don't remember me, feel free to disregard this message—"

Holly heard the unmistakable click of a phone coming off the hook.

"Holly?" said Jack.

"Hi. I didn't know you were there."

"I just walked in the door."

"Oh. Sorry. I can call back later if that would be better."

"No. No need. What's up?"

Holly's mind went blank. Amanda had emailed her Jack's phone number that afternoon, which struck her at the time as bizarre, and maybe even a little perverse, but at that moment, with Jack's question hanging unanswered in the air, Holly saw it for what it was. Pity. Amanda pitied her. There was no other explanation for it. She pitied her for being alone, for being divorced, for being at a place in her life where doing something like this, calling up a man she barely knew and asking him out on a date, was even on the table as a reasonable course of action.

"I was just wondering if maybe you would like to do something with me. Have dinner or something. Sometime. Whenever."

There was a long pause.

"Are you asking me out on a date?" Jack finally said.

Holly could feel her heart pounding. "Yes."

"Because I'm afraid I'm going to have to say no to that."

"Oh," said Holly. She felt a wave of almost primitive embarrassment wash over her, the kind of embarrassment normally associated with junior high, with bodily functions, with episodes of public nudity. *This is why you don't do things like this, Holly. This—this part right here, this exact moment—is why this was a bad idea.* "Okay. Well. Sorry to bother you."

"Because I would prefer it," said Jack, "if you would let me ask you out on a date."

"Oh."

"That's how I'd like to do it."

"Okay."

"Would you like to have dinner with me on Friday night?"

Holly smiled into the phone. "That would be good."

From Holly's seat she could see out the window into the night. It had started to rain a bit right after the wine arrived, and the townhouse across the street was up-lit with spotlights. It reminded Holly of Paris. She looked across the table at Jack, who appeared to be momentarily transfixed by his goat cheese tart. He looked up and caught her staring at him.

"What?" said Jack.

"Nothing," said Holly.

"What is it?"

Holly was quiet for a moment, and then said what she had been thinking all night, all week actually, ever since Amanda sent her Jack's phone number. "Isn't this sort of a peculiar situation?"

"In what way?"

"You and Amanda just cut it off completely? Just, one day, bam, cold turkey?"

"Amanda did. But I respected her decision," said Jack. "So, yes, I guess."

"Huh." That's all she said, just "huh," but she cocked her head to one side and examined him with undisguised skepticism. Jack looked right back at her, with a bemused expression on his face.

"So that's it?" Holly finally said. She sat back and folded her arms in front of her chest. "You just, one day, decide to stop talking to each other and it's over? Nobody's heart was broken, Mark never found out, and everybody just goes on with their lives like nothing ever happened?"

"What are you after here?" said Jack.

"I'm not sure."

"Take a stab at it."

"Okay, I guess my moralistic side, combined with the writer in me, the dramatist or whatever you'd call it." Holly reached for her wineglass and took an emboldening gulp. "It just feels like there should be consequences."

Jack nodded his head thoughtfully. "Of what sort?"

"Like if, say, Mark found out about it somehow and left her. Or Amanda turned out to be pregnant, and she didn't know whose baby it was. Or if she tried to end things and then you went all psycho on her and threatened to tell her husband. *Fatal Attraction, Crimes and Misdemeanors.* That movie where Diane Lane is cheating on Richard Gere, and then he ends up sort of accidentally killing that sexy actor whose name I cannot remember and rolling him up in a rug."

"Those are pretty big consequences."

"Okay, maybe not that big," said Holly. "I'm just saying, something should *happen.*"

"That would make you feel better?"

"No! It would be horrible," said Holly. "But at least I'd feel like there was some moral center somewhere, like we lived in a universe where things made sense. Instead, in this version, people do whatever the hell they want and everybody gets off scot-free. Nothing bad happens, nobody gets in trouble, a few weeks pass and then, hidey ho, what do you know, you and I end up out on a date!"

Jack settled back in his chair and looked across the table at her for a long silent moment.

"What?" said Holly.

"You realize it's just neurotic, don't you?"

"What is?"

"This moral outrage of yours," said Jack. "I read your novel. You think it comes from your good Christian upbringing, but it doesn't anymore."

"What are you talking about?"

"This. All this," said Jack, and he waved his hand in the air, like there was a fog between them, like the atmosphere was thick with something suspect. "Your inflexible, puritanical attitude. It's a common attribute of the truly neurotic. Along with wanting everybody to like you and waking up in the middle of the night."

"It is not."

"Trust me," he said. "We can go back to the Strand. I'll buy you a book about it."

"Are you serious?"

"I'm afraid so."

"That is really depressing," said Holly.

It was depressing. Holly had long ago come to terms with the fact that she was a tad on the nutty side, but this — the thought that one of the most fundamental aspects of her personality might be nothing more than yet another neurotic quirk — well, it was actually pretty disturbing.

"If it helps at all, you should know, I do feel bad about it," Jack said. "The stuff that went on with Amanda."

"You do?"

"Like you said last time. At the very least, it was unethical. Unlike you" — he smiled a nice smile here — "I'm happy that Mark didn't kill me and roll me up in a Turkish rug. And, I'm happy," Jack paused here, eased back in his chair, and looked across the table at Holly, "that I'm out on a date, with you."

After dinner, Jack hailed a cab and escorted Holly across town to her apartment. He walked her to her door, and when they got there, he took her hand in his and brought it up to his mouth and kissed it. His lips were soft and warm, and she felt a flicker of something promising, a hopeful feeling she hadn't had in as long as she could remember.

"Let's do this," Jack said, "again and again and again."

Spence Samuelson was standing in the hallway outside his apartment trying unsuccessfully to open his door. He could hear his phone ringing inside and it was making him nervous. He'd stopped off at a bar after a bad blind date, and now he was having difficulty putting his key into the lock. The ringing stopped, but as he swung open the door, it started up again. He looked at the clock in the kitchen. It was 12:48 a.m.

He picked up the receiver and heard an angry voice barreling through the line. "*What* did you do?"

"Mom?"

"What did you *do?*"

"What are you talking about, Mom?"

"Joan called her mother when she got home and she was hysterical."

"What?"

"*Hysterical.*"

"Why?"

"She says you made a face."

"*What?*" Spence sat down on his couch, still in his overcoat.

"She says you made a face."

"You're going to have to be clearer than that, Mom, because I have no idea what you're talking about."

"Joan told her mother that when she walked into the restaurant you looked up and you saw her and you made a face."

"Mom, I didn't make a face. I promise you, I *swear* to you, I did not make a face."

Had he made a face? It was certainly possible. Spence had been sitting at the bar, halfway through a martini, waiting for his blind date to show up when a mountain of a woman walked in with a nervous, expectant look on her face, and a voice deep inside of him shouted, "Nooo." He supposed that sentiment could have come with an attendant facial expression.

"She says you did," Vera said. "She says it was all she could do not to run out of the restaurant crying, it was such a nasty face."

"I'm sorry, it must have been her imagination, because I did not make a face."

"Well, she says you did," Vera said, signaling she was surrendering no ground, "and she said all you talked about all night was breasts."

"*What?*"

"Breasts breasts breasts. Apparently, that's all my son is interested in. Big humongous breasts. So much so that he thinks talking about them is polite dinner conversation."

"Honestly, Mom, I have no idea why she would say such a thing."

"You think she's making it up? You think this sweet girl goes on a date and then calls up her mother and tells lies to her?"

"Maybe. I don't know." Spence scrolled through his memory of the conversation until he landed on something. "We did talk about Pamela Anderson at one point. Her name came up. It's possible the topic of her chest came up in the course of the conversation, but I don't remember."

"I have to sit down."

"But it was an extremely small part of the overall conversation."

"I just don't understand how you find the subject of Pamela Anderson's breasts appropriate to talk about on a first date. I'm sorry, it just doesn't make sense to me. Plus you drank too much, and then you didn't even take her home."

"I didn't pick her up. We met at the restaurant. It wasn't a take-home kind of situation."

"Joan told her mother that after dinner you flagged down a cab and jumped in and left her standing alone on the sidewalk."

"She told me she *wanted* to walk home, she needed some air, listen, Mom, this is why I didn't want to do this. This is why I said no to this scheme of yours about twenty times. This is exactly the scenario I was looking to avoid."

"You need to call Joan tomorrow morning and apologize and ask her out on another date."

"No way."

"Spencer, I am extremely embarrassed by this entire episode."

"I'll apologize," said Spence, "but I'm not going to ask her out again."

"Just one more quick dinner."

"Mom, if she came home from our date crying, I'm pretty sure she won't want to go out with me again."

"Harriet said that Joan said that she would say yes if you asked her out again."

Spence sighed a big sigh.

"Tomorrow," his mother said, and she hung up the phone.

Spence sat back on his couch and tried to reconstruct the chain of events that led to this phone call. A little while back, his mother had called him and said she had met somebody she thought he would like. "I'm not going on a blind date," he'd said. "She's beautiful," his mother told him. Not pretty, not attractive, not good-looking—*beautiful*. Over and over again, his mother told him how beautiful this woman was. "Her name is Joan, and she is stunningly beautiful." "I don't care, Mom, I don't want to do it." "Just one dinner," she said. "For me, Spencer," she said. And somehow he had gotten it in his head that going out to dinner with his mother's neighbor's stunningly beautiful daughter Joan would be a relatively painless way to make his mother happy, like remembering to send her flowers on Mother's Day or noticing when she did something new with her hair. So he said yes.

Joan turned out to be so far from beautiful that Spence spent the first fifteen minutes of their date in a state of mild bafflement, trying to make sense of the woman who was before him. She was, as promised, in her midthirties, and she had nice shoulder-length brown hair — good hair, really, Spence had to admit — and she had a pleasant, open, smiling face that nonetheless reminded him of a coconut cream pie. Her breasts were enormous, and they were hoisted up to such an improbable height that they brought to mind pulleys and counterbalances and steel girding. She was clearly proud of them, in the misguided way that Spence found that all fat women are impressed with their own breasts. She was at least forty pounds overweight. Could be as much as seventy. (Spence was no good at guessing the weight of fat people — it was a question of density.) Is this what a pair of sixty-year-old women find beautiful? Spence found himself wondering. Is that even possible? Or had they deliberately tricked him? Too late, he remembered his mother's penchant for overselling. For months, he'd listened to her rave about the frozen hot chocolate they served at the ice-cream parlor out in Kimmswick. How he just had to go with her the next time he was visiting and taste this amazing frozen hot chocolate. Last Thanksgiving, she made a plan for them to go get some together the next day, and all morning she gave it a nonstop big buildup, to such a degree that he found himself, as he sat waiting in the red leather booth, actually anticipating the wondrous culinary delight he was about to partake of. And what did the waitress place before him? A fudge milkshake in a latte mug.

All in all, he thought the date had gone quite well, for what it was. What it was was a two-hour-long, three-course meal shared by two people who would never kiss, never touch, and with any luck, never lay eyes on each other ever again. He'd felt quite proud of himself, like he had done, well, not a good deed exactly, but at least that he had comported himself as a grown-up. He wasn't going to call her and apologize. He didn't have anything to apologize for. And he most definitely wasn't going to ask her out again. He didn't care what his mother said.

give me that much

Eight days later, Spence showed up at the restaurant Joan had suggested, an overpriced Italian bistro which was around the corner from her apartment. There had indeed been a phone call. There had been an apology, which Joan proceeded to assert was not necessary, not at all, but with a palpable edge to her voice that sort of frightened him. Somehow—and Spence still wasn't entirely clear on how it had happened, except that his mother had everything to do with it—there had been talk of doing it again sometime. Then came a midweek email exchange, as the two settled on a time and a place. Spence couldn't help feeling, as he shrugged off his overcoat and handed it to the hostess, that he had been outplayed entirely.

He scanned the room and spotted Joan. She was seated at a banquette with a small rectangular table pulled in tight in front of her, the dimensions of the table seeming to emphasize her impressive girth. Again, the boobs were out. Acres of cleavage were on display. It was, Spence thought as he made his way over to the table, the kind of cleavage that makes you think you could reach down in and pull out a ham sandwich.

"I'm sorry, am I late?" he said.

"I was early."

"Good. I hate to be late," he said. He leaned in over the table and gave her a sort of kiss, he kissed her hair really, while he clutched her right shoulder. It was like grabbing a deboned chicken carcass. He sat down on the chair across from her and smoothed his shirt front and his tie, like he was preening, like he was trying to make a good impression. "Good to see you. You're looking well. You got a little sun this week?"

"I don't think so," said Joan.

"Really? Well, you're all aglow." Okay, buddy, ratchet it down a bit, Spence said to himself as he opened his menu. "Have you had a chance to look?"

"Yes." Clipped.

"Good, well, I'm easy." He scanned the menu. "I'll get the pasta arrabiata. Just because I like saying it." He rolled his *r*'s. "Arrabiata."

Nothing from Joan. Not even a smile.

"Shall we order a bottle of wine?"

"Are you sure you wouldn't prefer your martinis?" said Joan. Not "a martini." Martinis plural. Was it just his imagination, or was this some sort of a slam? Spence had had three on their last date, four if you counted the one he'd tossed back before she showed up. He had, when he first saw her, more or less instantaneously reached the point where he knew the date wasn't going to end up anyplace interesting, and he'd decided to salvage his half of the evening by getting quickly and pleasantly soused.

"I'll do wine if you'll do wine."

"Fine," she said. Her face was a freckled pie. It was completely expressionless. This was not at all like last time, Spence was starting to realize. Last time, Joan had been smiling and tilting her head, playing with her hair, fondling the ruffled edges of her plunging neckline. Now she was just sitting there, massive, looming, like one of those statues on Easter Island.

"Red or white?"

"I prefer white," said Joan.

"White, white, I love white. Glad you said white." He indicated the wine list, which was housed in a massive leather-bound portfolio. "Shall I?"

"Be my guest."

His eyes scanned the wine list, but nothing was registering. He was just going to pick the second cheapest on the list like he always did, but he pretended to be absorbed because it gave him time to collect his thoughts. His date was giving off a very peculiar vibe this evening. Last time, some innate feminine quality—of being pleasing, of being receptive and warm and pliable—was on display. Now she was just a large, angry woman. And he had been called on to give a command performance.

"Where did you go to college?" Spence asked after ordering the wine.

"I told you that last time."

"You did. Of course you did. Don't help me. It was one of those little brainy schools. Bryn Mawr? Middlebury…?"

"Swarthmore."

"Swarthmore. Right. The Garnet Tide."

"Your friend Cliff went there," she said flatly. "And you went to Brown."

"Yes. Yes I did. Bad mascot, Brown. Plus bad school colors. There's nothing worse than a Brown University sweatshirt. That's why you never see anybody wearing one. Central Park on a Saturday, you'll see Penn, you'll see Harvard, you'll see Cornell, but never Brown." He was simply babbling now. He had to keep off subjects that might have been covered during their disastrous three-(okay, four)-martini date. He felt like

Princess Leia dancing in front of Jabba the Hutt, spinning around, faster and faster. "We've got good famous students, though. Laura Linney"—flat chested!—"Leelee Sobieski—" Flat as a board!

"I've seen people wearing sweatshirts from Brown."

Spence looked at her with a faint smile frozen on his face.

"A guy at my gym," said Joan. "And there's a girl in my building who wears one on the weekends."

"Well, that shoots my theory," Spence said. He laughed a forced laugh. "I guess I'll have to retire that one. The 'nobody wears sweatshirts from Brown' bit. Into the trash heap it goes."

A grim silence fell over the table. The waiter arrived with the wine and took their orders.

"Is everything all right?" Spence said once the waiter crossed off.

"What do you mean?"

"It seems to me that maybe you don't really want to be here," said Spence.

"Why would you say that?"

"Well, I don't know, it's just a sense I have. And if you want to cut this short, just let me know."

"Do *you* want to cut this short?" said Joan.

A trick question. He knew if he said he wanted to cut it short, it would go straight back to Harriet and his mother. Well, fuck those two old biddies. If they don't want to understand something as basic as, as, as *what kind of woman he was entitled to,* well—

"I'm having a wonderful time," said Spence.

"Good."

"So."

"So."

"So, did you have a nice week?" Spence said.

"I did."

"Did you do anything interesting?"

"I went to that thing I told you about. At the museum."

Spence felt like he was taking a blue book exam for an eight o'clock class he'd repeatedly slept through. Museum. Thing at a museum. "Really? Great. How'd that turn out?"

"You know. Pretty much what you'd expect," she said. She took a hearty pull from her glass of Chenin Blanc. "Lots of frogs."

Was she fucking with him? For a moment that seemed a distinct possibility. Frogs at a museum. Or maybe it was a frog museum? Do we have a frog museum in Manhattan?

"That sounds wild," he said.

"It was at night, so the frogs were a lot more active than they are during the day when most people get to go see them," said Joan. "It was kind of cool, actually."

A lightbulb went off. The Museum of Natural History. The big frog exhibit. *Saved!*

"I love that museum," said Spence. "I used to go there all the time to look at the nature dioramas. It feels kind of like being in a time warp. Like it's a museum of a museum."

"Exactly."

"So, it was just kind of a party there at night to see the frogs?"

"Like I said last time," she said, her freckled pie face completely unreadable, "it was a fund-raiser for this program I volunteer for that helps disadvantaged kids go to Catholic high schools in the city. I was on the committee in charge of the event. The kids were there, and we try to get as many possible sponsors to go, too, so they can meet the kids and connect with what we're trying to do and hopefully write big checks."

"Did you raise very much money?"

"Just under fifty thousand dollars."

"That's amazing. Good for you. Let me send in a check." What was he saying? Now he was paying this woman? Two nights of his life weren't enough?

"You don't have to."

"I *want* to. Really," said Spence. "I wouldn't suggest it if I didn't. I don't have time to go to enough of those things and I think it's really important that people, you know, *give back*."

"I'll email you my address tomorrow."

"Do that."

There was another long silence. Spence elected not to fill it. Instead, he took an enormous forkful of penne arrabiata and set about chewing. Time for Big Joan to carry a little water on this date. He entertained a fantasy, in which he put his fork down and looked into her eyes and said, shouldn't we be honest about what's going on here? We both know what went wrong with our last date. I am never going to date a woman like you. And you're mad at me for it. You're angry at me, and at all men, and I don't blame you for it, really I don't, but can't you just see that this is the way of the world and, oh, I don't know, maybe lose some weight and then maybe, well, who was he kidding, he still wouldn't have gone out with her, she was too old and those freckles, but surely *somebody* would. Might. But instead of accepting that, you go home and *tell your mommy on me!*

Joan was talking like a good fund-raiser, repeating a conversation she'd probably had a hundred times before. "In this city, it's the kids in the middle that fall through the cracks," she said. "If an underprivileged kid is a genius, the city will move him to a magnet school, where he will be challenged and get extra support, and there've been all sorts of lawsuits and legislation in the past decade on behalf of the slow ones, so they get special teachers and small classes and early interventions, but the kids we help are just ordinary, average students who would get lost otherwise. They get a mentor and tuition to go to a parochial school. Most of them end up going to college. Their lives are turned around completely, and it only costs about four thousand dollars a year."

"I'm not sure if we covered this before," Spence tiptoed into dangerous ground, "but did you go to Catholic school?"

"All twelve years."

Ah-ha, thought Spence. Perhaps that explains tonight's new, slightly sadistic side of Big Joan.

"Really?" he said. "Twelve years? What was that like?"

And on that he got her really rolling. He could finally relax a bit, and just lob in a laugh, a shocked expression, a question about corporal punishment, a suggestive (but not too suggestive!) comment about knee socks and plaid skirts.

"I don't think it's quite as intense as it was when I was growing up, you know, the religious part of it, but I don't really know," she said. "Did you go to church growing up?"

"A few times. Christmas and Easter, some years. It wasn't a big thing in my family."

"Do you believe in God?" she asked.

Spence did not believe in God. In fact, Spence knew that there wasn't a God. He was certain of it. He found, to his great surprise, that this was not a popular position to take these days, even smack-dab in the middle of Manhattan, even among the elite pie slice of his peers, that group of thirtysomething

strivers who seemed to be the most godless, soulless, materi-
alistic human beings on the face of the earth. If atheism was
unfashionable here, no wonder they were teaching creationism
in Texas, Spence sometimes found himself thinking. If atheism was uncool in Manhattan, what hope was there for the rest
of the country?

It was, though. It was uncool. Everyone claimed to be spiritual. "Spiritual, but not religious" was the way ninety percent of
the women Spence met characterized themselves, and the men,
well, Spence never discussed such things with men, but he was
pretty sure, by the level of horror and revulsion he encountered
when he announced to his dates that he was an atheist, that the
men were running around town saying the same thing. Spiritual but not religious! Who came up with that nonsense?! Yet
they all said it, and exactly the same way, too. As though they
were *searching* for just the right words, trying to pull them out
of the ether, implying that they had explored the traditional
routes to God through the world's great religions, found them
all lacking, and instead cultivated a private and palpable connection to the divine. Spence had been known to grill his dates
on precisely what they meant by this, and he had come away
with the understanding that "spiritual but not religious" meant
the following: they comforted themselves with the notion that
there was a God but they never bothered to investigate the
proposition or even think about it all that much. Like believing
in Santa Claus.

"I don't," he said.

"Not at all?"

"No," said Spence. "Well, I suppose, on some level, I'm
willing to accept that there is, maybe — *possibly* — some kind of

a force out there, but not that it is intelligent or benevolent or the least bit interested in mankind."

"What kind of force?"

"The force that's in a tree. Or inside a slab of steel."

"And that's God?"

"No. It's a force," said Spence. "And even if you want to call it God, the truth is, it has none of the characteristics that humans attribute to God. But that's as far as I'll go."

"That's kind of bleak."

"Yeah, well," said Spence, as he mopped up the last bit of arrabiata sauce with a stubby piece of focaccia, "life is bleak."

Spence picked up the check—one hundred and twelve dollars plus tip—and offered to walk Joan home. He figured the walk home was the last requirement of this date, his mother would have nothing to harangue him about, and that once he deposited Joan at her front door he would be free to never see or speak to or even think about her ever again.

"You know, your mother is really into you," Joan said, once they got out on the sidewalk.

"What do you mean?"

"I mean, she's really into you. To be perfectly honest, I was curious to meet you, just to see what kind of a man has a mother who is that in love with him."

"My mother is not *in love* with me."

"Well, maybe that's not the right phrase," said Joan. "She's obsessed with you. She talks about you all the time."

"She was trying to fix you up with me," said Spence. "She was trying to make me sound good so you'd want to go out with me."

"No, no. This is way beyond that. You wouldn't believe the things I know about you."

"Give me an example."

Joan stopped walking, as though so deep in thought that further locomotion was impossible. "Well, I know your espresso machine, which you use to make yourself a double espresso every morning before work, cost fourteen hundred dollars."

"My mother told you that?"

"I'm afraid so," Joan said. She started walking again, and Spence trailed along a half step behind.

"Why on earth would she tell you that?"

"That's just it. It makes no sense. My mom says she does it all the time. She's always talking about your stuff, and how much money you make, and how successful you are. Stupid things. Like how expensive your ties are. It drives my mother crazy."

"My dad died three years ago," said Spence. "She doesn't have very much to talk about."

"It's no big deal. I was just curious," she said.

"She's lonely," said Spence. "She doesn't have a whole lot of her own going on right now."

"That's probably all it is," said Joan. She stopped in front of a brownstone with a big pot of geraniums on the front stoop. "Well. This is me."

"Nice building," said Spence.

"Thanks," said Joan. "I'll email you the address tomorrow."

"The address?"

"So you can send in the check. They'll send you a receipt at tax time."

"Right. Great."

"So."

"Well," said Spence. He went in for the awkward half hug because he couldn't think of anything else to do. "Good night."

"Good night."

Spence walked to the corner of Sixth Avenue and flagged down a passing cab. As he sank into the backseat, a feeling of immense heaviness overtook him, like molten lead had been poured into his chest and throughout his body, and for a moment he felt like it would be impossible to move his arms and legs. He looked down at his left hand and moved it a few inches along the vinyl seat just to see if he could. He could. He couldn't have put it into words, that would have been beyond him, but Joan had somehow confirmed a suspicion he had, a suspicion that something about his life wasn't quite right.

"You know who I'm becoming?" Lucas said. "Guy Who Puts Tabasco on Everything."

Holly and Lucas were at the tiny Greek diner a few blocks from her apartment, eating an early Sunday brunch. It was the place she went when she couldn't think of another place to go, with unmemorable food and vaguely hostile service but blissfully short, neighborhood-defying brunch lines.

"Yesterday, I put Tabasco on a mango," Lucas said. He shook a spring storm of Tabasco droplets over his scrambled eggs and home fries and Canadian bacon. "And you know what? It wasn't bad."

Holly had gone out with Jack again, the night before. It was their second date, another good one, with a kiss on her doorstep that made her knees go weak. When she got inside, there was a message on her answering machine from Lucas. He was at a bar around the corner with some friends and wanted to stop by. Holly found herself in a moral quandary. Could she go out on a date with Jack and then, less than an hour later, hop into bed with Lucas? Was that an okay thing to do? She thought about what Jack had said on their first date, about her puritanicalism being nothing more than a neurotic tic, and then she dialed Lucas's number and told him to come over. And she felt the way she always felt when she found herself involved in something like this, sort of, impressed with her own moxie, like a teenager who cuts class *and* smokes cigarettes *and* drinks vodka stolen from her parents' liquor cabinet, all at the same time. And even if the only rules she was breaking were in her own head — she'd been on just two dates with Jack, and a single kiss, no matter how weak-kneed it had left her, was not, she realized, in the end, binding, while the loose and forgiving parameters of her sexual relationship with Lucas were crystal clear to all involved — still, she felt a little bit like a rebel.

But now it was the next morning, and Holly found, in the glare of the spring sunlight, that she was back to her old self.

"I think we need to stop this," she said.

"Stop what?" said Lucas.

"Stop seeing each other."

"What makes you say that?"

"I just think we do."

"Okay," said Lucas. He slowly and purposefully screwed the little red cap back on the bottle of hot sauce. "Where is this coming from?"

"What do you mean? It's coming from me, where else would it be coming from?"

"I mean, why are you doing this now? Why are we having

this conversation today? Is it because you found out your ex-husband is getting remarried? Because I don't think that's a reason to stop seeing me."

"It's not because of that."

"Because that," Lucas's face turned stern and serious, and Holly had a flash of what he would look like at forty, "would be a very stupid thing to do."

"It's not that."

"What is it, then?"

Holly took a deep breath and sank back into the cool leather of the booth. "I think I might have met someone."

"Ah." Lucas picked up his coffee cup and then put it down again. "Ah ah ah. Who is he?"

"You don't know him. He's not important."

"He sounds pretty important if he's why you're breaking up with me."

"Lucas, we were never, I mean, this wasn't…"

"This wasn't what?"

"I'm just saying, we both knew this was temporary. It was a temporary situation."

"Listen, Holly, you can say something isn't a relationship, but that doesn't change the fact that it is. So yes, you are breaking up with me. That's what this is. Give me that much, at least."

"Okay. I'm breaking up with you."

"Thank you."

"But we weren't in a committed relationship."

"Apparently not."

Lucas scooped some eggs onto a piece of toast and took a big bite. He chewed and looked directly into Holly's eyes. His chewing went on forever.

"I'm not going to start feeling bad here," said Holly. "I was always very clear about things. From the very beginning, I was clear."

"Yes, you were." He took another bite and chewed some more. "So, what is he? Old?"

"He's older than you, yes. He's older than me, too. Not by much, I mean, he's in the same general generation that I'm in, and we're at the same place in our lives and we want the same things."

"What do you want that I don't want?"

"Oh, I don't know, kids?"

"I want kids."

"Right now?"

"You're saying this guy you just met wants to have a baby with you right now?"

"I'm not saying that," said Holly. "But it would be on the horizon, I suppose, if things worked out, it would be on the near horizon. It would be in the foreground of the horizon."

"Well, I think you're making a mistake."

"That's entirely possible."

Lucas looked down at the half-eaten food on his plate. His hair had gotten longer, Holly noticed, and he had unruly curls everywhere. *He's adorable,* Holly found herself thinking. *I want to pick him up and put him in my pocket.*

"Well, say something," Holly finally said.

"What would you like me to say?"

"I don't know. Something. Anything."

Lucas got up from the table and pulled some cash out of his wallet. He put a few bills down on the table.

"Good luck to you."

And he left.

exhibit a

I'm sort of surprised that reincarnation hasn't been a bigger hit in America."

Holly was stretched out naked alongside Jack in his bed, and she realized, once the words were out of her mouth, that she had violated her rule about being the first one to speak after sex. It could be argued that Holly and Jack had reached the point where rules like that were no longer necessary—they'd been dating pretty consistently for six weeks now, really dating-dating, doing the kind of stuff that feels like an exquisitely romantic preamble to the kind of relationship where you buy one another toiletries and wear each other's cozy pants—but Holly wasn't so sure.

The thing about sex that always surprised Holly was that it was so darn intimate. Really, it was such a strangely personal thing to do with somebody else. *Who came up with this?* she often found herself thinking. And while the sex that night with Jack had been good—both parties had reached a satisfactory, albeit not simultaneous, conclusion—there was a moment near the end there—past the end for Holly, not to put too fine a point on it, but before the end for Jack—when Holly ended up stretched across the bed, on her knees and forearms, with her rear in the air and her right ear pressed to the mattress. She opened her eyes and found herself almost unconsciously scanning the spines of the books stacked on Jack's nightstand. *The Cloud of Unknowing. The Path Is the Goal. Reincarnation and Karma.* She knew this wasn't kosher, sexually speaking, but she couldn't help herself: if words were in front of Holly's face, she read them.

"What do you mean?" said Jack.

"Reincarnation is such an appealing idea, when you really think about it. Getting to come back and do this again and again and again," said Holly. She nestled a little deeper into the crook of his arm. "Talk all you want about life being suffering, I think the idea of complete nonexistence is much worse. The idea that you die and, poof, you're gone."

"Reincarnation isn't necessarily a positive thing."

"I know. You can come back as a cockroach," said Holly. "But I think it's interesting that both Buddhism and Christianity have this idea that you, the essence of you, will continue more or less *forever.* Not just blend into a giant anonymous force field of 'light' or 'energy' or even 'love' — that there is a specific part of you that will go on. In Christianity you have the immortality of the soul and even the resurrection of the body, and in Buddhism you have the idea, so far as I can tell, that the essence of you goes back down to earth into a different body, or an animal's body, or a bug's, or whatever."

"Until you achieve enlightenment and become a Buddha. Then you more or less blend into the 'anonymous force field' as you call it," said Jack.

"I guess it developed in a time, and in a part of the world where, you know, suffering was really *suffering.* That's my point about America. Nobody really wants it to end. I'm miserable half the time, and still there isn't the smallest part of me that wants to stop existing."

"Do you ever meditate?"

"I've tried it," said Holly.

"And?"

"I don't know. It feels a little too much like self-improvement. Religion as stress relief. All I ever want is the bliss."

"The bliss is beside the point in Buddhism."

"Yeah, okay, what is the point of Buddhism?" said Holly. "I can't really wrap my head around it. All I think of is, reincarnation and, you know, don't kill bugs."

"How about, I buy you a book."

"Okay," said Holly. "I can't promise I'll finish reading it, though."

"Why wouldn't you?"

Holly reached for one of the pillows that had fallen to the floor and scrunched it up under her head.

"I don't know," said Holly. "I guess I just can't get behind a religion that doesn't have a God."

"It's not that there isn't a God in Buddhism, exactly," said Jack.

"What is it, then?"

"Well, Pema Chödrön puts it this way," said Jack. "She says that in Buddhism, God is left as an open question."

"An open question?"

"There might be a God, or there might not be one. It's a mystery."

"Yeah, no, I don't like that," said Holly. She disentangled herself from his arm and sat up.

"Why not?"

"Because in all of life, God is an open question. You look at the ocean, and God is an open question. You stand on a mountaintop, and God is an open question. The point of religion is to *answer* that question."

Holly leaned back against the headboard and used her pillow to cover herself.

"I will, however, say one thing on behalf of your religion," said Holly. She paused somewhat dramatically for a moment, to make sure she had his full attention, and then she said, "The funny thing about reincarnation is, it *sounds* crazy, but it doesn't *feel* crazy."

"What do you mean?"

"I mean, when you hear about it, you're like, whaaah? You expect me to swallow this? That *this* guy used to be *that* guy? That this Lama was that Lama who was that Lama a long time ago? That's crazy! But then, your own experience of yourself as a person makes it feel sort of right, the thought that you've been around forever and you're going to exist forever. That *feels* more true than the idea that tomorrow you could get hit by a bus and then completely cease to exist."

"You know what your problem is?" said Jack. "You're a spiritual person with no spiritual practice. Go back to church if you can't meditate."

"I can't go back to church."

"Why not?" he said.

"I don't fit in anymore."

"So? Who cares?"

"Believe me, it matters," said Holly. "Plus I'm sinning left and right, and I have no intention of slowing down any time soon."

"What are you talking about?"

"Exhibit A," said Holly. She gestured to all of it, the tangle of sheets, their two naked bodies. "That's the main one,

I guess. But, you know, I got a divorce, and I wrote that book and it has the f-word in it, like, a hundred times, and it wasn't an altogether complimentary portrait of my religious upbringing. Nope, I pretty much burned my bridges back to my own people with that one."

"What about finding a church that's Christian, but not so..."

"Not so evangelical?"

"Not so conservative, I was going to say."

"Like, what, one of those Episcopal churches that has an openly gay priest?" said Holly.

"Why not?"

"With the clothes drive in the narthex and the transgendered support group in the basement, antiwar sloganeering from the pulpit, potlucks featuring mung bean and tofu chili, hymns addressed to God our Mother, that sort of thing?"

"In that general neighborhood, yes."

"I can't do it," said Holly. "It's completely foreign to me. It's worse than foreign. It pushes more buttons."

"What do you mean?"

"I sit in a church like that and I start to feel like Jerry Falwell. It brings out every long-discarded fundamentalist impulse in me," Holly confessed. "I find myself flipping back through Leviticus and searching for injunctions against sodomy. Honestly, I'm sort of stuck. I can't go forward and I can't go back."

"You could go forward," said Jack.

"I honestly don't see how."

Jack rolled over and kissed her, sweetly, on her hip.

"Sometimes I think this," said Holly. "Sometimes I think, I'm a Christian, but I'm a horrible one. You know, maybe that's just what it comes down to. I'm not a very good person. My character has not been transformed. And I have no impulse whatsoever to make anyone else a Christian, I have no evangelical zeal, which is really one of the most fundamental aspects of Christianity. I've squandered this rich inheritance, this spiritual education and what were some objectively pretty powerful mystical experiences because, what — it's not cool? Is that my problem with Christianity, fundamentally? And I'm too lazy and self-involved to do anything rigorous, to think about any of it too hard, to pin myself down on anything specific. But, you know, if the plane starts to go down, I pray to Jesus. If I think I feel a lump in my breast, it all comes rushing back to me."

Jack rolled out of bed and headed towards the bathroom. "That's not really being a Christian, though, is it?"

the freudian
business model

Amanda showed up at lunch with a new purse.

"What do you think?" she said, holding it up in the air for Holly to admire.

"It's beautiful," said Holly.

"It cost twelve hundred dollars."

"What?!"

"I know," said Amanda. "Mark is going to kill me."

"I don't get it," said Holly. "You spent twelve hundred dollars on a purse?"

"Let me explain why it makes sense," said Amanda. She set the purse on the table, just to the right of her knife and spoon, in the place of honor usually reserved for her cell phone. "Most of the purses I buy cost what? Three hundred bucks, on average. Which means this is really just the equivalent of four purses. And I won't buy the other three purses, because I'm so in love with this one, which means I come out even. Ahead, really, because this one will last forever. At my funeral, I'll be looking down at everybody and I'll see my daughter, and she'll be carrying this purse."

"You are really rich."

"Yeah, well, Mark's bonus was good this year, that's all."

"How rich *are* you guys?"

"Holly, you can't ask people questions like that."

"Why not? I'm curious."

"You just can't."

"Okay," said Holly. "Sorry."

Holly sat back in her chair.

"You don't have to be sorry."

"That's good," said Holly, "because I'm not really sorry."

Amanda rolled her eyes.

"I can't help it if I find money interesting. That's why I like Victorian novels. Trollope always tells you exactly how much money everybody has. It makes everything clear." Holly reached for her menu and then said quietly, almost to herself, "In real life, I never have any idea what the hell is going on."

Holly once read somewhere that people who suffer from vertigo actually have a strong unconscious wish to jump. The vertigo, it turns out, is the psyche's way of protecting them from themselves, of keeping them from hurling themselves off bridges and balconies, from taking a flying leap when they visit the Cliffs of Moher or the north rim of the Grand Canyon. Holly wasn't sure if this was a fact or just a theory, but that didn't seem to matter, she found that if a person wanted to intensify the overall potency of their vertigo, to up the dose as it were, learning that particular tidbit will do the trick. Now, whenever she found herself standing someplace high, and gripped with that familiar fear, she discovered that the voice in her head had come up with something new to say: don't jump.

That's how Holly felt at that moment. She knew she had to tell Amanda she was dating Jack, and she was afraid—that Amanda would be upset, that their friendship would be over—and yet, a part of her, a part she didn't understand, wanted to jump.

"I've got some news," said Holly.

"What is it?"

"This is kind of, I don't know," said Holly. "I don't know how to talk about this."

Amanda's eyes narrowed. "You're not still sleeping with that twenty-two-year-old are you?"

"No. That's over."

"Good."

"It's just," Holly said, "I'm seeing someone."

"Yay. *Finally*," said Amanda. "What's his name? What does he do?"

Holly screwed up her face. "It's Jack. You know, your Jack."

"You're dating Jack?" Amanda said. Her eyes opened even wider than usual.

Holly nodded, her face still scrunched up. "Like you suggested. On the phone that time, remember?"

"Of course I remember. Why didn't you tell me about it?"

"Because it's weird."

"It is a little weird," said Amanda. She nodded her head slowly, as if absorbing the weirdness of it all. "But it's good. Good for you, sweetie. I mean it. Good for you."

"You're not upset?"

"No."

"Really?"

"I'm happy for you," said Amanda. "I'm happy for Jack, too. Listen, I wasn't going to break up my marriage. I don't want to be that person. Mark drives me crazy sometimes but I'm not ready to throw my entire world away."

"It was just your life spirit," said Holly. "Bubbling up."

"I'm aware you think that's bullshit, but I'm not ashamed of it. And I don't have any regrets," said Amanda. She opened up her menu. "I'm starving. What are you going to get?"

It wasn't until later that afternoon, on her way to go pick up Chester from the vet, that Holly found herself thinking about what Amanda had said. The part about having no regrets. How was that possible? It seemed to Holly that this was an excellent time for Amanda to entertain a few regrets. Her best friend was dating a man that she had had an affair with, an affair that put her marriage and family in jeopardy, an affair that her husband was unaware ever took place. At the very least, it was going to make double-dating tricky. Was it true, Holly found herself wondering, that if you could keep from feeling bad about something bad that you'd done, and you never got caught, then it didn't really count?

The more she thought about it, the more Holly wondered if anybody ever had any regrets anymore. She bet you could have asked Christopher Reeve, back when he was still alive, if he regretted saddling up that horse on that fateful day, and he would have talked about all of the lessons he'd learned and how his life, while truly challenging, was actually much richer now, and how he was who he was and the horse was who the *horse* was, and then he would have blown into his straw and wheeled off into the sunset. To regret anything had become almost un-American. Instead, there was this: everything happens for a reason. Something bad happens to you? Well, there's a reason. There are no accidents. It is all order in the universe. Once, just once, Holly wanted to hear someone say that everything happens for a reason, but it doesn't really matter, because in the end, we're all, every last one of us, going to die.

Two Feathers was as dark and gleaming and blue-tinged as ever, but instead of his usual expression — the one that made Holly think of smallpox-laden blankets and wampum trades gone sour — on this day, he greeted Holly with a big smile.

"I just got Chester's latest round of tests back."

"How is he?"

"His blood tests came back normal, the MRI is completely clear. The tumor is gone and it looks like it won't be making a comeback. That's why I kept him the extra day. The results were so positive, I wanted to make sure the lab didn't make a mistake."

"Are you serious?"

"I've never seen a dog respond this quickly to treatment. We'll keep a close eye on him for the next year or so, but there's no reason to think anything will change."

"I don't understand," said Holly. "Does that mean no more radiation?"

"No more radiation. Just bring him by in, oh, say about four months and we'll take another look around, but strictly as a precaution," said Two Feathers. "He's as good as new."

Lately, Spence found himself reflecting on a conversation he'd had with Cathleen a few months earlier, shortly after the onset of The Troubles, back when she was still willing to talk to him. It was back in her weepy-needy-angry phase, when she seemed to be holding out hope that there had been some mistake or, at the very least, that he might change. She'd asked him to go see a therapist.

"I've *been* in therapy, Cathleen," said Spence. "I know all about it."

"I'm just asking you to try again."

"I'm not saying there's anything wrong with it," he'd said. "It's just not for me."

Spence had gone to therapy, a few years earlier, at the behest of his girlfriend at the time, whose name was Minnie and who was now married to a pediatric oncologist and was the mother of twin boys. Spence and Minnie had been dating for just over a year when he had begun "acting out," as she put it—getting home at three a.m., "accidentally" turning off his cell phone—and she was getting fed up. She didn't know the half of it, of course, but Spence agreed to go talk to someone if it would make her feel better.

Minnie's therapist wrote down the name of a colleague on the back of one of her cream-colored business cards, which Minnie handed to Spence over dinner, and which Spence managed, somehow, to lose somewhere between the restaurant and his front door. A week passed before Minnie saw her therapist again and a new card was issued, which Minnie kept possession of until she got Spence next to a phone, calendar in hand, during business hours.

Spence's therapist was named Lucinda, and she was short and zaftiggy with lots of curly black hair. She wore hippie gear, long skirts and big necklaces and clunky sandals, but you could tell she didn't start out that way, you could tell she came from someplace like Scranton and had middle-class, normal parents. She appeared to be well into her forties, and the third finger of her left hand was conspicuously bare, which got Spence to thinking. Every man he knew who was in therapy (a) had a female therapist and (b) was there because his girlfriend, who was in therapy herself, more or less forced him to go. Which meant that the entire therapeutic community was fueled by women who were dissatisfied in their relationships with men, who go into therapy in their thirties, become therapists in their forties, and, through it all, try to get the men who they're convinced are the source of all their problems into therapy themselves. It was the Freudian business model.

Spence liked therapy. He liked being able to talk about himself, relatively honestly, and not have to worry about it coming back to bite him in the ass the way it had when he had opened up with girlfriends in the past. He liked to see himself through the eyes of Lucinda, to sort of appreciate his own depth and complexity, to sit back and applaud his willingness to examine his relationship problems, to show up and "do the work." His first session was like a blind date, but a blind date in which he felt absolutely no obligation to ask the other person anything about herself whatsoever, which felt, if he were completely honest with himself, nicer than it probably should have. The second session was more of the same. By the third, he was starting to wonder what exactly he was supposed to be doing. He feared he had only two fifty-minute sessions' worth of autobiographical monologue in him, and he was in danger of repeating himself. He brought this up with Lucinda, and she reassured him and said, "Just say whatever pops into your mind." So he did that for a while. He talked about problems at work. And about the time his sister locked him in the basement. And how he had started to worry about his mother, who was sixty-two, dying. These thoughts were not, well, ever-present, but more like a worry stone he rubbed every once in a while. *My mother is old. She's going to die someday.*

"Sometimes, when our minds are overtaken by unexplained dark thoughts, something else is operating," said Lucinda.

"Like what?" said Spence.

"Well, to give one example, sometimes the dark thought can actually be a wish in disguise."

"What do you mean?"

She looked at him with an expressionless face.

"You think I *wish* that my mother would *die?*"

Therapeutic silence.

"I don't want my mother to die, ever. I *love* her. She's just old, and I worry about her, like a normal person worries about their mother."

The following week, Spence forgot to set his alarm and slept through his appointment. Lucinda charged him for the session, as was her stated policy, and he felt ill-used and pissed off. That was all he needed to know about psychotherapy. He felt fortunate, really, to have figured out the truth so quickly. He mailed Lucinda a check and never went back.

———

"Have you ever noticed that pictures of missing people are always bad?" said Leonard.

He and Holly were on their way to lunch, walking up Amsterdam Avenue, and they were stopped at a red light.

"What do you mean?" said Holly.

"Look at this," said Leonard. He pointed to a black-and-white flyer stapled to a telephone pole. Stacy Margiano, age twenty-four, had been missing since the previous Thursday. "What do you see?" he asked. "Two eyes. Sort of a mouth. That could be anybody."

"Maybe that's why they're missing," said Holly. "Nobody can find a good picture of them."

The light turned green and they crossed.

"Alex is getting married on Saturday," Holly said when they reached the sidewalk.

"You talked to him?" asked Leonard.

"I sort of accidentally happened to stumble across his wedding registry online."

"Here we go."

"Crate and Barrel," said Holly.

"—"

"Lots and lots of white plates."

"I thought you were over this."

"I am over it. I just find it interesting," said Holly. "I vowed to spend my whole life with this person, and now he's vowing to spend his life with this other person, a person I've never even met, and all I know about her is that she's southern and beautiful and apparently plans to be baking a great deal of bread." She explained: "They registered for a breadmaker.

"But—and here's the big 'but'—*I don't care*," said Holly. "I don't care! I actually feel sort of philosophical about it all. Everyone wants to make life so complicated, but I think I've come up with the secret: if I just do the right things, good things will eventually happen to me, and my life will turn out fine."

"I don't see how that follows," said Leonard.

"Okay, I'll give you an example. I adopted Chester, even though I knew he had a brain tumor, but I felt like it would be wrong to just let him die, and now, you know, this miracle happened. And I like to think I was at least instrumental in getting Amanda to stop having that affair with Jack. And I didn't have an ulterior motive, you might not believe me given how everything turned out, but it's true. I did it because it was the right thing to do. And now Jack and I are together and it feels like that stuff is ancient history. I told Amanda about it yesterday and she's actually happy for us."

"That's good," said Leonard.

"I feel like a scientist who's had all of these theories for all of these years, and finally everything is clicking into place. Even all that stuff with Alex. It was awful, but it's over. And now I feel like I'm finally coming up for air."

"Yes, well, it's been a very stressful time for both of us," said Leonard.

"How has it been stressful for you?" said Holly.

"I had that move."

Holly just looked at him.

"What," said Leonard.

"You moved apartments," said Holly.

"—"

"In the same *building*."

"All change," Leonard pronounced, "is experienced by the psyche as death."

They walked together in a thoughtful silence for a moment.

"Are you comparing the end of my marriage, the destruction of my five-year relationship, and the fact that my dog almost died of brain cancer, to your moving two floors down?"

"I'm just saying, they're both stressful," Leonard said. He ticked them off on his fingers. "Death, divorce, moving. There's a list."

small comforts

If Holly sometimes felt like she was trapped in an abusive relationship with New York City, then the month of August was when the city went on a bender and dragged her around by the hair. People who had done things differently along the way—chosen more lucrative careers, married well, inherited country houses—were out in the Hamptons or off to Nantucket, bicycling around little islands off the coast of Maine, breathing in sea air and eating steamed clams, but Holly was stuck in the city. At least you could get a table for brunch on the Upper West Side on a Sunday, she would remind herself. At least you could get a decent seat at the movies on a Friday night. Small comforts, these were, but clung to. Just when she started to entertain the idea of getting out permanently, with all of the running for the hills and throwing in the towel that that implied, September would roll around, all crisp-aired and new-penciled, and there she'd be, enchanted all over again.

"Where have you been?" Mark said to Holly. "You used to practically live on our couch, and now we never see you."

"You see me," said Holly. "You're seeing me now."

Mark studied her face for a second and then pronounced, "You're in love."

"What are you talking about?" Holly said. She could feel her face turning red.

"Amanda said you were seeing someone, but I didn't realize it was love already. Why haven't we met this guy?"

Holly blinked. "No reason."

"What's wrong with him?" said Mark. "Gay? Bald? Short? Humpback? Stutter? Missing limb? Come on, be honest."

"Nothing's wrong with him."

"Then bring him to dinner. You've been seeing him for a while," said Mark. "I think you're ready to ignore my opinion."

Amanda came in from the kitchen carrying a bowl of blue corn chips and a jar of salsa. "Why don't you ask him to come to the opera in the park thing with us next Thursday," she said.

"Really?" Holly said to Amanda. "You'd want him to come to that?"

Amanda handed the jar of salsa to Mark. "Why not? It's easy enough. We'll just throw down an extra blanket."

"Ah," said Mark. "So what I'm hearing is, this guy is so fat he needs his own blanket."

"He's a little sensitive about it, so try to act like you don't notice," said Holly.

"Say no more."

Mark went to open the jar of salsa but nothing seemed to happen. Then he really tried to open it, although he acted like he wasn't really trying. Still nothing. He tapped it on the edge of the coffee table a few times with a practiced air and went at it again.

"I don't need salsa," said Holly helpfully.

"Do we have a towel or something?" asked Mark.

Amanda handed him a blue and white striped dishrag she'd brought in from the kitchen, seemingly for just this eventuality. Mark put the towel over the lid and braced the jar between his thighs. He doubled over and let out the kind of grunt one associates with powerlifters in the Olympic games.

"I don't even really like salsa," said Holly.

Mark's face was red and the veins on his neck were popping out. "Why—do—you—do—this—to—me?"

Amanda turned to Holly. "Mark is convinced I go to the grocery store and pick out jars with lids that are screwed on extratight just to emasculate him."

"This happens a lot?" said Holly.

"Not a lot," said Mark. He paused to take a breather.

Amanda rested half a hip on the arm of the sofa. "Sometimes I have to take the jar down to the deli on the corner and ask the little old Vietnamese man behind the register to open it."

"Once," said Mark. "One time that happened."

"The guy just looked me up and down, popped it open, and handed it back. I think he thought I was trying to pick him up."

"He's a powerhouse, that guy," said Mark.

"He's seventy-eight years old," said Amanda.

"Why don't you just buy one of those jar-opener things?" said Holly.

Mark, with some theatrical flair, firmly placed the unopened jar down on the coffee table, stared over the rim of his glasses at his wife, and then turned to Holly. "Jar-opener things?"

"You just kind of slip it over the lid," Holly said, "and then there's a lever, and it just twists it off."

"There's a lever?" Mark turned to Amanda. "Good lord, woman, why have you been keeping this from me?"

"I haven't been keeping it from you," said Amanda. "I just never thought about it."

"Well, that's it. I'm on strike. No more jars until we get the thing."

Amanda gave him a weary, wifely look. "I'll go get some hummus for the chips."

"What opera are we seeing?" Holly asked.

Mark shrugged and shook his head. "Don't look at me."

"*Rigoletto*," Amanda called from the kitchen.

Holly thought for a second and then called to Amanda. "That's the one where the girl is dead, in the sack, but then she's sort of alive and she sticks her head out of the sack and sings one last bit and then dies again, right?"

Amanda came back bearing hummus. "I have no idea."

"That sounds good, though," said Mark. "Wake me up for that part. I like a person singing in a sack."

"Where did you go to school?" asked Betsy.

"Harvard," said Lonnie.

Betsy tried but failed to hide her surprise. "You went to Harvard?"

"And then Princeton for graduate school in American Studies. I never finished my dissertation, though, so I've got a master's but no PhD."

"Why didn't you finish?"

"Long story."

"We're on a date," said Betsy. "Dates are made for long stories."

Betsy and Lonnie were, in fact, on a date. How she ended up

on an actual date with the fat guy who worked at her gym, Betsy could not quite figure out herself, except for the simple fact that he kept asking her. Lonnie asked her out six times before she said yes. Six times! She finally said yes, for no other reason than it seemed like the only way to get him to stop. She had agreed to go see a movie on a Saturday afternoon with him, which seemed like a suitably friend-type activity, and afterwards, for some reason, she'd ended up agreeing to grab a quick bite to eat.

"Are you sure? It's not that interesting."

Betsy nodded yes.

"Okay, well, I'd finished all my course work, and I'd gotten a pretty good grant to write my dissertation, but my Super Secret Grand Plan was to use the time and the money to write a novel instead."

"Really?" said Betsy. "About what?"

"My college buddies and I had been emailing each other for years, and I'd saved all of it in this huge computer file, you know, eight years' worth of really funny stuff back and forth, and I figured I could just sort of paste it together and add a few transitions and it would make a really funny book. The great email epistolary novel. So I went out and bought a case of paper and printed it all out. It was, I don't know, six thousand pages long. Then I started reading through it, and I got incredibly depressed."

"How come?"

"Honestly?" Lonnie looked at Betsy. "I realized that people weren't going to want to read, 'Hey dude, check this out, it's a Japanese woman putting a fish in her anus.'"

Betsy laughed at this, in spite of herself. Lonnie took a gulp of his beer and said, "Turns out, that does not great literature make."

"Then I sort of...devolved for a while," he said. "The grant money eventually ran out, and I moved back home, into my parents' basement. It was a dark time up in Saddle River, let me tell you. My parents were pretty cool about it, but they got a little worried. Finally, I took a job as a substitute teacher just to keep them from institutionalizing me."

Betsy couldn't tell if he was overstating things. From the look on his face, she got the sense that he was not.

"So there I was, out in Jersey, 'subbing,' and living in my parents' basement. Let me tell you, the ladies love that. When they call you and your mother answers the phone? They eat that up. And the teaching was stressful, if you can call it teaching. Just walking into the classroom each period took guts. You never knew what you were going to face when you opened the door. It could be fifty maniacs or seven mild-mannered south Asian scholars," said Lonnie. "Finally, I went to see a shrink, and in my second session, I had an epiphany."

"What was it?"

"I realized it's okay to be an ordinary person and live an ordinary life."

Betsy looked across the table at Lonnie. He was ordinary. He was funnier than she'd thought and, it turned out, smart, and he seemed thoughtful and kind—but he was still ordinary. As her mother would say, *He's a nice guy, but the world's full of 'em.*

"And I knew I didn't need any more therapy," said Lonnie. "I just needed to drop the rock."

"So how did you..." Betsy began, trying to make sense of this story and connect it with the Lonnie she knew, the guy who sat behind the front desk at her gym. "I mean, what made you want to work at Crunch?"

"I thought it would help solve my other major problem, while I gave myself a chance to figure out what I wanted on the job front," said Lonnie. He sat back in his chair. "But, as it turns out, proximity to exercise equipment does not translate into weight loss."

Betsy smiled.

"My mother says I'm barrel chested but" — and here Lonnie grabbed two handfuls of gut — "this is not chest. Still, all things considered, working at the gym has been a good thing for me."

"How so?"

"I've been watching everybody as they parade in and out, the bankers and the anorexics and their grim determined faces, and thinking, this is not the way to live a life."

"What do you mean?"

"Here's the problem with this city. There are too many people living in one place, and all of them are suffering from excessive ego demands," said Lonnie. "The truth is, I want pretty simple things."

"Like what?"

"Like a grill," he said. "I'd like to have a backyard, and a grill, and a wife who loves me. Hopefully a couple of kids. And I'd like to live someplace that fits me more, someplace a little more relaxed, maybe warmer, with things like bike paths and Little League games. I think I could get into riding a bike."

"What do you want to do? Workwise, I mean."

"I'm not sure it matters all that much to me, actually," said Lonnie. "I'll probably teach. I like it, and I'm good at it, so why not?"

"Right."

"I would like to clear one thing up," said Lonnie.

"What's that?"

"You probably think I've been asking you out because you're thin and pretty and all that, but that's not it."

"Why, then?"

"Because you seem like a nice person. A little, I don't know, maybe sad around the edges sometimes, but I can work with that. I've been sad before. I know what that's like."

Lonnie locked eyes with Betsy. She held his gaze for a moment and then looked away, down at her hands, which looked small and pale against the dark smooth wood of the table. "Even when you said no to me, you were always extremely nice about it. And so, I thought, you know, why not? Why not keep trying? What do I have to lose?

"I'm talking too much," he said. "What about you, Miss Betsy Silverstein? Why in the world are you still single?"

————

At the end of the evening, Amanda walked Holly out to wait for the elevator. There were just two apartments on the floor, and, as if to drive this point home, Amanda and her neighbor had joined forces and rather aggressively decorated the little vestibule they shared, with not just the usual plants and mirrors and prints and umbrella stands, but also a slipper sofa with matching end tables and candlestick lamps and a collection of leather-bound poetry books. The whole thing seemed designed to give the impression that someone might get off the elevator and feel the need to read Walt Whitman *right now*.

"Are you sure about this?" Holly said to Amanda. "Inviting Jack to the park next week?"

"Of course I'm sure. It's weird that we haven't been seeing you."

Holly lowered her voice. "Yeah, but won't it be strange for you?"

"Who knows? Maybe a little bit," said Amanda, "but I'll be fine."

"Because I feel bad enough about all of this as it is," said Holly in a quiet voice. "It's really, you know, it's really an odd situation, and you and I never really talked about it. I'm not sure I did the right thing in getting involved with Jack, after you two—"

"Hush," said Amanda. "That was temporary insanity on my part. I was out of my mind, you said so yourself. Honestly, it feels like the whole thing happened to somebody else."

"And you're not upset that we're seeing each other? I mean, I know you said it was okay, but I thought that maybe it would be different for you, now that things seem to be moving forward the way they are."

"I'm happy for you guys. Listen, I wasn't going to throw away my life on a thing that I had no idea would work. You'd been moping around about Alex, and then you were wasting all your time on that twenty-two-year-old. Jack is a good guy, and he wants something real," said Amanda. "Besides, I'm a married woman. I can't be putting single guys off-limits for my friends."

"Okay, but, you really want me to bring Jack to the opera in the park?"

"I do," said Amanda. "Honestly. We'll just do it and get any awkwardness out of the way, and everything will be normal."

The elevator doors opened, and Holly gave Amanda a quick hug. "This is one of those times when my life feels too grown-up for me," she said.

"I know what you mean," said Amanda.

"I feel vaguely European."

———————————

"You know, I want to kiss you, but I don't want you to run screaming from the room or anything," said Lonnie.

It was late. Lonnie and Betsy were sitting together on Betsy's couch, still talking. Betsy didn't really know how that had happened, how Lonnie ended up in her apartment after dinner, what made her offer him coffee, coffee that neither of them ended up drinking. None of it made sense to her, except that, for some reason, she hadn't wanted the date to end.

"Can I just," Betsy began, and then she edged her body close to him and rested her head lightly on his chest. He was leaning back, with his arms stretched along the tops of the cushions, and his sweater, which had looked all evening like an ordinary charcoal gray wool V-neck, turned out to be cashmere and impossibly soft. He smelled good, and, Betsy thought, well, *familiar*, like dried leaves and firewood, like rain on cement, like loam or peat or dirt, but clean dirt, the kind you'd like to sink your hands deep into or use to grow heirloom tomatoes. His chest moved up and down with each breath, and his belly did, too, and Betsy found herself breathing with him, slower and deeper than she was used to. She stayed just like that for quite a while, breathing deeply with her head on Lonnie's chest, and she could feel something inside of her start to unclench, to unspool — her mind flashing on her mother, all sharp angles and papery skin, and then on her father, who'd stopped hugging her when she turned eleven. After a while, she found herself moving her hands over his chest, slowly and tentatively at first, and then with some boldness. He felt more solid than she would have expected, if she had even allowed herself to expect, but the one thing she'd never planned for was this: Lonnie, on her couch at midnight, with her burrowing into him like a small animal seeking safety in a cave, his arms now strong around her, for once with nothing to prove, for once not scared of it all, her heart opening just a crack with this glimpse of what it could be like, what it might, maybe, be like.

"I'm so afraid," she finally said, quietly, and into his sweater really, but he heard her and smoothed her hair with his hand.

"I know," Lonnie said. "I know."

the girl in the sack

T his is Jack," said Holly.

Amanda and Mark were sprawled out on top of an old quilt, and they had spread out a black and yellow Mexican yoga blanket beside them, to save a space for Holly and Jack. The park was packed. The light was fading fast, but it was still warm and muggy, and Holly felt sweaty and a little on edge.

"Hi, Jack," said Mark. "I'm Mark. I'd get up to shake your hand, but I'm incredibly comfortable."

"Don't worry about it," said Jack. "It's good to meet you."

"I'm Amanda," Amanda said. She was staring boldly at Jack with a faint, impersonal smile on her face. "Nice to meet you."

"Nice to meet you, too," said Jack.

"Sorry we're so late," said Holly. She was trying hard to be normal, trying hard to act like this was a normal social engagement devoid of undercurrents and subtext. "I went to Fairway straight from work, and then I had to go home to pick up Chester."

Amanda poked through the bags Holly brought with her. "Yay," said Amanda. "Good cheese choices."

"Some old lady rammed into my ankles with her shopping cart," said Holly. "And then she didn't even apologize. She actually glared at me. Like it was my fault that I happened to be *walking around in a grocery store*."

"Well, we appreciate your sacrifices in order to bring us the truffled Moliterno," said Amanda.

"And I finally get to meet Cancer Dog," Mark said. "Come here, boy."

Chester made his way over to Mark, who started to pet him. Chester stretched himself out in the grass next to him, knowing a good thing when he saw it.

"Did Holly tell you the story of how she adopted a dog with a brain tumor?" Mark asked Jack. "It's both incredibly sweet and deeply disturbing."

"She told me," said Jack. "It seems to have worked out all right in the end."

"Everyone thought I was going to end up with a very expensive, very dead dog," said Holly. "But I proved them wrong. We proved them wrong, didn't we, Chester?"

Amanda handed around plastic cups filled with white wine. Mark lifted his and offered a toast.

"To Chester," said Mark.

"To Chester," everyone said.

The strains of an orchestra tuning up, amplified loud enough to be heard in New Jersey, filled the air. Holly lit a few candles, Amanda unwrapped the cheese, Chester thumped his tail. Applause rippled through the crowd as, off in the distance, the singers walked out onstage.

If there's something good in New York, people know about it. When there's music in a park, people show up for it. Hordes, throngs, packs of them, always arriving hours before the performance actually starts, staking out their territory, putting up helium balloons so their late-coming friends can spot them, glaring at people who try to squeeze in front of them, who accidentally step on a corner of what they deem to be the eight-foot square of the park their picnic blanket entitles them to for the evening. At some point, a sane person is forced to ask himself: this is supposed to be relaxing?

But it was. It was relaxing, eventually. Once you managed to buy your cheese, once you made it to the park, once you found the friends who were saving your spot somewhere in the vast sea of picnic blankets, you began to relax. And then the music started, and it cooled off a bit, and the sky slowly darkened, and a few distant stars came out. As long as you didn't expect to be able to actually *see* the performers on the stage, as long as you were content to simply posit that there was a real-live conductor up there conducting real-live world-class musicians even though the music that actually entered your eardrums was being pumped out of speakers that belonged at a U2 concert, as long as you didn't have to go to the bathroom and the grass wasn't damp and you hadn't forgotten to bring a sweater and the bugs weren't out and the babies weren't crying, it was magic.

It was nearly eleven by the time the girl in the sack finally died and then sang and then died again—only the opera, since it was being put on outside, wasn't fully staged, so there was no sack, and the girl was just standing up in the middle of the platform like the rest of the performers, which Holly and Mark both found kind of disappointing. Then there were some fireworks, and pretty soon the mass of people started packing up and heading for the exits. Mark and Amanda were going to catch a cab on the east side, so the foursome said their good-byes in the middle of the great lawn. Holly and Jack found themselves on the path leading out of the park at Seventy-ninth Street.

"What did you think?" Holly said.

"It was nice," said Jack. "The music was great."

"I always feel the same way when I go to the opera, sort of ashamed of myself for getting excited when I hear the one bit of music I recognize, feeling my heart leap in recognition, and then realizing that the only reason I know it is because I heard it in a spaghetti sauce commercial."

The crowd was moving slowly, and Chester made his way over to a lamppost and started to pee.

"Mark seems like a nice guy," said Jack.

Holly looked at his face. "Was that too strange for you? Meeting him?"

"No. He's pretty much what I expected."

"What about seeing Amanda?"

"No," said Jack. "It was fine."

"Good," said Holly. "You're staying over, right?"

"If you'll have me."

A little ways up ahead of them, in the slow flow of the crowd, there was a small boy dozing in his father's arms. He opened his eyes sleepily and said, "That's my dog!"

"No, sweetie," his mother said, in that annoying voice that parents now all seem to use with their children. "That's *their* dog."

"No. Mine. Mine!" The kid's eyes opened wide and he pointed straight at Chester.

"That's those nice people's puppy," the woman said,

employing the universal parenting voice, and then they walked off in the opposite direction, crossing the street quickly and heading south.

————————

Later, when Holly and Jack were back at her apartment, and they got into bed, she turned to him and said, "Can I ask you something?"

"Be my guest," said Jack.

Holly took a deep breath. "Explain the cheeseburger."

"Okay, yes, well, the cheeseburger," said Jack. "Typically, it involves a grilled patty of ground beef, served on a bun and topped with a slice of melted cheese —"

"The first time we met, you ordered a cheeseburger. At the diner with Amanda that day. It's kind of been bugging me this whole time."

"Because I'm a Buddhist."

"Yes, because you're a Buddhist. That seems sort of fundamental."

"Okay, well, first of all, in my defense," said Jack, "the Dalai Lama eats meat."

"He *does?*"

"He does."

"People know this?" said Holly. "This is known?"

"He's been a vegetarian for short periods, at different times in his life, but he eats meat and fish now. His doctors have told him to, for his health. Have you ever seen pictures of Tibet?"

"I can't remember," said Holly. "Probably."

"There's not a lot of greenery. Meat is a huge part of their diet, so the tradition of vegetarianism didn't really develop in Tibetan Buddhism the way it did in, say, Japan."

"Huh."

"But, you know, it's one of those things that could change," said Jack. "I leave open the possibility."

Jack turned out the lights.

"If I was a Buddhist, I'd have to be a vegetarian," Holly said. "I'd have to be a vegan, come to think of it. It wouldn't matter how sickly and pale I got, my hair could be falling out in clumps, but I wouldn't be able to take the thought of all that bad karma being chalked up against me. I mean, as it is, half the time I'm walking around, I'm just waiting for God to punish me."

"Punish you for what?" said Jack.

"Everything! Nothing. I don't know. That's the problem," said Holly. "That's what happens when you grow up the way I did. You spend the rest of your life just waiting for God to smite the shit out of you."

Jack smoothed her hair with his hand.

"And at the same time, I have this memory," said Holly. She was lying on her back, looking up at the ceiling, which, in the darkness, seemed strangely far away. "I was in the car, riding home with my family from church one day, I must have been about thirteen or fourteen, at the height of my personal religious fervor—I was going to church three or four times a week, reading my Bible every morning, committing entire chapters of it to memory, the whole deal, and I wasn't just going through the motions, I really believed, I mean, I was a *believer*—and I looked out the car window and saw an old

Snickers wrapper lying in the gutter. And I remember thinking, I mean, really being struck by the thought, that nothing
up in heaven was going to be anywhere near as good as that."

Jack was quiet for a moment, and then he rolled over on
his side and looked at Holly's face.

"It's interesting," said Jack.

"What is?"

"You believe in God," he said. "You just don't believe that
God is good."

london, baby

After enduring weeks and weeks of radio silence, Spence came home from work late one night and discovered a letter in his mailbox, postmarked Boulder, on Cathleen's trademark sage green stationery. He rode up the elevator to the thirty-seventh floor aware that his heart was beating quickly, and he poured himself a vodka tonic before sitting down at his glass-topped dining table and opening the envelope. The letter was quite formal and measured in tone—"reasonable Cathleen," as Spence liked to think of her, was apparently back on the scene—and it proposed that, on the advice of her therapist Mona (who had, although Spence never did find this out, dictated this very letter), the two of them begin talking on the phone again, for one hour only, every Sunday night at eight o'clock her time, ten o'clock his time. He read the letter through twice before deciding that it was the crack in the door he'd been waiting for, and his heart leapt.

Six weeks earlier, Cathleen had handed the reins of her emotional life over to Mona, a move that necessitated increasing her sessions from one to three times a week. Mona had been a more or less silent, eyebrow-raising witness to Cathleen's most recent disastrous relationships—the eight months she'd spent sleeping with her Intro to Native Trees and Shrubs professor, who claimed he was separated from his wife of eighteen years ("He sleeps in the guest room. No, no, he really does!"); the clinically depressed social worker who verbally abused her and self-medicated with pot he bought from one of his parolee clients—and this time, she was going to earn her pay. Mona had insisted that Cathleen cut off all contact with Spence, quit returning Crazy Molly's calls and emails, and stop talking to Holly Frick, and Cathleen had obliged on all fronts. She spent six weeks going around and around and around the whole Spence thing on Mona's couch for an hour every Monday, Wednesday, and Friday, trying to make sense of it. Just when it looked like she might be running out of things to talk about, Mona gave her permission to resume contact with Spence again, as long as it was in a controlled setting and did not lead to undue obsessing; hence, the letter.

It isn't altogether clear what Mona's motivation was, midafternoon therapy sessions being notoriously difficult to fill and Cathleen's self-employed status making it possible for her to show up at two, three, or four p.m., depending on Mona's availability. To be fair, Cathleen's relationships had always exploded without much rhyme or reason, the Shrub Professor disappearing on what turned out to be a fourteen-day Mediterranean cruise with his wife, the pot smoker offering Cathleen no more data than a cold look and the words "I'm done"—so perhaps this phone call business was designed to give Cathleen a measure of closure or clarity, a portion of the understanding that seemed forever to elude her. She had confessed in her very first session that whenever she was in a relationship, it felt like she was turning the crank of a jack-in-the-box—the happy song played and everything was fine until, completely out of the blue, the clown burst out of the top and everything was over. Just like when her father disappeared when she was nine!

Anyhow, Spence and Cathleen started talking again. They spoke to one another in soft, small voices, the tender talk of two soldiers wounded on the battlefield of love. They had the feeling that they had learned something, passed through some fire together somehow, and were still standing. There were, at the end of the very first call, mutual I-love-you's. By the third Sunday, they were weaving their dreams together: could Cathleen stand to live in New York for a few years, would Spence be willing to move to Colorado, what about kids, private schools, what's your position on childhood vaccinations, organic babies, the family bed? That Spence had spent the past six weeks going about his usual romantic business (two dates with Big Joan and a few rounds of rollicking, lighthearted sex with the bucktoothed Scottish oil rig worker, who was much cuter than she sounds) and that he had more or less written off Cathleen after she stopped returning his calls — none of that ever came up. They made a plan for Cathleen to fly out right away, so they could celebrate their reunion face to face.

———

Leonard was on his way home from the vitamin store when his cell phone rang.

"Are you sitting down?"

It was Jake, his agent, calling from LA.

"I'm walking down Seventh Avenue."

"I don't care. Sit down. At the very least, lean up against something heavy," said Jake. "I've got big news."

"What's up?"

There was a pause, and then Jake, employing an uncharacteristically singsong tone of voice, said, "How do you feel about London?"

"I've only been to Heathrow," said Leonard. "I had a four-hour layover on my way to Rome last summer."

"Would you be interested in going?"

"To London? I guess so."

Again with the singsong: "What would you think about living there for a while?"

Leonard had no idea where this conversation was headed, and he was beginning to feel strangely unmoored inside of it. "What are you talking about?"

"Here's the real question," said Jake. There was a dramatic Hollywood pause. "How would you like to move to London in order to be the head writer and executive producer of a little show you wrote a while back called *Sweet Fancy Moses*?"

"Are you serious?"

"I've got an offer in hand."

"I thought that pilot was dead."

"There's no such thing as dead when I'm your agent, baby."

Leonard clutched his fish oil. Jake hadn't called him "baby" in a *very* long time.

"What? How...?" There were a million things about this conversation that didn't make sense, but Leonard seized upon the most glaring: "Why London?"

"Sky Television wants to start producing half hours with more of an international sensibility, which in this climate means 'American.' The president flew out here last week looking for finished scripts to jump-start the process."

"I didn't even know I was up for that."

"Of course you were up for it. Do I tell you everything I put you up for? You were up to direct *Spider-Man 4*. You don't need to hear about all the jobs you don't get. I'm here to protect you from all that."

"You put me up to direct *Spider-Man 4*?"

"The point is this," Jake said. "The *point* is, America has stopped producing sitcoms, yet the only sitcoms the rest of the world wants to watch are American sitcoms, so the Brits have decided to start making them. American sitcoms. I know, I know, it doesn't make a hell of a lot of sense, but that's their concept, and you are set to be the prime beneficiary of it."

"I still don't understand how this even happened."

"What do you mean? I made it happen. What do you think, these things happen by magic?"

Actually, these things do happen by magic. And the way this one happened was, Nigel Blankly, the president of Sky TV, flew to Los Angeles and sat at the head of four long conference tables at the four major talent agencies and laid out what he was looking for: an original half-hour comedy script which had been developed for an American studio and network but never produced, whose rights had reverted to the creator, by a writer/producer who was willing to relocate to London indefinitely. Preferably with a strong male lead, a sophisticated sensibility, and broad appeal. Something outside the box, but still near the box. By the time he got back to Shutters, a four-foot stack of fifty-page scripts had been hand-delivered to his suite, unproduced pilots being as much an unsavory by-product of Los Angeles as unemployed actors or bumper-to-bumper traffic. It was a sheer stroke of luck that the script Nigel happened to grab on his way to the bathroom at midnight was written by Leonard four years ago as part of an otherwise glaringly fruitless overall deal at Sony, and also

Leonard's luck that Nigel had ordered the jhinga vindaloo at dinner, and, although it is unclear if it was the fault of the jhinga or the vindaloo, was detained long enough to read the entire script from cover to cover, twice.

"I always loved that script," Jake continued. "I kept it on the corner of my desk for the past two years. You don't know that, but it's true. I can tell you don't believe me." Jake called to his assistant, "Heather, is it true that I kept *Sweet Fancy Moses* on the corner of my desk for the past two years?"

A perky voice piped up in the fuzzy speakerphone distance. "It's true. On the corner of his desk! It was the first thing he had me read when I came to work for him."

"See?" said Jake. "You don't even know how much I love you. Pack your bags. You're going to London, baby."

Two babies in one call.

Leonard flipped his phone closed and stood motionless in the middle of the sidewalk, parting the sea of humanity which flowed and eddied around him. Could life really change this quickly? Could it be as simple as that? That something big, and good, and completely unexpected could drop from above and into one's lap?

And in a flash, Leonard saw this for what it was: a reprieve. A pardon, even. Temporary, maybe, but it was entirely possible that that much, at least, was up to him. And the part that depended on him, well, he decided right then and there, he wasn't going to disappoint. He really did want to do something good, to *make* something good, and if being good was required of him, or at least striving for some modicum of consciousness and clarity and engagement with the world and his work, well, then, he would do that, too. He was being given a second chance, not one that he deserved, certainly, he was well aware of that fact, but that only made it all the sweeter. He felt a profound sense of gratitude, way down in the deepest part of him, a part that he didn't even know existed. *Thank you.*

And, with that, he turned on his heels and headed back to the vitamin store. He was going to need more than just the fish oil. He was going to need all the help he could get.

———————

Meanwhile, all the way uptown, Holly and Chester were taking a walk in Central Park. Over the past several months, the two of them had developed a handful of comforting little rituals, most of them involving what they did on their walks. They had the Long City Walk, a lengthy jaunt down Columbus and then up either Amsterdam or Broadway, anchored by a visit to a dog boutique that dispensed liver-flavored dog treats, and the Short City Walk (a two-block rectangle that was sufficient for Chester to take care of business), and the Short Park Walk (in at Eighty-fifth Street with a quick loop to the pine barrens and back), but the Long Park Walk was special. The Long Park Walk had two rules. First, they couldn't follow a route they had ever followed before, and second, they weren't allowed to return home until they had encountered something unexpected and extraordinary. Some days, after an hour of uneventful meandering, "unexpected and extraordinary" had to be interpreted rather broadly, forgivingly even—a purple crocus poking through a crust of snow, a pair of squirrels having sex in a tree—but they had managed to spot the red-tailed hawks a few times, and once, Woody and Soon-Yi.

On this particular day, they started on the equestrian path, circling around the reservoir, past the Japanese cherry trees and through a stand of towering maples, and then they kept heading north, to where the park is nearly deserted, up where bad things have been known to happen. Holly liked it up there. The tourists were afraid to venture that far, and most sensible New Yorkers kept themselves to the more populated sections of the park, which meant that it was one of the only places on the island of Manhattan where it was possible to be outside and yet feel completely and utterly alone. They had been walking for quite a while when Holly first saw them. Birds, more than seemed possible, hundreds, thousands even, each one small and pitch-black, flying through the sky in a great whirling dark cloud. Chester was excited at first, straining at his leash, but, as the flock overtook and then enveloped them, he froze and started to tremble. Holly crouched down and put her arms around him and watched in awed silence as the birds swarmed and squawked, pecking at the grass, each hopping forward a few feet and then pecking some more, blanketing the ground as they had filled the sky, some darting in and out of tree branches, the flock suddenly taking flight in a single great whoosh, only to return to the earth again a few moments later. The whole thing, Holly found herself thinking, had the quality of a dream. It wasn't until much later that she would recognize it for the omen that it was.

When Holly and Chester got home, there was a woman sitting on the front stoop. Holly didn't recognize her at first, couldn't remember having seen her before, and that was probably just as well, because if she had, she probably would have just kept walking. Instead, Holly climbed the steps, and as she did, the stranger slowly got to her feet.

"I'm here," the woman said, "to throw myself on your mercy."

bad people

J ack came over to Holly's apartment straight from work just like he'd promised. She was in the middle of unloading the dishwasher when he showed up, and she opened the door with a damp dishrag slung over her shoulder and an old china teacup in one hand.

"You're not going to believe what happened to me today," Holly said to him. "I won't even make you try to guess, because you wouldn't be able to, not in a million years."

"I have something I want to talk to you about, too," said Jack.

"Okay, but I've got to go first, because this one won't wait," said Holly. She headed back into the kitchen to the dishwasher while Jack took off his coat and hung it in the hall closet.

"Remember that woman from the park the other night?" she called. "The one with the little kid who thought Chester was his dog?"

"Yeah."

"Well, it turns out, Chester *was* his dog. She's the woman who put him in the shelter."

"You're kidding."

"All this time, I've been trying to fathom what sort of person would do that to their dog, and today the answer showed up on my doorstep."

Jack sat down on one of the bar stools. "She showed up here? How come?"

"She wants me to give Chester back!" said Holly. "Can you believe that? I mean it, what is going on in this world? I really feel like I'm unequipped to deal with humanity at this point. Who are these people that think this is an acceptable way to live?"

"Did she say why?"

"*Apparently,*" and Holly leaned on this word mightily, as if to drive home the point that whatever came after it was highly improbable, "after her kid saw Chester in the park he got hysterical and started crying all the time, so they took him to a shrink, and the shrink decides that the kid is worried his parents are going to give *him* away or some crap like that, so now this woman is offering to pay me whatever I spent on Chester, and even more 'for my trouble.' For my trouble! She tried to bribe me! Do I look like the kind of person who would be susceptible to a bribe?" said Holly. She paused long enough to look at Jack and see if he was getting it, if he was absorbing the monumental outrageousness of it all. "What is it? You seem distracted."

"Nothing. No. Keep going."

"I mean, these people were willing to let Chester *die* because they didn't want to spend their precious *money,* and I save his life, and now that he's all healthy and fixed they want him back? Uh-uh, sorry, I don't think so," said Holly. She started in on the silverware, the clinking and clattering providing unneeded emphasis. "And they aren't poor, either, let me tell you. They live on West End in the Eighties, I know because she gave me her card 'in case I had a change of heart,' and she was wearing those Prada slip-ons with the red stripe on the heel that say to the world 'I spend three hundred bucks on my run-around shoes.'"

"I feel a little bad for the kid, though."

"Maybe this is a good lesson for him, about his parents. Better to learn it now. If I were him, I wouldn't get too comfortable," said Holly. "Besides, I love my dog. I'm not giving him up."

"It's a bad situation, that's all I'm saying."

"It's not my bad situation," said Holly. She crouched down and kissed Chester, who'd wandered in from the living room looking for a treat. "And you know what else? I don't care. Even if it is the right thing to do. I don't care! I'm not going to do it!"

"Well. There you go, I guess."

"Yes," said Holly. "So, what is it you wanted to tell me?"

"Maybe it can wait."

"No, no, I'll calm down. Let me take a breath." Holly closed her eyes and took a long, cleansing breath, and then opened them and looked over at Jack. He was perched somewhat awkwardly on one of the bar stools, tapping a penny against the granite countertop. "What's up?"

"This isn't easy," said Jack. He tapped the penny a few times. "I'm just, I'm trying to be honest and up-front about everything."

"Okay…" Holly said. She didn't like the sound of this, a person she was in a relationship with nervously attempting honesty and up-frontness. "What is it?"

Jack let out a big breath. "Amanda and I have been talking again."

"What do you mean, talking?" Holly said. "Talking about what?"

"Everything. Us." For a moment, Holly assumed the "us" referred to her and Jack. That they were the "us" that Jack and Amanda had been discussing. But then Jack said, "I'm afraid I'm still in love with her."

"What?" said Holly. "You are?" She slumped back against the refrigerator door. "I thought that was over."

"It was. At least, I thought it was. But then we saw each other that night in the park and, I don't know. Something happened."

"What do you mean, something happened? What? What happened?" Holly flashed on that night in the park. Luke-warm wine, thick muggy air, *Rigoletto* blaring from speakers the size of Volkswagens. It had been a tad awkward when she and Jack first walked up and saw Amanda and Mark sprawled out on the picnic blanket, there had been an undercurrent of tension, but this? How was it possible?

"I don't really know what it was," said Jack. "The point is, we've been talking again."

"So, I don't get it," said Holly. "This, us, is over? Is that what you're telling me? And you and Amanda are just going to pick up where you left off?"

"I feel really horrible about this, Holly."

"And the fact that she's married to someone else? Doesn't that pose some sort of problem for you?"

"She wants to leave Mark."

"This is crazy. You're both crazy," Holly said. She started to pace around the kitchen, which wasn't easy, because it was so small. "You've lost your minds. I feel like I should knock your heads together like my dad used to do with my sister and me, and snap you both out of it. How did this...has it been going on all along? Have you been sleeping with her behind my back?"

"No. No. Absolutely not. That's why I wanted to tell you right away, so there wouldn't be any lies."

"Well, as long as there aren't any *lies*," Holly said. "I think you're in the clear, destroying a family, ruining a little kid's life, I mean, as long as you're honest and up-front about it all."

"Amanda was going to leave Mark anyway," said Jack. "She met with a lawyer a long time ago. Before I was even in the picture."

Holly snorted. "I seriously doubt that."

"Why is that?"

"She's just telling you that so you don't freak out when she leaves her husband for you. I've known Amanda for a long time. The woman likes to swing from vine to vine. She doesn't waste time, you know, walking around on the jungle floor."

"I feel really bad about all of this."

"Yeah, well, you should feel bad. That's exactly what you should feel," said Holly. "You guys both tell me it's over, you both tell me I'm the one you actually like, I start to really fall for you, and now this? I mean, what about..." Holly stood there in the middle of the kitchen and thought of a million different things to say but stopped herself each time. Jack was just sitting there, watching her, like he had braced himself for this and probably for much worse.

Finally, she said, "I mean, am I the crazy one? I thought things were going good between us. We really get along and we like the same kind of things and we have interesting conversations and good sex, and now you tell me you want

Amanda instead of me? I don't even get what you guys see in each other. I mean it, really. I'm completely confused here."

"These things don't always make sense," said Jack. "Honestly, I'm as surprised by this as anyone."

"Well, you're not as surprised as me," said Holly. "Or as much as Mark is going to be when he finds out. Or Jacob, when his parents move into different houses, I'm guessing he'll be a bit on the surprised side."

"I'm sorry, Holly," said Jack. "I really am."

"Yeah, me too. And if you'll excuse me," said Holly, "I'd like to be alone with my dog."

————

Spence was in his kitchen, mixing up a batch of martinis. Cathleen had arrived from Boulder the night before, and they'd spent the day wandering around in Brooklyn together, trying to get a feel for the place. Spence was trying to find a part of the city that Cathleen could see herself actually living in, even if it was for only a few years. She seemed to like Brooklyn, sort of, Cobble Hill and Carroll Gardens at least, with the stipulation that she could have her own garden, which was apparently one of her nonnegotiables. Spence noticed, as he led her down the wide, tree-lined streets, as they popped into stores displaying weird hats and trendy shoes, a knitting shop, the organic grocery store, a yoga studio that also, rather inexplicably, sold baby clothes—Brooklyn!—that he found himself, for once, strangely eager to please.

"Why did you lie to me about the plant?" said Cathleen. She had materialized in the doorway, and she was holding a small potted plant.

"What do you mean?" said Spence. "I'm not, um, sure—"

"The plant, Spence. This is not the plant I bought you."

"It isn't?" Spence's face assumed an expression of almost preternatural guilelessness, a blend of confusion and surprise at this piece of information, his head cocked a little to one side, eyebrows pulled together and just a tiny bit up.

Cathleen let out a big sigh. "No, it's not, Spence. It's not the same plant."

She put the pot down on the kitchen counter. Spence flipped a leaf over and examined the pattern of the veins. "Are you sure?"

"Come on, Spence, please, just stop it."

Spence let go of the leaf.

"I forgot to water the plant," he finally admitted. His shoulders dropped a few inches. "And when we started talking on the phone again, you asked me how it was and I said fine, and then you asked me again and I said fine, and then when you said you were coming I went out and bought another plant."

Cathleen folded her arms in front of her chest.

"I shouldn't have lied to you about it."

"No, Spence, you shouldn't have."

"I didn't want to hurt your feelings," he said. "Since you bought me the plant. It seemed like the easiest thing to do."

Cathleen just stared at him, silently, and then began to nod her head ever so slowly, like it was all becoming clear to her, like the pieces of a puzzle that had been scattered across the floor were finally together and the picture was, at long last, unmistakable. It looked for all the world like this had finally done it, the plant deception was the last straw, and all of her questions about Spence had been asked and answered and then answered again, and there was only one possible thing for her to do. Spence watched as all of this crossed her face and felt a clench of deep, almost bottomless fear. He had finally done it, whatever it is he always managed to do, for whatever reason he always did it, he didn't understand it, he couldn't make sense of it, and at the same time he had a moment of searing clarity: that Cathleen, sweet Cathleen—with her dopey hand-felted purses and her impossibly long hair, with her clunky Boulder shoes and the world's tiniest waist, with her boundless capacity for understanding and what up until that moment had seemed to be a limitless ocean of love for him—was his last, best chance for happiness.

"I need to know," Cathleen said, finally, "if you're going to stop being such an idiot."

———

Holly was standing outside Amanda's gym, leaning up against the brick wall, waiting for Amanda's class to get out. It was dusk, and most of the people walking by were on their way home from work, distracted and tired, about half of them talking into their cell phones. Holly watched as Amanda passed through the revolving glass door, in black capris and a gray sweatshirt, with a gym bag slung over her shoulder.

"You're a crappy friend," said Holly.

Amanda turned around and saw Holly. She took a breath and then said, "You talked to Jack."

"Yes I talked to Jack," said Holly. "What the hell is going on with you two?"

"How did you know I was here?"

"I called your house. The new nanny told me," said Holly. "FYI? She's pretty indiscreet."

"I feel horrible about this, Holly."

"Well, good, apparently we all feel horrible."

"I'm in love with him."

"Argh." Holly put her hands on the sides of her head and squeezed. "Could you two please stop using that word to describe this. I don't know what it is, but I am unwilling to concede that this is love."

"I think I've been in love with him all along," said Amanda.

"Then why the hell did you tell me to go out with him?" said Holly. "I'm serious, Amanda. That was a shitty thing to do. You sent me his phone number! I don't get it."

"I don't blame you for being upset—"

"Upset?! I'm furious!" said Holly. She gestured wildly. "This is me, being furious. You put me in a horrible position!"

"I thought it was over," said Amanda. "I wanted it to be over."

"So you could cheat on your husband, but you didn't think you'd cheat on your best friend? You thought tossing me into the middle of everything would keep you from seeing him again?"

"It wasn't quite as deliberate as that, Holly." And here Amanda sighed a big sigh. "But, yeah, probably something like that."

"This is crazy," said Holly. "You're married, Amanda. And I really like him! I do! And I haven't liked anybody in a very long time."

Amanda just stood there for a moment. "I've made such a mess of things," she finally said. "I mean it, really, this is such a huge awful mess."

There was a park bench on the sidewalk outside a small pharmacy, meant for customers only, according to the sign, but Holly and Amanda sat down. Amanda seemed to shrink a bit into herself. She was sweaty from the gym, and her hair was sort of stuck to her head, and Holly thought she looked like an eleven-year-old boy.

"So what are you saying, you're going to leave Mark?"

Amanda nodded a small nod.

"And move to Brooklyn into Jack's tiny apartment, and take Jacob to his dad's house on the weekends?"

"Maybe."

"And you're going to, what, take up Buddhism? And give up shopping at Barneys and put Jacob into day care while you go to work selling real estate or, I don't know, another one of those divorced-women jobs?"

"It's possible. I don't know. I haven't thought that far ahead."

"That's not that far ahead, Amanda. That's what happens when you tell Mark you're in love with somebody else."

"I haven't figured out the details yet."

Holly cocked her head. "You do realize that Jack works for a nonprofit," she said. "He has a job wherein, in the actual name, it is indicated that he doesn't make very much money."

"I don't care about money."

"You don't care about money," Holly repeated flatly.

"You're obsessed with money, Holly. Sex and money and religion. All the things you're not supposed to talk about in polite company."

"Because those are the interesting parts of life! And this is one of those rare occasions when all three collide," said Holly. "I mean it, Amanda. Look at what you're doing to everyone. Forget about me for a second, not that I needed this in my life right now, but what about Jacob? You're going to ruin his life."

"Children would rather be from a broken home than live in one."

"Not true! Completely not true! There've been studies that prove it! Kids are better off in every way if their parents stay together. Besides, your marriage wasn't unhappy until you started screwing around behind Mark's back."

"That's not the way it works. Everybody knows that. People don't go looking for another person unless things aren't working inside their marriages."

"Some people do."

"Oh, yeah?"

"Bad people do! For example."

"I don't need to listen to this," said Amanda. She got up off the bench and hurried towards the traffic and stuck her arm in the air to hail a cab.

"I think you do," said Holly. She trailed along behind Amanda. "I think it's exactly what you need. I think you never hear anything remotely like it and one of the reasons I was placed on this planet is so that I could be the one to say it to you."

"You are so self-righteous, you know that?"

"Whatever happened to just plain 'righteous'?" said Holly. "Whatever happened to that designation? Because I think it could apply here."

"Jesus, Holly—"

"I'm semiserious! Am I the only person who's trying to do the right thing? Is that just me? And, you know, a few lunatics in the red states? I mean, have an ounce of integrity, at least. Consider some value bigger than yourself and what you, at this moment in time, *want*."

A cab pulled up and stopped. Amanda opened the door

and put her gym bag on the backseat. Then she turned and looked at Holly.

"I can't imagine not having met him. I can't imagine not having had this. And I don't want to spend the rest of my life without it," said Amanda. "I don't love Mark anymore. I'm not sure when it stopped, or why, but that's the truth. And I'm sorry if you can't understand it, and if you think I'm doing the wrong thing, but this is my life, Holly. This is it. This is all I get. And I'm going to take it."

Amanda got into the cab and shut the door. Holly stood there and watched as it pulled away from the curb and returned to the flow of traffic, blending into the great heart of the city, until all she could see was a stream of red lights.

edelweiss

West End Avenue has a very distinctive feel, especially for a street that doesn't have anything all that distinctive about it. There's no commerce to speak of at street level, and the traffic goes both ways, and the stoplights seem to take forever to change, but that isn't enough to explain the feeling. Holly always thought that it seemed oddly out of sync with time—not like it belonged in an earlier century, or even in a different decade, but more like, well, when you got there, you found yourself inside a different day of the week than the one you were in before. Like it was Wednesday on Broadway, but a few hundred feet away, over on West End, somehow, it was Sunday.

After Chester's operation, when he came home from the hospital, his head had been bandaged up, and one of Holly's duties was to change the gauze and clean the incisions. She had to do it once a day, and it wasn't easy, mostly because at that point Chester barely knew her. She'd had him less than a week before he had to go in for his surgery, because Two Feathers thought it would be best not to delay. The first time she went to change the bandage, she could tell Chester was frightened, and she found herself singing to him in an effort to calm him down. Holly had a horrible voice, and she didn't know the words to very many songs, but the one

that happened to bubble up from inside her was, for some
unknown reason, "Edelweiss." She changed the word *home-
land* to *Chester* and ended up singing it in a circular round, the
way that song demands to be sung, and it worked almost like
a drug. Once his radiation treatments started, Holly sang to
him first thing each morning and at night right before they
went to sleep, snuggled up together in bed. Each morning
her Marimekko sheets, a wedding present from the crazier of
Alex's two aunts, smelled of dog, and each night she drifted
off to sleep worrying if Amanda was right, if she was torturing him, if she was doing the wrong thing. She even sang it
in front of Jack, once, accidentally. She thought he was in the
shower, but when she looked up, she saw him standing in the
doorway with his arms folded, watching her, silently, with a
smile on his face.

She found herself reflecting on all this, once she was back
in the elevator and on her way down, after she had left Chester to his new life, or to his old life—to his life without her.
Looking back on it, "Edelweiss" was not a bad choice. You
don't encounter "Edelweiss" a lot these days, not unless you're
watching *The Sound of Music,* and if you're going to associate
a song, for the rest of your life, with a deep and tender sad-
ness, with a loss that is so surprisingly painful it feels almost
embarrassing, it's best probably to pick one that you can
avoid simply by changing the channel whenever you see Julie
Andrews spinning around on an impossibly green hilltop. If
she could keep herself away from that and, let's see, coffee-
houses with kitschy Viennese themes and choral concerts
put on by junior-highers, Holly figured she was probably in
the clear.

six apples

A few months later, Mark called Holly and asked her if she'd like to get a cup of coffee. "A coffee of the abandoned" is how he'd put it, like this was a common phrase, the way one would say "the day of the dead." They had both been abandoned, that much was true. After Amanda said good-bye to Holly outside the gym, she went home and lobbed a grenade into the middle of her marriage and blew the entire thing up. It all happened incredibly quickly, with no marriage counseling, no second and third tries. It didn't seem like it should be that easy to end a marriage, but Amanda made it look that way, like she just shed one skin and put on another.

Holly got to the café early. She was sitting at a round table, alone, fighting the urge to clean out her purse, but she didn't want to have a bunch of old receipts and tissues and gum wrappers heaped in a pile in front of her when Mark showed up. She needn't have worried. When Mark arrived, he was wearing a pair of khakis that bagged at the knees and a crinkled orange sweater. He had always been in danger of losing his hair, but now it seemed to be coming out in great wild clumps, and the tufts that remained made him look somewhat birdlike. It was a little disconcerting to look at, like unhealthy levels of radiation had been involved, or someone, in a fit of pique, had pulled out handfuls at random. Holly

felt sorry for him. It was almost like his hair decided to kick
him while he was down.

"How are you?" Holly asked once he sat down.

Mark shrugged his shoulders and said, "Eh."

"Eh's good. Eh's great," said Holly. Her voice sounded
annoying even to her, artificially peppy and upbeat, like she
was encouraging a toddler. She took a breath and willed it to
drop down to a more honest register. "When Alex left me, it
was a month before I could tie my shoes."

"Is that true?"

Holly nodded yes. "I would have killed for just 'eh.'"

"Well, that's something, then."

"Just so you know, I'm not really in contact with Amanda
anymore, so anything you say to me won't get back to her. Not
that I'm picking sides," said Holly. "I'm just, not on hers."

"Because she ran off with your boyfriend?"

Holly realized, in a sudden burst of clarity, that Mark
believed just that: that Amanda had stolen Jack from her.
He was missing huge chunks of the story—the part about
Amanda and Jack's earlier affair, and just how Holly ended up
in the middle of it—and she had an overwhelming urge to fill
him in on all the juicy particulars. As quickly as the thought
came to her, she forced herself to let it go. What did it matter,
now? It wouldn't do him any good, it wouldn't give him what
he needed, it would just make him feel foolish and stupid and
blind, and he probably felt like that already. Besides, Holly
thought, it wasn't, in the end, her business.

"No, just, you know, the whole thing," she said.

"You don't approve."

"No, actually, I don't."

"I wouldn't be too hard on her if I were you."

Holly blinked. "Why not?"

"Sometimes I think, in these types of situations, it's just a race to see who can find somebody else first," said Mark. "Who knows, two years from now, it might have been me who met someone and ended up leaving her."

"What are you talking about? What types of situations?" Holly examined his face. "Were you having affairs, too?"

"I wouldn't call them affairs," he said. "Let's just say, my antennae were up. And I was less than a hundred percent committed to my marriage. I didn't want to break things up while Jacob was this young, but that's not to say I wouldn't have if the right person had come along."

"Gosh," said Holly. "I had no idea."

"It's hard for a marriage to end without a third party involved," said Mark. "In fact, I'd go so far as to say it's impossible."

"It's so weird, hearing this," said Holly. "I always thought you guys were happy."

Mark sat back and thought about it for a second. "We were as happy as two people could be who both ended up married to the wrong person."

"Is that true, do you think? That you guys should never have gotten married?"

"I don't think I'd say that, even after all of this," said Mark. "We got Jacob out of the deal."

"How is he doing?"

Mark had surprised himself and everybody else by insisting on joint custody, and Amanda had agreed. Jacob spent every weekend with Mark, just the two of them, as well as every other Wednesday night. Mark told Holly that he kept his schedule clear when his son was staying with him, he put his BlackBerry in a sock drawer, and he did all the hands-on stuff he had once found so mind-numbing, the unending cycle of meals and diapers and naps and baths, trips to the park and then back again, bedtime stories that Jacob insisted be read three times in a row. They spent hours on the living room rug together, Jacob sitting hunchbacked in his diaper, Mark stretched out on his belly, simulating crashes with Matchbox cars, the kind of thing that the old Mark would have been willing to put up with for about ten minutes tops.

"And, I joined a men's group," said Mark.

"You're in group therapy?"

Mark nodded yes. "Seven guys, all different ages, completely different walks of life, everybody's got their own set of problems. We have a talking stick we pass around." Holly figured Mark saw the incredulity she was experiencing on her face, because he said, "I'm completely serious. It's got feathers on top and everything." He paused for a moment and then continued in a thoughtful tone, "It's the kind of thing I never would have done in a million years, but it's been the best thing that's ever happened to me. I was sleeping through my life. And I'm not anymore."

"Good for you."

"Don't get me wrong. I was devastated when Amanda told me she was leaving. But that's one of the things I've learned from my group. Some people need to be devastated. Devastation," Mark said, "is an underrated experience."

Holly cocked her head to one side while she thought about this. It was true, probably. She might not have used those words, not exactly, but the mistake that people seem to make, the place where they seem to go wrong these days, is to *not* be devastated, for a while at least, by their devastating experience.

"In a different time, our marriage probably would have

lasted. But things are different now. People are less willing to put up with unhappiness."

"And yet, so many people are so unhappy."

"And therein," said Mark, "lies the rub."

After she said good-bye to Mark, Holly made her way up to Union Square to the farmers' market. It was already late in the fall, and the pickings were getting a bit slim—kale and squash and decorative corn, beets and turnips, things that needed to be braised—along with the usual suspects, the jars of honey and lavender sachets and the scary handmade soap. Holly was looking at the honey, wondering if she wanted to be the kind of woman who had special honey, when she heard someone call her name.

She looked up and saw Spence.

"Hi," said Holly.

"Hey," said Spence. "What are you doing here?"

"Nothing, really. I had an urge to make some soup, but now I'm not sure." She gestured towards the neighboring vegetable stand. "I don't feel like carrying home anything too gourd-y. What about you?"

"I was just walking by, and I saw all the stands, and I thought I'd like an apple. The guy wouldn't sell me just one, so now," Spence held up a small brown paper bag, "I've got six."

Holly nodded knowingly and said, "That's how they get you."

"It's kind of funny," said Spence. "I was walking along, and thinking about it, and I realized I've never owned six apples, at the same time, in my entire life."

They stepped away from the honey stand and stood there, together, in the center of the market.

"How are you?" Holly asked him.

"Not bad, actually."

"Whatever happened to that girl?" said Holly. "What's-her-name. From Boulder."

"Cathleen," Spence said helpfully.

"*Cathleen,*" said Holly. "She was a freak show. Do you ever hear from her?"

"Actually, we're engaged."

"Oh my gosh," Holly said. She scrunched her eyes closed tight. "I am so sorry I just said that. I had no idea."

"No, it's okay," said Spence. "She's embarrassed about all of that. Calling you up."

"She was upset. And it was fine," said Holly. "I liked her. I liked her spirit."

"She liked you, too."

"So, how did that…how did it…?"

"Resolve itself?"

"Exactly."

"I'm still not entirely sure myself," said Spence. "We didn't talk at all for a while, and then we did, and somewhere in the middle of all of that, it was like this fog lifted and everything became clear."

"Oh. I almost forgot," said Holly. She hit him, pretty hard actually, on his left shoulder. His face registered his surprise. "That's for cheating on me in Italy," she explained.

"I really thought I told you about that," said Spence. He rubbed his shoulder.

"Are you being serious?" said Holly. "I mean it. Is that really true?"

"It is. Honestly. I thought I told you."

Holly stood there and looked at him. She had to look up, because he was so tall. She remembered how nice it was to have a tall boyfriend.

"Did you know me at all, Spence?" Holly finally said. She was joking, at least the tone of her voice was, but she found that she really wanted to know the answer to the question. "Did you ever even know who I *was*?"

"What do you mean?"

"Describe the scene wherein you told me that you had sex with someone on your trip to Italy. Just, refresh my memory. How did I react?" said Holly. "Did I scream at you? Did I kick you out? Did I throw something breakable at your head?"

"You're making the point," said Spence, "for why I apparently didn't tell you."

They walked out of the market proper and ended up standing in the middle of a wide expanse of gray asphalt. In the summer, when there were more vendors, the market sprawled out all over the place, but this time of year there were these pockets of open space.

"But, you know, I think you may be on to something," said Spence.

"On to what?"

"I don't think we knew each other," said Spence. "I think that's exactly it. I think that was our problem."

"What makes you say that?"

"Okay, well, I read your book and, the funny thing was — it wasn't me. The outsides were me, the stuff I did, the things I liked, and the schools I went to and all that, but you got my insides all wrong."

"I did?"

"It was actually kind of strange, reading it. It's almost like you couldn't even *imagine* me or something. You couldn't bring yourself to understand what it felt like to be me. I mean it, Holly, you've got to cut people some slack," said Spence. He looked down at her face — her eyes were open wide, and unblinking, like she was taking this in — and he forged ahead. "I don't want to overstep things here, but Cathleen told me about what happened with your husband, how he just walked out one day for no reason, and, you know, maybe this is part of it. You've got to let people be just, you know, *people*. Everyone does bad things sometimes, for all sorts of reasons. You've got to try to at least understand."

Holly just stood there.

"Even now, I just lied to you," Spence confessed. "I knew I hadn't told you about what happened in Italy. I just didn't want to deal with your…whatever. Whatever it was going to be, I didn't want to deal with it."

A man walked by with a little girl sitting on his shoulders. A woman in a down vest was trailing along behind them, wheeling off a huge pumpkin in a red Radio Flyer wagon.

"And I'm not saying it's all your fault," said Spence. "Admittedly, I have some problems with the truth. Historically, certainly, that has been the case. But I'm working on it."

"You are?"

Spence nodded. "I don't want to die alone." He held up his bag. "I want to be a six-apple guy."

Holly nodded her head.

"I am sorry about Italy," said Spence. "I owed you, at the very least, the truth about it."

"It's okay. Thanks, though," said Holly. "And I'm sorry if I upset you with my book."

"Don't worry about it. Here. Have an apple."

Spence handed her an apple, and she polished it on her sleeve.

"Whatever happened with the other girl?" Holly asked. "The one who took the pictures."

"Molly?" said Spence. "She was institutionalized. Briefly. I heard she's doing better."

There was a guy roasting chestnuts on the street corner, and the smell wafted over, hinting at the coming winter, but in a good way, in the way that makes you think about Christmas and snow days and fires crackling away in fireplaces.

"Well. Wow," said Holly. "So, you're actually getting married. I'm proud of you, Spence."

"I think there's something in the air right now. You remember Betsy Silverstein? She eloped with this guy she met at her gym," said Spence. "They're moving to Austin next month. Her little brother Lucas moved out there and they visited a few times and they love it."

Sometimes Holly could start to see the order in things, she got a glimmer of a pattern. And that thing everyone seems to say these days, about how things always happen for a reason—Holly was getting closer to being willing to concede that that was maybe, possibly true. That idea of a person's life being a tapestry, and it wasn't until late in the day that you could see all of the threads linking one part to another, all of the strange and random connections, how everyone impacts each other in seemingly small but important ways. Or, maybe you start with the messy side of the tapestry, and you flip it over when you die, and then you see the gigantic white unicorn sitting inside the enchanted bower with the pear tree behind it. That was how the metaphor was usually employed, she knew, but Holly found she liked thinking about the strings. For now, maybe, she would focus on the strings and not worry so much about the unicorn. The unicorn could probably take care of itself.

"Do me a favor," said Spence. "Don't write about this."

"About what?"

"This. All this. Cathleen calling you. Molly. Me."

Holly thought about it for a moment and then nodded her head slowly. "It would make a good story."

"Holly."

"And it has a happy ending. For you and Cathleen, at least. You get to walk off into the sunset," said Holly. "My life has been short on happy endings lately."

Spence looked at her face and sighed. "Well, if you do, at least change me around more this time."

"I would."

"I don't want to be getting any angry phone calls from my mother."

"You'd be completely unrecognizable. I promise."

"And don't put in anything embarrassing."

Holly took a big bite of her apple, chewed, and then swallowed.

"Can I put in the part where you cry every time you watch *Extreme Makeover: Home Edition?*"

"No way. Absolutely not," said Spence. He looked at her. "How did you even know about that?"

"Cathleen told me on the phone one night."

"Sweet Jesus."

"Cathleen told me," Holly said, biting into her apple and smiling at the same time, "quite a lot."

kids on leashes

A few days after she bumped into Spence at the market, Holly's phone rang.

"I heard about what happened with Chester," said Two Feathers. "I just wanted you to know that I think you did the right thing."

"Thank you."

"I imagine that was pretty difficult for you."

"Yeah, well, in the end, I couldn't do it to that little boy," said Holly. "It wasn't his fault. And Chester, too. I couldn't do it to him, either."

It was true. When they started walking down West End, Chester had strained at the leash and more or less dragged Holly to the address printed on the card the woman had left with her a few weeks earlier. When they entered the lobby, his little toenails scratched on the marble floor, trying to get traction, and Holly let herself be pulled into the elevator, which was open and waiting. The doorman had smiled a big smile and shouted helpfully, "Apartment eight B." It wasn't until she saw Chester rolling around on the floor with the little boy, who's name turned out to be Malcolm, that she knew for certain she was doing the right thing. But that can be small comfort, really, when it means giving up something you love.

"I was thinking you might be ready for another dog," said Two Feathers.

"No way."

"Why not?"

"I can't go through that again," said Holly. "It was too painful. I'm done with dogs."

"Well. Give it some thought," said Two Feathers. "Actually, I have one in mind."

"You've got a dog you want me to adopt?"

"I do."

"What's wrong with him?" Holly said flatly.

"Nothing. His owner is being transferred to Jakarta and has to give him up. He's a beagle, still a puppy, really. I think you'd like him."

"Yeah, no, I don't think so, but thanks."

"I could bring him by some day after work. We could go for a quick walk in the park. No pressure."

Holly was silent for a moment. "You can bring him by," she finally said, "but I'm not going to be adopting another dog, that much I can assure you."

Leonard had asked Holly to move to London to write for his show again. He asked her every week, during their standing Sunday-night phone call, but this time there were actual dollar figures involved along with some impassioned pleading. It was tempting. She'd flown out to visit him when they shot the pilot, and she was surprised and pleased when she realized that one of the main characters was based on her. It was a funny show, and as much as he complained about everything—the network, the studio, the actors; the traffic, the English, the damp—Holly could tell that Leonard was thriving. He actually had a boyfriend, a real one, a sweet guy named James who had some kind of big finance job in the City and liked to cook, and who had a slight mother-hen quality that Holly found reassuring. James seemed to enjoy looking after Leonard, and Leonard, whatever else was true about him, tended to benefit from some looking after.

Holly spent a week in London. At night, she hung out with Leonard and James, and during the day she wandered around aimlessly, poking into bookshops and antiques stores, only twice doing anything overtly cultural, a visit to the Tate and one to Keats's house in Hampstead. She found herself returning again and again to something Jack had said to her, right before they broke up: that she believed in God, but didn't believe that God was good. It seemed to her that that was exactly it. She *didn't* believe that God was good, not really, not in a way that counted. Not the God she grew up with, anyway, the one who took up residence inside her consciousness all those years ago and stubbornly refused to leave. And if God isn't good, then only a fool or a masochist would follow him, right? If you don't believe that God is good, then the healthy thing, the life-affirming thing, is to go your own way.

She was starting to come to terms with the fact that she had a religious personality. It was looking like that part of her wasn't going to change. More and more often these days, though, Holly found herself thinking that perhaps what God wanted was not to be feared or obeyed or even to be worshipped — but maybe God just wanted to be *wondered* about. Wasn't that at least a possibility? Why else would all of this be so confusing? Why else would there be so many different ways, and so many conflicting ideas, everybody so convinced that they're right and everybody else is wrong, and the people without anything unwilling to even look for something, because the people *with* something seem so darn unappealing? And, who knows, maybe it is a gift to be able to believe in God and still get tripped up on the how. *Because where there is a path, it is someone else's path.*

And the journey from "knowing" to "not knowing" wasn't the same thing as losing your faith. It wasn't the same as believing in nothing, either. Even if it might look like that from the outside, from the inside, Holly knew for sure, it was different. Faith should take you further and further into life, and give you a way to engage, somehow, with the mystery behind it all, and if she was going to live a life without the comforts of dogma — and, yes, she missed her dogma sometimes, the warm soft blanket of complete and utter certainty — well, the least she could do for herself was figure out a way to go forward. She didn't have to go back, but she did have to go forward.

When Two Feathers showed up, he was wearing a pale yellow oxford shirt and a pair of beat-up 501s. His hair was out of the ponytail, and it hung straight down and just barely brushed the tops of his shoulders. Somehow, without the white coat, and with his hair freed from the ponytail, Two Feathers looked different. Holly couldn't put her finger on it, and after a minute she stopped trying to. The puppy he'd brought along with him was cute, she had to admit, big-pawed and floppy-eared with a shiny black nose. Two Feathers offered her the leash, but she refused it. She would walk, she had agreed to that much, but that was as far as this was going to go.

"I'm always surprised you don't see more kids on leashes," Two Feathers said.

They were heading for the park, and they'd just managed

to make their way past a pair of twin boys meandering aimlessly down the sidewalk. Their mother was doing her best to shepherd them along while she hauled groceries in their double stroller.

Holly thought about it a second. "It seems like you should either see no kids on leashes, or every kid on a leash."

"Exactly. It should be either illegal, or compulsory."

"I vote for compulsory," said Holly. "Leash laws for toddlers in Manhattan."

When they crossed into the park, Two Feathers handed Holly the puppy's leash, and this time, she took it. It was scratchy blue nylon, and quite long, and she found herself looping it around her wrist and then grasping it, the way she always did. She felt the tug at the other end and, for a moment, she missed Chester so much she could barely breathe. But she kept walking, and she kept breathing. A lot of life, it seemed to Holly, was turning out to be just like that. You keep walking, and you keep breathing, and then one day you notice, again, the feel of the wind on your cheek.

It was a while before Holly finally asked, "What's his name?"

"Panty."

Holly looked at him. "Please tell me you're joking."

"I'm afraid," Two Feathers said, "that I'm not."

"Panty?" said Holly. "Who names their dog Panty?"

The dog looked back over his shoulder at Holly but kept right on walking.

"I think it's because he pants a lot," said Two Feathers. "When he exercises. I don't think it has anything to do with, um, panties."

Panty was panting, that much was true. He had a spring in

his step, and his entire body seemed to bounce up and down as he walked. It looked, at times, like all four paws were off the ground at once.

"Well, I wouldn't be able to change it," Holly said quietly, almost to herself. "It'd be too confusing to him. He clearly knows his name." She tested him by calling out, "Panty," and watched as he stopped in his tracks and gave her an expectant look. "See? That's not fair to do to a puppy. Which means I'd be stuck with a dog named Panty for the rest of my life. Everyone will assume I made it up, that I'm the sort of person who, who"—Holly scrambled around for the end of this thought—"who names their dog 'Panty.' And I don't even know what kind of person that *is*."

"If it's any help, the guy who named him Panty, the one who got transferred to Jakarta, seemed relatively normal."

They made a right turn and started down one of the footpaths that winds along the western edge of the park. It had rained earlier in the day, and everything was wet and shiny, and the leaves were bright against the flat gray sky. Panty just kept trotting along. His tongue was out, pale pink and flopping. He seemed happy. It would be nice, Holly found herself thinking, to have a happy dog.

"He does pant a lot," Holly said.

"That he does."

"Is that normal?"

"In my medical opinion?" said Two Feathers. "I'd say he's on the pant-y side of normal. But still normal."

Up ahead, there were a couple of out-of-towners standing very still, taking pictures of a squirrel. Holly stopped walking so Panty wouldn't startle their subject.

"It's very difficult for me," Holly said, "you know, being

here in the park with you, not to ask if you can do that thing where you walk over dried leaves and twigs and sticks and things without making any sound."

"It's difficult for you not to ask me that?" said Two Feathers.

"Painfully so," Holly admitted.

"Well, then I'll answer it," he said. "I have no idea. I've never even thought about it."

"Really? Never?"

Two Feathers smiled at her. "I'd like it if you'd have dinner with me," he said.

"Panty and I will be incredibly quiet," said Holly, smiling right back at him, "if you feel like giving it a try."

"I was thinking Friday night."

Holly bent down to pet the dog. She started to scratch him behind the ears, but he immediately flipped over onto his back, paws lolling in the air, angling for a belly rub. She knelt down beside him on the grass, which was wet, and she could feel it slowly soak through the knees of her jeans. She rubbed and scratched and rubbed some more, while Panty threw his head back with what looked like pure and sheer delight.

"I am," said Holly, "such a sucker."

THE GOOD, THE BAD AND THE DUMPED

Jenny Colgan

Now, you obviously, would never, ever look up your exes on
Facebook. Nooo. And even if you did, you most certainly wouldn't
run off trying to track them down, risking your job, family and
happiness in the process. Posy Fairweather, on the other hand . . .

Posy is delighted when Matt proposes - on top of a mountain, in a
gale, in full-on romantic mode. But a few days later disaster strikes:
he backs out of the engagement. Crushed and humiliated, Posy
starts thinking. Why has her love life always ended in total disaster?
Determined to discover how she got to this point, Posy resolves to
get online and track down her exes. Can she learn from past
mistakes? And what if she has let Mr Right slip through her fingers
on the way?

'A Jenny Colgan novel is as essential for a week in the sun as Alka
Seltzer, aftersun and far too many pairs of sandals'
Heat

978-0-7515-4030-7

DIAMONDS ARE A GIRL'S BEST FRIEND

Jenny Colgan

Sophie Chesterton has been living the high life of glamorous parties, men and new clothes, never thinking about tomorrow. But after one shocking evening, she comes back down to earth with the cruellest of bumps. Facing up to life in the real world for the first time, Sophie quickly realises that when you've hit rock bottom, the only way is up.

Join her as she starts life all over again: from cleaning toilets for a living to the joys of bring-your-own-booze parties; from squeezing out that last piece of lip gloss from the tube to bargaining with bus drivers.

For anyone who's ever been scared of losing it all, this book is here to show you money can't buy you love, and best friends are so much more fun than diamonds . . .

'Jenny Colgan always writes an unputdownable, page-turning bestseller – she's the queen of modern chick-lit'
Louise Bagshawe

978-0-7515-4031-4

OPERATION SUNSHINE

Jenny Colgan

Evie needs a good holiday. Not just because she's been working all hours in her job, but also because every holiday she has ever been on has involved sunburn, arguments and projectile vomiting – sometimes all three at once. Why can't she have a normal holiday, like other people seem to have – some sun, sand, sea and (hopefully) sex?

So when her employers invite her to attend a conference with them in the South of France, she can't believe her luck. It's certainly going to be the holiday of a lifetime – but not quite in the way Evie imagines!

'Colgan at her warm, down-to-earth best'
Cosmopolitan

978-0-7515-3762-8

WEST END GIRLS

Jenny Colgan

The streets of London are paved with gold . . . allegedly.

They may be twin sisters, but Lizzie and Penny Berry are complete opposites – Penny is blonde, thin and outrageous; Lizzie quiet, thoughtful and definitely not thin. The one trait they do share is a desire to DO something with their lives and, as far as they're concerned, the place to get noticed is London.

Out of the blue they discover they have a grandmother living in Chelsea – and when she has to go into hospital, they find themselves flat-sitting on the King's Road. But, as they discover, it's not as easy to become It Girls as they'd imagined, and West End Boys aren't at all like Hugh Grant . . .

'A brilliant novel from the mistress of chick-lit'
Eve

978-0-7515-4332-2

Other bestselling titles available by mail